Ballroom Fever

by

Natalie Cross

Dancesport Mystery Series

Ballroom Fever

Cover Art by *Diana Carlile*

The Wild Rose Press, Inc.
PO Box 708
Adams Basin, NY 14410-0708
Visit us at www.thewildrosepress.com

Publishing History
First Edition, 2023
Trade Paperback ISBN 978-1-5092-5014-1
Digital ISBN 978-1-5092-5015-8

Dancesport Mystery Series
Published in the United States of America

Drowning in his own melancholy, he turned his gaze back to the darkened parking lot. His eyes narrowed. This was new.

Two white vans, with their lights off, drove into the parking lot behind the studio, reversed into the spots in front of the antiques store, and idled there.

He cocked his head, his mind whirling. Nothing good ever came from an unmarked white van. He opened the camera app on his phone and tried to zoom in on the front bumpers, but there were none. While Pennsylvania didn't require front license plates, it was possible they had been removed and it was an out-of-state car.

His mind whirred, preferring the mystery to the wallowing.

"What are you looking at?"

Startled, he whipped his head around and noted Anita standing behind him, holding an enamel tray with a bowl of soup and a large glass of iced water. She peered over his shoulder.

"Do you see those vans?" He pointed. "It seems a little weird that they're outside the antiques shop so late on a Saturday night. They pulled in without their lights on. Does she do online orders?"

Anita snorted in response to his question. "Mrs. DeVeaux?"

"It might explain why they're here, if she has to ship items by a certain time." Though Patrick didn't think that was it at all.

Anita shook her head. "Mrs. DeVeaux stopped by earlier and said she was expecting a delivery. I've never really paid attention to when her deliveries arrive or leave." She pulled up a side table and set the tray upon it.

Dedication

To those out there who feel like they need to be something they are not. You are wonderful, and you are enough.

Prologue

Lucy Knight tossed her hair over her shoulder, regaling her very bored boyfriend with the finer points of the murder podcast she'd been listening to before he'd dragged her to this party. Whatever. Junior year was not for staying with lame-ass, tool boyfriends, even if he was the best Standard dancer in the Lewis High ballroom club.

She hadn't been down to Lewis Creek in ages. Not since her older brother had gone through his "Greatest Catch" phase, which had lasted barely longer than the time it took to bait a hook. The creek wasn't deep enough to swim in, so its primary use was for scenery, idle fishermen who didn't mind snagging guppies too small to eat, and rowdy teenage parties.

She had certainly never been at Lewis Creek after dinner, when the sunlight had turned from postcard-perfect October into murdery dark forest in the space of a finger snap. The moon was a scimitar, slicing through the thick velvet night. Autumn in Lewis, Pennsylvania was a weird, almost mystical time of earlier nightfall, eighty-degree days and thirty-degree nights.

She couldn't wait to leave.

Tonight was like something out of one of those angsty teen dramas she streamed after she had finished her homework, only seedier and less well-lit. Lucy hadn't really expected more. Life was never the same as the movies. Groups of people standing around the open trunks of SUVs, holding red plastic cups and chatting. The music sucked a lot more, too. On TV, they always played the right kind of music. The kind you could dance all sultry to if you wanted, or you could stand around looking cool, laughing with your friends.

It sure as hell wasn't this whiny emo music with the tinny feedback from the 1980s-era boombox.

"I don't get why you listen to such morbid shit." Daniel Riley rolled his eyes. He wasn't paying any attention to her. He was focused on the group thirty yards away, gathered around the open trunk of a brand-new silver SUV. The car didn't hold his attention. That honor belonged to one very handsome, very uninterested individual.

Lucy should have known. Jeremy Nguyen was football captain and head of the drama club, and regarded by ninety-eight percent of the student populace as the hottest guy in school. Lucy fell in the other two percent. Maybe he could be bored by Daniel's inane habits, like pretending he read James Joyce for fun. Lucy had dated him long enough to know he had never made it past page three. That was what happened when you dated the guy your parents chose.

She sipped from her bottle of sparkling water and surveyed the scene. Cataloguing any and all details would be good practice for her future criminology degree. Bunch of sticks, group of kids lighting up, pile of leaves, future college crew team wannabes… There. About twenty feet away, hiding in a grove of trees, she spied a woefully underdressed Sophie MacAllister. Perfect.

"Where are you going?" Daniel called as she

moved away from him.

She didn't bother looking back, just held up a hand in supposed farewell. "To talk to someone who listens." She didn't particularly care if anyone heard her.

A few feet from her, also watching Jeremy Nguyen to no one's surprise, Sophie stepped on a branch, the snap crackling through the air like a firework. She froze, foot lifted in midair.

Poor kid. She clearly didn't know anyone. A gust of wind snapped Lucy's long, black hair against her face.

"Hey, Soph!" She waved energetically. Everyone needed help now and then, and she wasn't one to leave a fellow ballroom club member alone in the literal forest.

"Hi, Lucy." Sophie nodded shyly at her. She shivered, tightening her denim jacket around her exposed midriff.

Lucy softened. Sophie clearly had come out tonight wanting to party but didn't quite know how things were done. Happened to everyone. "Having fun?" She unwound the multi-colored scarf from her neck and offered it to Sophie, who blushed and shook her head.

"It's great. Yeah." Sophie stared at the ground, digging her toe into a patch of pine needles. "How about you?"

Who did Sophie usually hang with? Lucy didn't typically pay attention, but thought she was friendly with some of the other ballroom girls. Why hadn't any of them come with her?

Daniel, who for some unknown reason had followed her, rolled his eyes. "Lucy listened to a podcast about some serial killer, and she's talking about it to everyone we meet." Seriously. If Lucy could figure out how to break up with him without having to find a new dance partner, she would. But the Ivy League liked champions and commitment.

Lucy flipped her hand at him and focused on Sophie. She was used to Daniel's passive aggression when it came to her interests.

"It's fascinating." Seriously, why did she need to defend herself about this? "About the Golden State Killer? Daniel doesn't like me talking about it, but I think it's important to know as much as we can so we can protect ourselves."

"It's a weird hobby." Daniel yawned, not bothering to hide it. Yeah. Tonight. Maybe on the ride home. It couldn't be that hard to break up with someone and find a new dance partner. Her teacher Patrick or his girlfriend Anita could probably help her with auditions.

Sophie shifted from foot to foot. "I get that. Did you hear about the drug ring they busted up here in town? We live just a street over from that house, the one where they were storing the drugs." She bit her lip, as if worried she had shared too much.

Lucy nodded to relieve Sophie's anxiety and could see the sophomore's shoulders relax. "Totally. Here I was, thinking nothing exciting ever happens here, and then boom. Small town drug ring."

Daniel yawned again, more pointed this time. "My dad runs the real estate office, the one where that agent worked. You know, who made up the false staging company so she could hide drugs? He was *pissed.*" He shrugged and checked the time on his phone. "Lucy, we've gotta head out. I have golf practice early tomorrow before school."

Damn Daniel and his stupid golf practice. He could go to it newly single.

Lucy noticed Sophie staring over their shoulders, likely at Jeremy Nguyen. She couldn't leave her now, not if Sophie was going to throw herself at the hottest guy in school while his sometime ex-girlfriend, Madison of the original Resting Bitch Face, watched. It would be like releasing a goldfish into a shark tank.

"Let's stay a few more minutes, Daniel."

"But, Lucy—"

Lucy sidestepped him and moved next to Sophie, wrapping her arm around the girl's thin, chilly shoulders. Lucy elbowed her softly in the ribs. "You have good taste, Soph. Go talk to him."

"I can't. I mean, he's with Madison." Sophie bit her lip again. At the rate she was going, she wouldn't have any lips left.

Lucy shrugged. "Not really. They're going through a rough patch, and he can do so much better than Madison." She elbowed Sophie again and could practically feel the girl squee. It really was so much easier to build people up than drag them down.

"Can we go or what?" Daniel yawned again. "I'm done." Clearly Daniel didn't see it her way.

Someone moved in the dark shadows of the grove by the creek. It was Adam Greenwood, current editor of the school newspaper. He and his group stood in a tight circle, smoking and drinking. He was watching Sophie, his eyes flicking up and down, but not in a predatory way. Lucy's spine tingled. Adam Greenwood would be better for Sophie than Jeremy. No heinous beast Madison lurking in the background, waiting to pounce.

"Hey, look." She nudged Sophie and nodded at

Adam. "Adam Greenwood is checking you out."

"Adam Greenwood?" Even in the dim light by the creek, Lucy could see Sophie's cheek redden. "No, no he couldn't possibly be looking at me."

"He is totally looking at you. He's a great guy. Go have fun!"

Daniel sighed and ran his hand over his perfectly gelled hair. "Seriously, how long do I have to listen to this? If we're going, let's go."

Lucy rolled her eyes. "Cool it, Golf Pro Ken. This is important stuff." Adam moved away from his friends, holding a vape in one hand and waving shyly toward Sophie with the other. *Perfect*. Lucy didn't love vaping or matchmaking, but this seemed very worthwhile.

"I think I'll stay for a bit longer." Sophie bit her lip again, her gaze on Adam's approach. "I'll be fine."

"Good. Lucy, come on." Daniel stalked toward his parents' luxury sedan.

Sophie looked okay. Nervous, but excited. She would be fine. This was quintessential coming of age stuff, right? Talking to someone you liked. It didn't stop a curl of trepidation from gathering at the back of Lucy's neck. She was suddenly indecisive, a feeling with which she was not familiar and did not in any way care for.

"Sophie—"

"Lucy! Come on, or I'm leaving without you!" Daniel slammed the driver's side door loud enough to echo through the trees.

Sophie half-smiled at her. "I'll be fine, Lucy. Really. Thank you."

The trepidation wouldn't let her go, and she did not entirely think it was due to the inevitable breakup five minutes into her future. Maybe it was the darkness by the creek. It felt foreboding, like the start of a thriller novel. "If you're not, or you feel worried in any way, call me. Please."

"I will. Don't worry. I'll be fine. I'm just going to have a little fun, right?"

"Lucy!"

Damn it, Daniel really was a categorical ass. Why her parents had wanted them to date was beyond her.

"Okay." Lucy wrapped her in a quick, tight hug. "Have fun. Call me if you change your mind about the ride." Sophie smelled a bit like woodsmoke and drugstore perfume. It soothed the nervous tingle along her spine. Sophie would be all right.

She glanced over her shoulder as she walked toward Daniel's car. Sophie stood there, chatting with Adam. She would be fine. Wouldn't she?

Chapter One

Patrick O'Leary paced the floorboards of his girlfriend Anita's apartment. And paced. Maybe he should go and pace the dance floor downstairs. There was more acreage.

He thumbed the little box in his pocket until he was nearly convinced he had rubbed a hole in it. He briefly considered throwing it across the room but that would defeat its original purpose entirely.

Moaning, Patrick sank onto Anita's comfy couch and covered his face with his hands. It was supposed to be so easy. He needed to bend on one knee in his most dramatic Gene Kelly impersonation, take her hands in his, and say, "Anita—"

Patrick mouthed the words, but he could not make them come. They kept getting caught somewhere between his diaphragm and his vocal cords.

Patrick removed the little black box from his pocket and turned it over and over in his hands. The edges of the velvet wrapping were starting to look a bit worn and weary. Probably because he couldn't stop worrying at it.

Was he doing the right thing? Was this even the right time? Maybe he had missed his chance. His timing had been off before.

The water turned off in the bathroom, and the door swung open, releasing a cloud of steam. Patrick hastily shoved the box back into the pocket of his pants, but he could not quite rouse himself from his seat on the bed. It was too hot in the apartment. He should drink some water. Maybe have a beer, or go for a run. Anything to ease the ache in his chest.

He turned on the TV, the remote shaking in his hand.

The local news station showed an image of Christina Blake, the woman who haunted his dreams. His pulse raced as he flipped to the next channel. This time there was a news van and police cars parked by Lewis Creek. Perfect. Great night all around.

Patrick turned the TV off, though it took him four tries, since his hand trembled so badly. Why in the world did Anita still pay for cable? She should go full streaming. Maybe if he focused on this thought, he could avoid what came next. What had been happening more and more often over the last six months.

He leapt off the couch and attempted a few jumping jacks, but the lactic acid in his body from the panic made the exercise frenetic.

He slumped back on the couch and tapped the black jewelry box in his pocket repeatedly. He needed to get this under control. He had to be strong for Anita, for himself.

Maybe a change of scenery. Patrick checked the window, which looked out onto the parking lot shared by Lewis Dancesport and the antiques store. Half the lights were burned out, particularly on the antiques store side. The shadows there twirled and leapt. His heart throbbed, and a tight hand closed around his lungs. That wasn't safe, to have such shoddy lighting. Not in the least. What if something happened—

The rush of blood in his ears was loud enough to drown out the sounds of Anita padding softly across the room.

The dark. Arms tied to the bed, musk and too-sweet tuberose clouding out all other sensation—

He couldn't breathe. He was definitely having a heart attack. Maybe he should call an ambulance. No, no ambulance. It would take him to the hospital, and he was ninety percent certain his mom was working tonight. He'd rather have a heart attack than explain himself to her.

As if on cue, an ambulance raced down Main Street, sirens and lights blaring through the still small town.

The periphery of his vision darkened, leaving him only a thin circle of light in the center. How was he supposed to see? How was he supposed to do anything? Damn it, he was going to die before he had a chance to ask Anita to marry him. He was too young for this. If only he could see her one last time, dance with her—

Then she wrapped her arms around him, enveloping him in the scent of hibiscus and grapefruit. His muscles unclenched and his breathing eased. He settled against her body, lining himself with her warm comfort, with her strength. His vision cleared as his heart rate slowed to a more sustainable pace.

"Hey." She nuzzled into the side of his neck. Patrick reflexively tightened his arms around her towel-clad waist. Six months into this new phase of their relationship, and he still could not believe his luck. He rested his cheek against her damp blonde hair, inhaling her.

He didn't need a doctor. He didn't need a hospital.

He needed Anita.

Also, around this time, other parts of his body became aware that she was only wearing a towel, and his fingertips drifted down to explore the creamy thigh underneath the hem.

Anita laughed and drew away from him. Her blue eyes twinkled like the crystals on one of her ballroom gowns. "Patrick, stop. We have to get ready for the party."

"No party." He flipped her onto her back on the couch and kissed her, reveling in her taste and the feel of her underneath him. "Let's stay in." This was a much better idea. Why go out into the dark night where— *things*—could happen, when they could stay in, make out, then watch that Swedish murder show he liked? He licked down the curve of her neck, the anxiety receding as he got closer to the line of the towel covering her chest. Genius. He was a freaking genius.

"Patrick." She threaded her hands into the hair along his temples, his skin sparking beneath her touch.

At least until she pulled his protesting lips from her body.

"Patrick, you have to go to the party. It's for John and Katie." The cute little furrow between her brows deepened.

Patrick kissed it. "How many parties do they need? They've already had an engagement party, a bridal shower, a groom sprinkle, which was merely an excuse to get drunk and watch the Eagles/Giants game, and the bachelor/bachelorette stuff coming up."

Anita laughed and pushed him away. She sat up on the couch and, unfortunately, fixed her towel. He huffed and sat back on the couch. He had to listen when

Anita had her stern-teacher expression in place. It gave him some fantastic ideas for role play.

Anita smiled, her mouth soft. "You're a groomsman. You're supposed to go to all the parties. And Katie's the only girl with four brothers. Her family's excited for this barbecue."

A supportive, loving family. Yeah, the idea of that really made Patrick want to leave the house. He slumped into the profusion of throw pillows on Anita's couch, the ring box digging into his hip. Maybe this was a good time to ask her. It would certainly distract her from her intention of going out.

Though Anita took her commitments very seriously.

Another ambulance siren winged through the open window as it sped down Main Street. Patrick followed its path idly.

"What's going on tonight? That's a lot of ambulances in a short period of time."

Anita glanced out the window, her damp hair hanging over her bare shoulders. "I don't know. But I do know what you're doing."

"What *I'm* doing?" Patrick pasted on his most innocent expression. "I haven't the foggiest idea what you're talking about."

She stood from the couch, shaking her head. A water droplet smacked him in the cheek. She headed for the bedroom. "Every time we need to go out lately, you do everything in your power to shut it down."

His phone buzzed on the table.

"It's not my fault I have remarkable powers of persuasion." So what if he liked staying home? He went out when it was absolutely necessary, like when he had to work or they were invited to showcases or competitions. He was a complete idiot for posting that video of their Hozier show dance at the Keystone Star Ball. He had intended to advertise the dance studio, but it was possible to do a job too well. The invites had been nonstop since that thing went viral.

Dimly, he registered that since he still ran a successful lifestyle brand, he ought to be thrilled that something he had posted had gone viral. But everyone went through slumps, right?

His phone buzzed again, and he checked the text message

—*Groomzilla: Are you at the party yet?*—

Patrick blanched. Not that John Flaherty would care, but Patrick was still in basketball shorts and a too-tight Phillies T-shirt. Not exactly appropriate pre-wedding party attire. What were they calling this barbecue? Friends and Family Pre-Wedding Get-To-Know-You? Altogether too many hyphens.

His phone buzzed a third angry time, reminding him that he still hadn't answered his friend. His fingers flew over the keypad.

—*Just getting ready.*—

For a fleeting second, he considered blaming Anita and how long it took her to get dressed. But that was A) blatantly false and B) a total dick move.

On cue, Anita stepped from the bedroom, already dressed in a peach A-line dress with chains along the shoulders instead of straps. How was that barbecue attire? Or was this one of those fancy barbecues with a dress code like South Beach So Hot? He should have paid more attention to the invite. He was a terrible friend.

Patrick re-focused. Anita had her hands on her hips, like she was losing patience. Which had happened exactly never. "Patrick, get dressed. We have to go."

He collected his tongue from where it had fallen on the floor. "You look amazing."

She rolled her eyes and ran a brush through her long blonde hair. "You're stalling. Put some clothes on that actually fit." She disappeared back into the bedroom.

Patrick frowned at his T-shirt. He should get a new one. Just because it was the last thing his dad had given him before hightailing it for greener pastures didn't mean he had to cling to it forever.

His phone buzzed again.

—*Groomzilla: I'm working. When you get there, can you spread the word? Can't call Katie. She put her phone in the freezer since the caterers kept calling and stressing her out. I'll try to be there ASAP*—

A mission. Patrick could manage a mission. He stood up from the Patrick-sized divot in the couch and stretched.

He sent John a thumbs-up emoji and a GIF from *The Hangover*, then walked into the bedroom.

Anita sat at her vanity, polishing her flawless makeup. He was the luckiest damn guy in the entire world. No, the universe. "I'm going to get dressed." He headed for his side of the closet. They weren't officially living together yet, but the ring box implied that wasn't too far off, right?

"Patrick."

The stern timbre of her voice made him turn. Her usually light, affable expression was now edged with concern. "Patrick, are you sure you're okay?"

The panic tensed in his gut, but he shoved it away. "Fine. Just fine. Everything's fine, Anita. Let's go to the party."

Maybe if he said it enough, it would eventually be true.

Chapter Two

Anita sipped from her glass of white wine, letting the cool liquid calm her nerves. What was going on with Patrick?

The backyard of Katie and John's house looked gorgeous, complete with fairy lights and a bonfire currently manned by Katie's four brothers. The night air smelled like fall should, with the aromas of crisp apple cider and cozy fireplace. It was practically an I Love Autumn candle.

It would be better if Patrick weren't shaking like a live wire beside her. If only he would go to therapy, but he wouldn't even admit to her that something was wrong. He hadn't dealt with what Christina Blake had done to him, to them, and ignored wounds festered until they rotted.

She sighed. This wasn't the place or time to think about festering wounds. This was about celebrating with friends.

So she pasted on her best friendly smile, gripped Patrick's elbow, and dragged him to make the social rounds with her.

"I don't really feel like small talk. You're the one who's mad good at it," he said as they left a group of Katie's friends from the local elementary school.

"That's not true. People adore you, but it's good to keep up the practice for both of us." Her heart heaved in her chest, and she scanned the group. "Perfect. There are Will and Bobby. You like them."

Will Forbes and his boyfriend Bobby approached them, bottles of local microbrew in their hands. Will engaged Patrick in some ritualized masculine version of a handshake. Whatever. At least he seemed a little less grumpy.

"Can I borrow your boyfriend for a moment?" Will asked. "Groomsman stuff."

"Of course." The corner of her mouth tilted, but it was a half gesture. Patrick's face was so pinched he was seventy-five percent crab. She couldn't deal with it now. She turned to Bobby, who was inspecting the partygoers with benign interest. "Having fun?"

He startled, as if lost in his thoughts. "Yeah. Everyone here is so nice."

"That's right. You're not from Lewis, are you?"

"No, I'm from Maine." He smiled in an apologetic type fashion, though she didn't see any reason to be sorry about that. "I went to law school at Penn. How's the studio? Will showed me some of your online videos. You and Patrick are insanely amazing."

Anita flushed. "Thanks. It's weird. I spent most of my life dancing and competing and blaming myself for not winning more often. I thought I was doing something wrong, and that's why I wasn't successful." That and her father's derogatory words ringing in her ears like the world's most pejorative gnat. "Then Patrick and I started partnering, and everything clicked." She gazed across the bonfire, where Patrick and Will stood beside a pensive-looking Katie. "He brings out the best in me."

"I know what you mean."

Anita turned, noting that Bobby's gaze was on Will and Patrick, too. A warm, fuzzy ball of hope curled in her chest. "You and Will are great together."

"Thanks." He readjusted his glasses on his nose. "I love him, you know? He's a bro-ish, sports-obsessed Neanderthal, and I cannot believe I get to be with him. He's not what I ever expected, and he's more than I deserve."

"I'm sure that's not true." Even if she felt exactly the same way about Patrick. "As long as you're happy, you deserve each other."

He tilted his head to one side. "I wish I could do some kind of grand gesture for him, you know? To show him how much he means to me?"

Anita nodded, lost in thought. Did she show Patrick how much he meant to her? Maybe that's why he wasn't acting like himself. Maybe she left him in doubt of her commitment.

Bobby sipped his beer and clinked the bottle against her glass. "What about you two? You have the ultimate rescue story. Diving in to save Patrick from a stalker's clutches."

If Anita turned any redder, she would combust like the bonfire. "I don't know. I panicked, honestly. The police were coming. I should have just waited."

"Waited for Patrick to be love bombed in the most awful, literal sense?'

Despite the apprehension steeling her spine, she laughed. It felt good, normal, to laugh. Like it was something she'd be able to repeat. "Well, when you put it that way."

They sipped their drinks companionably for a few moments, two almost-friends forced together by circumstances.

"Do you know where John is?" Bobby asked.

"No. Patrick said he got a message that he's stuck at a scene. But he heard ambulances earlier, heading out toward Lewis Creek." Her phone weighed heavily in her small shoulder purse. "I probably should have checked the news. I just can't really bear to watch it anymore."

"I get that." Bobby rubbed at the label on his beer bottle. "I hope everything's all right."

"Me, too. There's too much going on in Lewis lately."

"Tell me about it. I work with Dennis Rayner sometimes. You know, the accountant who was in that home invasion and drug bust a few months ago?" Bobby shook his head. "Crazy."

"Tell me about it." She knew all too well. Dennis and his girlfriend Tabitha were regulars at her dance studio. Nothing like tragedy to bring people together. The apprehension clenched around her spinal cord. "Bobby. Do you think it's possible for people to build lasting relationships, when they get together like Dennis and Tabitha?" Or her and Patrick, not that she was asking for herself or anything.

Bobby smiled, his face soft and kind. "You mean the Sandra Bullock *Speed* conundrum? I think so. All relationships take work. It's about finding substance beyond the adrenaline rush."

"That makes a lot of sense." She wished she felt it, though.

The DJ, a.k.a Katie's brother Declan, turned on a U2 mix. Katie jumped in the air, her eyes searching wildly before her enthusiasm deflated. She was probably wishing John was there.

Katie Bannion was the kind of girl Anita had always wanted to be, a genuinely kind, tiny ball of energy who talked at the speed of sound in her thick Delaware County accent. Though petite, she maintained a definite aura of authority that reminded Anita distinctly of her own third grade teacher, who could cut a fight in half with a single stare. It probably helped that Katie was an elementary school teacher.

Will and Patrick rejoined them, the latter threading his arm around her waist and pressing a kiss to her temple. "Everything okay?"

He smiled, but it was merely a fractured image of his usual self. "Right as rain."

"How's John?"

"He'll be delayed a bit longer." Will took a long pull from his beer, his brow furrowed.

"What's going on at the creek?" Bobby asked.

Anita snuggled against Patrick.

"I don't know." Patrick's entire body was tense, like someone had filled his spine with concrete. "Something about school kids getting into trouble?"

"Lewis isn't what it used to be." Will finished his beer and held the neck of the bottle between his thumb and forefinger.

Nothing was what it used to be. Anita sipped her wine, her gaze focused on Patrick.

Everything could change.

Chapter Three

The bell over the studio door clanged, and Anita glanced toward it, her good mood plummeting. It was going to be one of *those* mornings. "Hello, Mrs. DeVeaux."

Mrs. DeVeaux, the proprietress of the antiques store across the parking lot, was a fine, brittle sort of woman in a two-piece navy-blue suit complete with pearls, court shoes, and a Jackie O hat atop her perfectly coiffed silver curls. "Ms. Goodman, last Saturday the noise was simply unacceptable."

Anita tightened her ponytail and forced her lips into a thin smile. It was difficult to manage much more when dealing with her neighbor. "I am so sorry, Mrs. DeVeaux. We try to close it down before ten o'clock."

On the dance floor, John and Katie halted the rehearsal for their wedding dance, which was probably a good thing. John was an excellent deputy, but despite the choreography to maximize both of their strengths, he lacked confidence.

Oh right. Her neighbor was still talking.

Mrs. DeVeaux crossed her arms and scowled. "See that they do not also take all the parking spots. I get very important deliveries. The weekends are my busiest times."

"Of course." Anita nodded. She always posted signs detailing the parking restrictions. It wasn't like she could illuminate them with neon. And who got deliveries after ten on a weekend? Her neighbor had never met a complaint she hadn't filed. Literally. John Flaherty had told her once that Mrs. DeVeaux had called the police station to report "possible smoking in the parking lot."

Mrs. DeVeaux inspected the studio, a sneer curling one side of her trademark red-lipsticked mouth. With a tsk and a shake of her head, she stomped outside.

Anita sighed. If she had known the lease to the apartment and dance studio would come complete with an interfering neighbor…

"What was that about?"

Anita turned to see Patrick behind her. He was dressed in a soft green T-shirt and jeans, and she had never seen anyone look quite so enticing. Especially after being berated by the 1960s Junior League. "She said the party on Saturday was too loud and someone parked in some of her spaces."

Patrick rolled his eyes. "Someone breathes the same air as she does, and she brings it to the city council."

"You should run for city council, then," John said, sprawling his tall frame into a folding chair. He winced as he removed the no-scuff dress shoes and changed into a pair of sneakers.

Anita looped her arm around Patrick's waist, loving the feel of his muscles and warmth against her fingertips. "That's definitely what you need, honey. Yet another job."

She might have imagined it, but Patrick blanched ever so slightly then coughed, and it was as though nothing had changed. There he was, same old Patrick.

Handsome, dead sexy, thoughtful, funny, and hers. She still got shivers up her spine when she remembered that. Patrick was hers.

Even if she couldn't shake the feeling something was not completely right with him.

Now he was back to his usual joviality, saying he was going to run under the name "Honey O'Leary." Maybe it was just her, looking for problems where there were none. John certainly didn't seem to notice anything amiss, and she respected his investigative skills.

Anita moved back toward the check-in desk, watching Patrick from the periphery of her vision. It was not obvious, but there was a stiffness in his posture where before there had always been fluidity and strength. A hesitancy in his smile. It wasn't her imagination.

Something was definitely going on with Patrick.

****

"So you're coming tomorrow, right?" John asked with an undertone of urgency.

Tomorrow? Hell, he didn't even know what today was. "Absolutely!" Patrick replied, even if he could not recall to what he was agreeing. Hopefully nothing gross or involving fishing rods. "Wouldn't miss it for the world." He forced a smile. If he kept blathering platitudes for the next few minutes, it would either come to him or eventually John had to give him some specifics.

"Great, so we are meeting at eight thirty at the paintball field." John put an arm around Katie, who reached up on her tiptoes to peck his clean-shaven, brown-skinned cheek, and waved as they departed.

Patrick held up a feeble hand in farewell. At least he knew what he had agreed to do now. Even if the very idea made his stomach roil and skin crawl like he was lying in a pool full of non-poisonous spiders.

He hated paintball, he hated any sport that involved playing with weapons. It probably had something to do with his mother, but lately he was in no state of mental fortitude to open that can of long-buried worms.

Still. This was John, his friend, not to mention the deputy who helped convict Christina Blake after she had gone all movie psycho stalker/murderer. He could suck it up for his friend's bachelor party. He could. He might need to pre-game like the Eagles made it to the Super Bowl, but he could do this.

A warm hand slid around his shoulders, and Patrick's eyes closed. He wanted to revel in that feeling, just for a few moments. It was the only time all day he felt like himself. His shoulders lowered half an inch.

"Everything okay?" Anita asked. She rested her chin against his shoulder, and if he could bottle that image of her beautiful heart-shaped face looking up at him with those blue eyes that made him want to move to the Caribbean, he would be happy for the rest of his life. He should take her on vacation, somewhere warm, where they could swim all day and lie on a beach with frosty umbrella drinks. Or maybe somewhere cool, up in the mountains where they could cozy up under red-checked flannel blankets while drinking spiked hot cocoa.

He should ask her to marry him. That would be the sensible thing to do.

"Of course." He tested a smile and found it was

easier than he had anticipated. Her doing, no doubt. "John reminded me about the bachelor party tomorrow."

She raised her eyebrows. "Boys going to the wilderness for some 'team building'?" She mimicked air quotes.

"I think the correct term is devolution."

She laughed and leaned away from him, but the distance felt so vast, so cold and empty and bare, that he immediately pulled her close to him again. Yes, that was better. Her body pressed against his. U2 was still playing over the stereo, and Patrick swayed to the rhythm, his forehead resting on hers. He dropped his hands to her hips, letting the motion soothe him. She wrapped her arms around his neck and dropped her cheek to his chest. Warmth blossomed through him, starting at the locus where her skin touched his.

Sadness, and something like yearning, yawed within him. He pulled Anita closer, trying to wrap himself in her limbs, her scent. There. His breathing could slow. The empty pit at the edges of his vision seemed farther away now. Anita. All he needed was Anita.

Anita tightened her embrace around him, as though she could sense that he was falling apart. They had stopped dancing now. They were frozen in some awkward pattern where he clung desperately to her, because she was the one thing holding his fragile self in one piece.

He needed to pull his shit together. She would never want him like this. She would never want someone weak, spineless. That wasn't him. He was Patrick. He jumped into the fray, he pitched in, he got things done.

He did not fall apart. He led, not followed.

Patrick's breath hitched in his chest once, twice, a third time. He could barely get enough oxygen. Something was wrong—

He felt her hands slide along his jaw, and then she was drawing her face toward his.

"Look at me," she whispered.

He had not even realized his eyes were closed. He opened them and nearly dissolved when he saw the pity in her face. "I'm okay." If he said it enough times, eventually it would be true.

"What's going on?"

He was falling apart, and he did not know why or how to fix it. "Nothing." He brushed a quick kiss across her forehead, and though it caused him physical pain, he moved away from her and did a quick sailor shuffle. "See? I'm A-Okay. Right as rain. Fit as a fiddle."

Anita crossed her arms and stared at him, like she was trying to decide if he was going to spontaneously combust. He really hoped he wouldn't. Not before he asked her to marry him. Not that she would say yes with the way he was acting.

Instead, he pulled his muscles into motion and forced another grin. "Really, Anita, everything is one hundred percent fine. I'm just going to get some work done."

He escaped into the office where he could shut the door, put his head between his knees, and finally focus on his breathing.

Chapter Four

John Flaherty had his notepad open, his travel mug full of hot coffee by his side, and a splitting headache.

He would blame his imminent wedding for the increasing frequency of his migraines, but he didn't have any desire to put that on Katie's plate, too.

Sheriff Forbes played with her glasses across the small conference table. So she was upset, too. It had been challenging to learn her tells as she was a murderous poker player. Over the last few years of being a small-town deputy, John had figured them all. She never fidgeted unless she was disturbed.

Deputy Curtis Wyczenczak's presentation was nothing if not disturbing. Headache-inducing? Definitely.

Curtis ran one hand through his short-cropped hair, sighing. He sank into a chair at the end of the conference table, beside the whiteboard where he had been making notes. "I don't know what to make of it all." He was the baby in this room, barely a year out of the academy, but he cared, and John knew that was the most important thing.

Sheriff Forbes tilted back on her chair, raising the front two legs off the beige tile floor. "Let's talk this through. What do you think, John?"

John ran his fingers over his stubbled chin. He'd barely had time to kiss Katie goodbye this morning, let alone shave.

He unbent his prodigious height from his chair rather than rose. Something else he had adapted to over the years. At least the Lewis PD offices had ceilings that were twice the height of the ones he had dealt with on the submarine.

The photos of the high school students who had been found unconscious at the Lewis Creek party were plastered on the whiteboard, staring at him, their expressions accusatory.

"We interviewed anyone left there, but it was pretty obvious most of the partygoers had already fled the scene." John tapped the end of his pen against the dimple of his chin. "Tons of tire marks. The kids we interviewed were, well, less than forthcoming."

"Intoxicated?' Sheriff Forbes rotated her glasses over and over in her hands.

"No," Curtis responded. "They all got tested and, though some were positive for alcohol or marijuana, none were over the legal limit."

"They're teenagers," John said, trying to keep his tone even. "None of them should have been drinking."

Sheriff Forbes eyed him, and he knew exactly what she was thinking. He hadn't been a saint in his teenaged years, either.

"So either they didn't see anything," he said. "Which is entirely possible at a party like that. Or they saw what happened and don't want to say anything."

Sheriff Forbes sighed. "What do you mean, a party like that? Don't forget I'm an old lady."

"Never." A smile softened John's cheeks. "A creek party like that? Kids would be standing around in groups, the only light from individual cars. Everything else would be pitch black. We've had a lot of streetlight outages lately, and it's been particularly noticeable around the high school and the road to the creek. With daylight ending a lot sooner lately, it's a recipe for problems."

"I'll call the township and ask them to look at the lights." Curtis made a note on his tablet. John was more old school, preferring pen and paper. "Maybe they have a record of who last serviced them. In case it's connected."

Sheriff Forbes joined John beside the whiteboard. "What's on your mind, John?"

Nothing. Everything. He was supposed to go to his bachelor party tomorrow. How could he enjoy himself when people were suffering?

"I don't know. Something feels familiar about it, but I'm not sure why."

The sheriff nodded, her short hair flipping over her shoulders. "I get that. Let's check with Philly, New York, Baltimore, and see if they've noticed anything. We'll query the township database to see if there are any similar cases over the last six months."

John couldn't take his gaze off sophomore Sophie MacAllister's photo, front and center beside Adam Greenwood, junior. Both were good-looking kids, full of promise.

They could have been him. Before.

"And the toxicology reports aren't back yet from the hospital?"

Curtis flipped through screens on his tablet. "They expect the results tomorrow."

Sheriff Forbes placed a comforting hand on John's arm. "I'll take care of it, John. I know you're busy this weekend."

"I want to help." He winced as a lance of pain shot across his frontal lobe and lodged for one excruciating moment behind his left eye. Ibuprofen. He needed ibuprofen.

"I know. But you can't be all work and no play. Especially not right before your wedding." She elbowed him kindly in the ribs, though since she was over a foot shorter than he was, the blow hit closer to his hip. "Go on. Have fun with your friends. Spend time with Katie. Come back on Monday refreshed and ready to see a new perspective."

She was right; he knew it. It was what his own family had been telling him. He recognized how driven he was and how badly he wanted to succeed at this job. Ever since Sheriff Forbes had talked to his parents, who had subsequently set him on the straight and narrow, he had wanted to be a police officer. To help people. To help kids like he had been, to see them as they were.

Sophie MacAllister had a small spray of freckles beneath her left eye.

"Okay," John said. The pain behind his eye retreated slightly, probably with the idea of relaxation. It had been in short supply lately. "Maybe it will clear my mind and help me remember why this feels so familiar."

"Good plan." She looked over her shoulder at Curtis. "Let's get to work."

Chapter Five

"It's way too early for this." Patrick yawned and tugged the sleeves of his jacket over his hands. It was also way too cold, way too remote, and way too much testosterone for this time of the morning. Granted, it was ten a.m., but still.

He huffed out his breath, watching the little puff of air crystallize in the October chill. Damn global warming. It would be seventy degrees out in a few hours, and then he would have to find a place to put his jacket, which would be a huge pain in the ass.

Maybe some of the whiskey his friends were drinking would put him in a better mood. It certainly seemed to be working for them.

John Flaherty, Deputy Curtis Wyczenczak, their friend Will Forbes, and all four of Katie's Bannion brothers huddled together a few feet away from Patrick, whooping and hitting each other on the back and generally doing an excellent impression of William Wallace and his soldiers in *Braveheart*. Patrick could smell the rank scent of liquor wafting from the group like smoke off a barbecue.

His stomach rumbled. He should have eaten on the way, but he had woken up too late. Restorative sleep had been elusive lately.

He wrapped his arms around his torso in a hug and hopped up and down. Too damn cold.

John and Will beckoned him over, but he just waved an ineffectual hand at them. "I don't want to mess up your whole bro vibe over there," Patrick said.

"You have to join us, man!" Will held up both hands like a gymnast landing a vault at the Olympics. If the gymnast had already had three beers and a shot of whiskey.

"Getting right on that." Patrick flipped him a thumbs-up. A thumbs-up? He really was a train wreck.

"Really, man, a thumbs-up?" John rapped him on the shoulder. "Aren't you excited? I'm getting married!" He shouted the last word like he was a Viking about to charge into battle.

Patrick mustered his own feeble "Woot-woot." He could do this. He had to do this. This was normal. This was good. Christina Blake was in jail, and he was fine. Fucking *fine*, thank you very much.

It was just…why did it have to be paintball?

****

Paintball goddamn hurt. The signal went off to start the game, and it was as though every one of Patrick's friends were some sort of desert commando. In all fairness, John had actually been a commando, albeit a seafaring one. Katie's brothers were all former jocks, now respectably employed, except for the youngest Bannion, who was in his first year at Penn State. They weren't Army Rangers, but they were doing their best interpretation.

It was the Bannion brothers versus Patrick, John, Curtis, and Will. Patrick was not holding up his end of this game.

Patrick exhaled hard and ducked behind a wall, holding his paintball gun in trembling hands. He could have slept in this morning with Anita. He could be wrapped up in her, watching Scandinavian crime TV, and eating bagels, and instead he was freezing his ass off in a bad *Lord of the Flies* parody.

In all fairness, that was also untrue. Anita never slept in on Saturdays. It was the studio's busiest day.

"Hey, man, this is awesome." Will crouched beside him, turned, and shot off a round at one of Katie's brothers, Declan or Damon or David. It was impossible to tell any of the Bannions apart. They might as well be chestnut-haired shapeshifting demons.

Will clapped him on the shoulder, hard enough to bruise.

"Are you okay?" Will's handsome, open face twisted in concern.

"Of course." He just needed to focus on trying not to die. Or be hit by a paintball, though that rather seemed preferable at the moment to having his heart squeezed out of his ass.

"Look, man—"

But then Will unleashed a primal howl, launched himself upright, and fired with the abandon of one who has seen too many Jason Statham movies. Behind their barricade, Patrick could hear war whoops, and the horde of Katie's D-named brothers ululated like Irish banshees.

He mustered his paltry excuse for enthusiasm, but it would not rise. He tried to muster any feeling, really, besides the dull throbbing that was hammering behind his right eye at the moment. But he couldn't. He was out. He was done.

He should be better than this, better for his friend. Even remarkably understanding friends had limits. It was better that Patrick take one, literally, for the team before he had a massive nervous breakdown in the middle of the goddamned Pennsylvania woods.

He stood up, his gun hanging at his side. He would have left it there behind the barricade, but then someone would need to pick it up, and even if he was crushingly bored and languid, he was not one to defer work to someone else.

Above the barricade, the scene was chaos itself. Men—his supposed friends who now resembled extras in an old Hollywood war movie—holding paintball guns, exploding periodically in pockets of color.

Yeah. Patrick was definitely out.

He turned to go, and at that exact moment, Damon or Declan or David saw him, screamed "Huzzah!" and fired their gun. At the same moment, he stepped into a divot in the ground, twisting his ankle. The paintball exploded against his skin, torquing his lower leg, and a searing crack of pain lancinated through his limb.

As he crashed in a mercilessly undignified way, holding his neon-green, paint-splattered leg and groaning, all he could think of was how disappointed in him Anita was going to be.

Fucking goddamn paintball.

****

"Have a great afternoon!" Anita waved, maintaining the smile creasing her face until Lydia Swann disappeared into her neat little, two-seater coupe.

Once she was out of sight, Anita sighed and collapsed against the glass door of her studio. Thank goodness she was closing early this Saturday afternoon. It was always one of the busiest days for the studio, particularly since their viral video had opened up a whole new clientele. By this point in the day, her feet were sobbing for a break, and her back cried out for yoga and a hot bath.

She yawned and threw one of the three deadbolts installed on the door. Better safe than sorry. She had learned that the hard way.

When she removed her dance shoes, she changed into her more comfortable slippers and curled her toes in a stretch. All of the pain and effort was worth it. Students like Lydia were thriving, meeting new friends and partners, and trying new, more challenging choreography.

Just a few more things to do before she could sit on her couch and relax for a couple of hours. Patrick would probably be out all night at the bachelor party, so she had the place to herself. There was a new Katee Roberts calling her name.

She finished sweeping the studio floor and was collecting the trash when there was a knock on the door. Every hair on her body stood immediately to attention. She crouched low, her knuckles turning white on the plastic ties of the trash bag.

"We're closed!" She stayed in her crouch, muscles tensed, heart thumping away like a thoroughbred on the final stretch at Belmont. Why had this not gotten easier over the last few months?

"Ms. Goodman! Open up! I need to speak with you immediately."

Her muscles unclenched almost immediately, the release so intense and sudden that she thought she might pass out. Ugh. If she did faint, then Mrs. DeVeaux would never go away.

Dropping the trash bag and wiping the cold sweat from her hands onto her leggings, she moved swiftly across the studio floor.

She threw back the deadbolt, tightening her facial muscles into what she hoped was a smile. "Good evening, Mrs. DeVeaux. So sorry, the studio is closed this afternoon."

The woman had exchanged the neat little pillbox hat and vintage 60s suit for a heather-gray, belted New Look dress, complete with petticoats. Anita never wore that much flounce except on a Standard gown, but she begrudgingly admired the woman's panache.

Mrs. DeVeaux pursed her tiny mouth into a tight pucker. "Ms. Goodman, I do hope there is no nonsense this evening. I have several very important deliveries, and I need full use of the parking lot."

Anita merged her sigh into the tightness of her smile. Did the woman not own a phone? This could have taken twenty seconds of her time and one less panic attack. Now it was a production.

"Not a problem, Mrs. DeVeaux. It's going to be a quiet evening. As you can see, we're all shuttered for the day." Maybe she bothered Anita because she didn't seem to have anyone else. She had never taken a single vacation in the years Anita had been her neighbor.

Mrs. DeVeaux narrowed her eyes and peeked suspiciously through the doorway. It was incredible that she had nary a crow's foot. Some sort of dermatologic wizardry. "I don't see that boyfriend of yours."

Even though her words cut, her voice softened a bit, as most people's did when they spoke of Patrick.

"No, he's out tonight at a bachelor party." Maybe Mrs. DeVeaux was lonely. Anita had never seen family visit, no big holiday dinners or anything. That might explain some of her troublesome personality.

The antiques dealer sneered, the softness dropping from her voice. "Men and their peccadilloes. You watch that one. No man is perfect." Anita lost any nascent pity for her neighbor.

Mrs. DeVeaux didn't know Patrick, not like Anita did. Patrick would never, ever betray her.

"Sure. Sounds good. I'm just going to watch TV. Thanks for stopping by."

The woman arched her eyebrows and spun on one heel. Anita caught a breathy mutter, "Rotting the brains of the youth today."

At least she had lumped her in with the youth. Anita typically felt like she was of a far older generation, one who was easily overwhelmed by social media or the rapid shifts in technology. Oh well. She had other talents.

She waved goodbye to Mrs. DeVeaux's retreating backside and threw the three deadbolts on the door. Then unlocked and relocked them. She would double check that the security cameras Patrick had installed were recording. They had a funny way of turning off now and then.

She flicked off all the lights and headed for the stairs to her apartment. She was now in dire need of Cozy with a capital C, the kind of cozy that involved fleece, too many throw pillows, and chocolate mousse cake.

Mere steps from her relaxation dreams, her phone buzzed in her hands, and she swiped to accept the call.

"Hello?"

"Hello. Is this Anita Goodman?" A tinny voice

sounded in her ear.

"Yes. Who is this?"

"Ms. Goodman, I'm Dr. Lee at Downingtown General."

Anita's heart clenched. While the doctor spoke, she ran about the studio, gathering keys, shoes, and whatever supplies she or Patrick might need.

There went her Cozy evening.

Chapter Six

Patrick wasn't sure what was worse, the itching, the burning, the aching, or the disappointment that hunched his shoulders.

No, it was definitely the pain. Broken legs hurt like a beast.

He refused Anita's outstretched hand, preferring to wrestle his new crutches out the side of her little hatchback like some macho meathead. He was a meathead. Of all the stupid things he had done in his life, this had to take the cake.

This was going to make Anita resent him. What good was he to her now?

He finally managed to get his crutches out of the car and wrangled them underneath his armpits, only managing to whack himself in the head three times, which wasn't bad for his first attempt.

With a decidedly un-masculine groan, he pulled himself to his unsteady feet. His leg in its cast throbbed as the blood flowed back into it. But he was standing. He had conquered this first challenge.

Anita stood before him, arms crossed over her chest, a bemused grin playing around her mouth.

"What?" He winced at his tone, but she took it in stride. Because she was amazing, and he was a twit.

"Sometimes, you can let people help you." She linked her arm under his shoulder, her touch rocketing through him. He really didn't deserve her.

He hobbled awkwardly beside her as they walked through the studio and to the stairs. She paused at the bottom, chewing on her bottom lip. "Are you going to be okay on the steps?"

Something black and toxic coiled in his stomach. "Of course I'll be fine. I'm not a child."

She arched an eyebrow at him. "Yeah, that tone is very convincing. Would you rather I throw the blankets downstairs and you can sleep on the floor?"

His cheeks flushed, and he hung his head. He mumbled something even he couldn't understand and set to the task of hauling himself up the stairs.

She helped him despite his behavior. Because she was an Amazonian goddess with a neat little ponytail and he was an ogre.

After what felt like seven years, but in all likelihood was less than five minutes, he arrived at the landing, huffing and puffing, every muscle in his body screaming and crying and begging. Athletic, his ass. He was a glorified couch potato.

She held his arm, steadying him as he hobbled on his crutches toward the couch. This was going to take practice. He had never broken anything, not even when he had been slide tackled during a varsity soccer game in high school. He had needed ten stitches, but his bones had held.

All that strength and nothing, wasted. He was a waste, a melodramatic self-loathing pile of old banana peels and coffee grounds.

"I'll get your laptop from your apartment tomorrow morning." Anita cleared a hollow through the mass of throw pillows on her couch and nestled him into it. She put one hand on his broken leg, lifting it onto a pile of pillows. His skin thrilled traitorously despite his black mood. "Did you want something to eat?"

He shook his head. He was wallowing and seventy-five percent of him didn't care. His leg ached and burned and itched. It was beyond maddening.

She shrugged and sashayed into the kitchen, her oversize cardigan hanging around her hips in such a way to accentuate her perfect bottom. Under normal circumstances, he would move behind her, wrap his arms around her waist, and breathe in her scent. She would lean into him, like they belonged together.

But these were not normal circumstances, and he was stuck on the couch in this confusion of throw pillows with absolutely no way to relieve his angst.

Damn paintball.

He looked out the window, searching for anything to distract himself. Same old Lewis. Same old town he had known since he was seven. After his father had ditched them, his mom had moved them here from Nutley. On that street corner just across from where Patrick now sat, sixteen-year-old John Flaherty and Will Forbes had once launched a bag of flaming dog shit out the window of their self-proclaimed "shaggin' wagon." Different times.

He craned his neck, noting that the streetlight right outside the studio's small parking lot wasn't working. Shadows pooled and eddied, causing his stomach to clench and furl. He'd have to check it tomorrow, maybe call the township or take a look himself. Though, of course, that would necessitate descending the stairs, and his leg was currently screaming at him not to do something so completely idiotic.

He had had enough of his own idiocy.

He glanced at Anita. She was busy in the galley kitchen, turning on the kettle and heating up some soup on the small stove. She hummed to herself, her hips moving to her own tune. The pain softened in his leg as he watched her.

He should have asked her to marry him weeks ago. She probably wouldn't even have him now.

Drowning in his own melancholy, he turned his gaze back to the darkened parking lot. His eyes narrowed. This was new.

Two white vans, with their lights off, drove into the parking lot behind the studio, reversed into the spots in front of the antiques store, and idled there.

He cocked his head, his mind whirling. Nothing good ever came from an unmarked white van. He opened the camera app on his phone and tried to zoom in on the front bumpers, but there were none. While Pennsylvania didn't require front license plates, it was possible they had been removed and it was an out-of-state car.

His mind whirred, preferring the mystery to the wallowing.

"What are you looking at?"

Startled, he whipped his head around and noted Anita standing behind him, holding an enamel tray with a bowl of soup and a large glass of iced water. She peered over his shoulder.

"Do you see those vans?" He pointed. "It seems a little weird that they're outside the antiques shop so late on a Saturday night. They pulled in without their lights on. Does she do online orders?"

Anita snorted in response to his question. "Mrs.

DeVeaux?"

"It might explain why they're here, if she has to ship items by a certain time." Though Patrick didn't think that was it at all.

Anita shook her head. "Mrs. DeVeaux stopped by earlier and said she was expecting a delivery. I've never really paid attention to when her deliveries arrive or leave." She pulled up a side table and set the tray upon it.

"Unmarked white vans always seem super suspicious. They're not loading or unloading anything. They're just sitting there."

Anita followed his gaze, then set one of her hands reassuringly on his shoulder and kissed the top of his head. "I'm sure it's all right, Patrick. You've had a terrible day. Eat something. Rest. I'm sure it's nothing."

Patrick begrudgingly turned to his soup, ignoring the siren of pain in his leg. They had thought it was nothing when Christina Blake started stalking them, and she had caused more than her share of trouble. Even small-town Lewis could have its peace and tranquility thrown for a loop.

Chapter Seven

Anita yawned and rolled her ankles before stretching forward in a deep bend. It wasn't often she and Patrick slept apart since they had started dating, and it had not suited her. She missed his warmth and the reassuring scent of him on her sheets.

Patrick sleeping on the couch was untenable, even with his black mood. Not that she didn't totally understand his grumps.

She wandered to the studio door and peered through the glass. The antiques store façade stood as it always did, windows darkened around the edges with faux-smudge, lending a veneer of antiquation. A bulky armoire blocked most of the view, and heavy, velvet curtains made the window trapezoidal. She wondered if it was odd that she had never been inside. Not once in the years since she had opened the studio. Probably not. It wasn't like she could afford anything there.

No sign of the white vans, either.

She stopped snooping on the antiques shop and wrapped her long gray-and-black sweater coat tighter around herself. Maybe if Patrick had his laptop, he would feel better and stop being such an unmitigated ass. She could go pick it up before he woke and surprise him.

****

It didn't take long to walk the few blocks to his

44

seldom-used apartment, and there was no one else up and about at that hour on a cold Sunday. Watching Lewis wake up had long been one of her favorite activities. Maybe next week, when Patrick was feeling better, they could sit outside at Amore, the local coffee shop, and people watch.

She tugged at her ponytail, tightening it against the back of her skull. A broken leg. Laid up for at least six weeks, likely months of rehab afterward. Patrick was so active. He was going to despise all of this forced respite.

She jogged up the stairs to his apartment, her mind focused on rifling through the myriad keys in her hand, trying to find Patrick's. He would have some ridiculously generic one, so she had marked it with a heart in peacock-blue permanent marker. Ah, there it was.

She halted abruptly outside Patrick's door. It hung ajar, a sliver of light from within visible through the crack. Her heart pounded and flip-flopped like a dying fish on the sand.

She threaded the longest and sharpest of her keys into the webbed space between her second and third fingers and pushed the door a little farther open. She kept her back against the wall, the entire room in her line of vision. "Hello?"

A tall woman, with dark brown, curly hair streaked liberally with gray, stepped out from the kitchenette. She had the lines from a decades-long perma-frown worn into her familiar face and blue hospital scrubs. "Where's my son?"

This day was already going well. A flush rising up her neck, Anita holstered her keys in the pocket of her coat. "Ms. O'Leary! What a surprise."

Patrick's mother shifted her gaze about the room, her vision not resting on one thing for any particular amount of time, but clearly disliking everything. "I heard Patrick was hurt. I drove all the way over, and he's not even here. Where are all of his things, all the gifts I sent? Did the two of you move in together?" Only she could make it sound like an accusation. "Of course no one thinks to tell me. I'm only his mother."

Anita's stomach clenched and tightened, an unpleasant sensation climbing her spine like a rabid monkey. Patrick did spend most of his time at the studio or in her own apartment, but it wasn't necessarily his mother's business. It wasn't like Diane reached out to him. "I came by to pick up his laptop. While he's recuperating, we thought it would be easier for him to stay at my place."

"With all those stairs?" Diane O'Leary scoffed, folding the kitchen towel in her hands into a neat, tight little square. "How foolish. The boy needs room to breathe. He doesn't need to be smothered."

Who was smothering? Anita stifled her incipient eye roll. Had the woman missed the two flights and the non-functional elevator at Patrick's building? "I am so sorry. I didn't realize you were coming to his apartment. You can always call me or Patrick." It wasn't like she hadn't had the same phone number since she was seventeen and had given it to Patrick's mom at least four times.

She could see his laptop sitting on his sleek modern desk. So close to freedom from this conversation, and yet so far.

It was none of Diane's business if she and Patrick

moved in together. Would it be so terrible? No, absolutely not. It wouldn't be that different from their current status. She had never made such a commitment before, not that any of her prior relationships had gone as well at six months as the one with Patrick. Maybe it would be nice, to know he would be there no matter what, to meld their lives more closely together.

"What on earth are you doing, just standing there?" Diane rolled her eyes broadly. She scooped up the laptop and charger, shoving them at Anita. She continued muttering under her breath, something that sounded suspiciously like, "Ruining his life with this malarkey."

Anita would laugh at the word "malarkey" if what she had said was not obscenely offensive.

"I should get back to Patrick and make sure he gets something to eat." She tucked the laptop and charger into the beat-up canvas messenger bag sitting by the door. Another five minutes and she could breathe, hopefully far away from this woman.

Diane sighed loudly. "I'll drive you, I suppose."

Anita froze mid-step. "What?" Oh, hell to the no.

Patrick's mother moved beside her. "I want to see my son. I need to clap my eyes on him. He needs me. I am a trained nurse, Anita."

As if she needed reminding. She ignored the needling anxiety that crawled along her skin. This was Patrick's mother. The single mom who had raised him all on her own from the age of seven. Anita could put aside her own pettiness for when Patrick was in crisis.

She pasted a smile on her face. "That would be wonderful. He would love to see you," Anita lied.

****

Patrick groaned and pressed his arm over his eyes to block out the sunrise peeking through the curtains. Everything hurt. His leg, his ass, his neck, his head, his pride. How could anyone sleep when the cast felt like some sort of medieval torture device, burning and needling and itching and aching simultaneously?

He tried rolling onto his side but that was a massive mistake in seventeen hundred ways, so he tried the other side, which was worse.

Great. Just great. And, of course, he had to pee.

He grumbled. The last urge trumped all of the others.

He was a professional athlete and ran two successful businesses, the dance studio and his lifestyle blog, PhillyProud. He could figure out how to hobble through Anita's small one-bedroom apartment to the bathroom.

With a groan of effort, he finagled himself upright, though his back muscles screamed, and the blood flowing down through his injured leg made it burn like the fire of a thousand hells. He breathed through the pain for a few moments. A couple feet to the bathroom. He could pee and find the ibuprofen bottle. Maybe even collect the crutches from the galley kitchen.

He yanked himself to a standing position, cursing his injury like it was the Patriots playing his beloved Eagles. It *was* Sunday. Maybe the Eagles were playing. That thought buoyed him the smallest amount, enough to get him hopping from the couch to the opposite wall. He could cuddle on the couch with Anita, order pizza, maybe invite their friends. Katie, in particular, was a huge football fan, and had been known to overturn many a bowl of corn chips in her fervor.

That would make him feel better.

He managed to make it into the bathroom and onto the toilet, where he slumped like a jellyfish, the invertebrate with which he currently most identified. At least this was one indignity done, and he hadn't had to rely on Anita.

She would never look at him the same after this. Not only had he broken his leg barely two weeks before John and Katie's wedding, but it also put him out of the running for many of the winter competitions he and Anita had been planning.

He stood to wash his hands, but something was off. Either the floor was slippery or his balance was off because of the gigantic vise squeezing his leg, or maybe it was just the thought of disappointing Anita.

Whatever the cause, his good foot slipped out from underneath him, and he crashed ass-backward on the fake-tile floor.

He closed his eyes and succumbed to it, letting himself wallow. He stretched out on the bathroom floor and indulged in a good old-fashioned, primal moan.

"Do you see this?" a very familiar and unwelcome voice chastised. His heart clenched and spine tensed anew. This was not what he needed right now. Maybe the floor would melt away and he could be sucked into an alternate dimension. "This is why he should not be here with you, Anita. You have no medical training."

No luck on the alternate dimension, then.

"So sorry, Diane. He was sleeping when I left."

Maybe if he kept his eyes closed, all of this would turn out to be nothing but a terrible, weird, embarrassing dream. Like the ones he had in high school where suddenly he was playing soccer naked during a ballroom dance competition. Or when he would wake up in a tiny closet hidden in the wall.

Nope, no such luck. He could hear his mother tsking away in Anita's living room. Doubtless she was fidgeting with throw pillows or re-organizing Anita's romance novels, neither of which his beloved girlfriend would appreciate.

If he kept his eyes closed, he could lie here on this fake tile floor forever and pretend this entire thing never happened. But no. No, that was not for the likes of Patrick O'Leary.

Footsteps tap tapped on the bathroom floor, the unmistakable sound of hospital clogs.

He sighed and opened his eyes. Showtime.

Patrick pushed himself onto his elbows and tried to smile at the two women hovering over him like empathetic vultures. "Hi, Mom. Hi, Anita."

Anita glowered behind his mother, Diane. The latter looked as she always did, her once-pretty face pinched like she was sucking on hard candies. But that was unkind. She was his mom. He should muster some sort of enthusiasm for seeing her.

His mom clucked and ran her hands all over him, assessing just like when he was nine and had taken a soccer ball to the head. He did his best not to cringe as her fingers brushed his skin. "You're bruised all over!" She flipped a murderous glare at Anita, so Patrick redirected her attention. He knew well what his mom thought of Anita, though heaven help him if he understood why.

"It's fine, Mom. I played paintball yesterday. That's where I got the bruises."

She clucked again, the sound so reminiscent of his

childhood that it made him think of all the things he normally repressed for the sake of his own sanity. Any more surprises this weekend and he was going to need a short-term psychiatric hold.

"He needs ice." His mom dropped her hands from him abruptly and went toward the kitchen. "I doubt you'll have frozen peas, but they really would be best."

"Of course I have peas, Diane." Anita crouched beside him and put her mouth toward his ear. For the first time all morning, he relaxed infinitesimally. This felt normal, Anita beside him, playful and conspiratorial. "Is there some medical study that proves that frozen peas are the best? Who would pay for such ridiculous research?" She kept her voice soft, meant just for him.

All the hurt and ache eased within his body as he breathed in her scent. "Just don't try frozen pearl onions. They've been shown to cause intense frostbite."

It was definitely not his best one-liner, but the hard edges of her mouth curled, and she looked at him, really looked at him, for the first time in twenty-four hours. This was what he needed. This was everything he needed.

"Let's get you up and back to the couch," Anita said.

She helped him to his feet, then steadied him against the wall while she went and fetched his crutches from the kitchen. His mom rifled through the tiny freezer, clucking disapprovingly at every bag of frozen vegetables, fruits, and dumplings. How anyone could find such food offensive, he would never know, but his mom was nothing if not particular.

He ignored it. He focused instead on the pressure

of Anita's steadying hand on his arm, the familiar lines of her body beside him. Using her as his guide, he maneuvered back to the couch and plopped into the nest of throw pillows and the Patrick-shaped hollow where he had slept the night before.

His mother bustled toward him, wrapping a kitchen towel around a freezer bag. "I suppose you did have peas. These will defrost quickly, though. I'll have to buy some more. Though it really would be easier if Patrick would just come home with me."

"No." The word escaped his mouth faster than he had intended, and a flush curled up his neck. His mother's hazel eyes narrowed and hardened. The nine-year-old Patrick inside of him flinched, but he was an adult now. He could make his own decisions, even if they weren't always the greatest ones. "Sorry, Mom. I would love it, really I would. It's just…that I'm already set up here, and I don't need much. It's only a broken leg. I can handle it."

Anita moved away, her lovely lips pressed in contemplation. What was going on in her mind?

His mom knelt beside him, suddenly solicitous, her manner earnest. Her bedside manipulation manner. "Honey, you know I would take off a whole day to take care of you. It would be hard, of course. You know how understaffed the hospital is, especially with the rise in ODs we have been seeing. My goodness, you would not believe the incompetence I have to deal with every day. They almost re-assigned me to the maternity ward, can you imagine? As if I could leave my floor. But I would stay with you, if you think I need to."

He patted her hand and tried to smile. "Really, Mom. I'll be fine here. I don't need anything."

She stood abruptly and twisted toward Anita. "That remains to be seen. I'll bring some of my famous vegetarian lasagna for dinner."

Anita guffawed and hid it behind a cough, busying herself in the kitchen with the French press. "Thanks, Diane."

Fabulous. Her famously inedible vegetarian lasagna. Patrick smiled weakly. "That would be great. Thanks, Mom. I'll be up and back to normal in no time."

She bent and pressed a thin kiss to his forehead. "See that you do. Bye, sweetie." She straightened and kept her back to Anita. "Goodbye, Anita."

"Bye, Ms. O'Leary."

The tension in the apartment dissolved once his mom slammed the door.

Anita hummed, and he could smell the life-giving aroma of his favorite drink. "Why are you making coffee? You don't drink it anymore."

She shrugged and poured hot water over her green tea bag. "But you do."

She was the best thing in the entire world, and he was a neurotic suckerfish. "I love you, Anita."

She rolled her eyes, but he could tell her smile was now finally genuine. "I love you, too, you idiot."

Patrick relaxed into his throw pillow cushion. Maybe everything wouldn't be so bad after all.

Chapter Eight

"Well done tonight, Tabitha." Anita smiled as the statuesque woman wrapped a luxurious cashmere coat around herself.

"Thanks for the lesson." Tabitha's boyfriend and dance partner, Dennis, linked their fingers together.

"No problem." She went to the broom closet while they collected their belongings. Always time for a quick sweep.

Tabitha's phone chimed loudly, and the woman's face looked pinched, which was not a typical expression for her.

"Is everything all right?" Anita asked.

"Yes." Tabitha slipped the phone into her bright-red leather tote bag. "I signed up for news notifications, about the...thing?" Her voice halted, but Dennis squeezed her hand, and when she spoke again, she sounded more resolved. "I guess there's a story."

"Oh." Ice trickled down Anita's spine. "Do you mean about those kids? The ones who got sick at the creek? Do they know if it was something in the water?"

"No." Tabitha sighed, clicking through the link on her phone. "Drugs. It looks like they overdosed, but the police aren't disclosing what caused it."

Dennis's pale face whitened even more. "I heard from a friend at the hospital that there have been a lot of fentanyl and PCP overdoses lately."

"That's awful." Anita leaned the broom against the check-in desk. She'd been avoiding the news without fully registering that she was avoiding it. "I hope they're okay."

"It is awful." Tabitha exchanged a glance with Dennis. "We should go. We have a dinner reservation."

"Of course. Have a great night." She walked them to the door and stood, waving, as Dennis held the door open for his girlfriend.

Anita smiled, a light and fuzzy emotion working itself through her. There was something heartwarming in seeing other people fall in love. She hadn't realized it until she and Patrick had finally gotten together, but now she wanted everyone to feel like she did. Everyone should have what she had. A person. A best friend.

And at the same time, she should mind her own business. She was a professional dancer, after all. People did not come to her for her matchmaking services. Though it was far more pleasant to think about love than drug overdoses.

The sight of Mrs. DeVeaux's antique store through the studio window caught her gaze. The ancient maple to the right of the front entrance had dropped its leaves already, and its bare branches curled menacingly over the building. It looked more like the entrance to a haunted house, not that Mrs. DeVeaux would or had ever decorated for Halloween.

Which reminded her. No Halloween party at the studio this year as it would conflict with John and Katie's wedding. But that didn't mean she couldn't set up a few pumpkins and whatnots. Her clients liked to mark the seasons at the studio.

She had just turned away from the window when

three loud, sharp knocks rattled the glass of the door. She clenched her hand over her heart to still its runaway-train thrumming.

She focused on her *ujjayi* breathing, hard gained after several hundred hours of yoga, and turned back to the door, tightening her ponytail. How had she not seen who it was? She had let herself get distracted, damn it. She should know better by now.

At least the tall man in the dark suit was one hundred percent not Christina Blake.

She clung to her paranoia, though. It was not the century for a traveling salesman.

"Can I help you?" She opened the door no more than two inches, keeping her distance.

He smiled, a rakish sort of grin that was accentuated by the thin, almost artistic lines of the facial hair around his mouth. His eyes were a light gray color, like the sky on a wintry morning. A chill ran up Anita's spine, but she couldn't tell if it was the gust of October wind or the stranger's presence.

"Hi. Is this Lewis Dancesport?" His voice was deep, lightly accented but not from Pennsylvania. More southern U.S.

"Yes. But we're closed for the weekend." Anita kept the door ajar, her spine tensed and ready.

"Shit." He chuckled, the lines of his face creasing in a geometric sort of way. "Just my luck. I hit traffic on Route 30, so I got here later than I anticipated. Do you have a card or something?"

"We're a dance studio. All of our information is online." At least it was now that Patrick had revamped and upgraded her website. Her previous one might as well have boasted stick figure drawings.

He placed his hands in his pockets, his stance intentionally non-threatening, every gesture seeming practiced to reassure her. She had trained herself not to succumb to such obvious chicanery. "I'm so sorry to inconvenience you, Miss—"

She hesitated. Just because Christina Blake had been a bad apple, that did not mean that everyone was up to no good. He was asking about the studio. Hopefully this was just a business thing. "Goodman. Anita Goodman. I'm the owner."

His posture relaxed. "I'm Steve. Steve Barnes. I'm a host over at Home Squared? The home shopping channel? We're based over in Downingtown."

What on earth was she supposed to say to that? She pulled the cuffs of her sweater over her hands. "Do you need something?"

"I really am sorry to bother you. I heard this was the best place around for dance lessons. I've been meaning to try it for a long time, but I only just gathered up my courage today."

"We're closing. Please check us out on the internet, give us a call or email, and we can discuss lesson times." The weight of her phone in her pocket comforted her. A few quick taps and she could call 911 or Patrick.

He nodded, his shock of ash-and-soot-streaked hair bobbing with the movement. "I get it. Really, I do. I'm just so busy during the week, and my schedule is so erratic. Sometimes I'm on nights, sometimes days. I really, really want to learn, and I had some time today. Is there really no chance of an intro? I'll pay extra for the inconvenience."

That should not be an enticement. She and Patrick

had spent the past six months trying to coach one another into being less polite. But she would be lying if she didn't need the extra money. With Patrick laid up, they wouldn't be able to swing the winter competition circuit, so cash flow would be tighter than she would like. And if this guy wouldn't even look at the website for the pricing information, how was that her fault? Maybe she could upcharge.

"Let me tell my boyfriend. He was expecting me." She closed the door in Steve Barnes's surprised face and quickly texted Patrick. At least he would know to send out a search party if she didn't come upstairs within the hour. Or an ambulance if this guy tried anything. Years of kickboxing practice had its benefits.

She tightened her ponytail again and opened the door, more widely this time. "Come in, Mr. Barnes. Did you bring an extra pair of shoes? Otherwise, I can offer you a rental pair."

****

Half an hour into the lesson, she regretted less adding on the last-minute lesson. Steve was charming, polite, kept his hands to himself, and listened well. Still, thirty minutes was about all the politeness she could muster tonight.

"Waltz is about the rise and fall." Anita turned on the practice music and danced around the room by herself, demonstrating the proper technique. "See? It comes from the core, and the dance flows from that. We will focus for now on the footwork, leading with the heel, sliding back the toe, etc. Foundation matters."

She moved to the check-in desk and picked up a printout of exercises, practice songs, and inspirational videos that she always gave to new students.

"Here." She handed it to Steve. He had removed his tailored pea coat and rolled up the sleeves of his white Oxford shirt.

He wore an expression of pleasant fatigue. "Thank you so much, Ms. Goodman. This was a great lesson. I had no idea it was so much fun."

"Well, you did great. Would you like to schedule another lesson?"

He smiled, a little shy, and kept his gaze on the desk before raising it quickly to her. Her hackles rose. "Maybe we could discuss it over a drink? Anywhere you recommend?"

Anita's professional smiled faded. "That will be one hundred and twenty dollars for the after-hours lesson, and twenty for the shoe rental. All future ones are seventy-five per hour. How would you prefer to pay?" She had overcharged him for the shoe rental. Under typical circumstances with less predatory clients, she lent them for free.

He didn't drop the sly smirk as he took out his credit card and handed it over to her. She rang him up with brutal, cold efficiency.

He watched her movements, too closely. The asshole.

She handed him back the credit card, and he languidly replaced it in his wallet.

Irritation prickled along her scalp. This was a waste of time. Patrick needed her.

Steve leered at her, but she stood up straighter and pasted on a banal expression.

"Mr. Barnes, you forgot the shoes." She pointed at his borrowed dance shoes.

"Of course." He slipped them off and as she leaned

down to pick them up, he leaned down at the same moment and the nearness of him was too much, too soon. His face was within inches of hers.

She jumped backward, holding the borrowed dance shoes to her chest. "Good evening, Mr. Barnes."

He straightened slowly, the move deliberate and calculated. "Thank you, Anita."

The minute he was out the door, she rushed over and threw all three deadbolts, then unlatched them and locked the door again.

She needed to talk to Patrick.

****

Patrick had perused every book in the apartment, and though work awaited him on his laptop, nothing quite captured his attention lately like the goings-on outside the window.

Tonight was no exception. He saw New Guy walking to his black luxury sedan, the exterior incongruously shiny in the autumn half-light. How did someone get their car that shiny? It reeked of newness.

The guy, too, fit his vehicle. Shiny and too-polished, too good-looking for quiet little Lewis, confidence practically shining out of his tailored ass.

A kernel of something petty and dark twisted deep in Patrick's gut. Was this the kind of guy Anita should be with? He even looked like an amalgamation of her ex-boyfriends.

Maybe Patrick should buy one of those telephoto lenses. He would be able to see better through this second-story window.

The door to the studio rattled open, and Anita sauntered in, pulling on her ponytail. She flopped beside him on the couch, drowning him with her sweet floral scent. "I am exhausted. Want to order tacos?"

"Tacos? Sure. Yeah. Whatever you want."

She kissed him lightly on the cheek, picked up her phone, and went into the kitchen to order. "Grilled chicken citrus salad, right?"

Boring. That's what Patrick was, with his grilled white meat salads. Shiny Guy probably had carne asada and talked all night about how "Oaxaca is the center of the Mexican food world." He probably drank prickly pear margaritas and compared them to the luxury tequila tasting he'd attended in Baja. He probably—

Patrick became acutely aware that Anita was staring at him, her long fingers poised over her phone, one eyebrow arched in apparent concern.

"Are you okay?" she asked.

"Of course." He pushed aside the tiny black kernel in his stomach. Shiny Guy wasn't here, was he? Patrick was. She had chosen Patrick. Even if it was just for the time being. "Everything is fine."

"Riiiiiight." She glanced back at her phone and re-opened the delivery app. "So chicken salad?"

"Surprise me."

"Surprise you? Patrick, you hate food surprises. That time at the deli when they switched the brand of yellow mustard they used? You had a conniption. We had to drive to Doylestown to buy the brand you liked so you could put it on your sandwich."

She had one hand on her hip. Exasperated. That's how she looked. Exasperated with him being all broken and predictable. He glanced out the window again, but Shiny Guy had driven his obnoxiously posh car away.

"I can feel like switching things up."

"Okay." There was a definite smirk lurking behind

her statement. He could almost hear the chances of her accepting his marriage proposal fluttering away on tiny sad wings. "What would you like then? Do you want to see the menu?"

He could picture the grilled chicken citrus salad, the little mandarin slices and the chili-lime vinaigrette, the rich avocado that balanced out all the tang. He swallowed and turned to Anita. "Something spicy. With meat. A lot of meat."

She rolled her eyes and said absolutely nothing.

****

He woke later that night, ruing the carne asada *al diablo* he had eaten. His stomach burned and roiled, as irritating as the incessant throbbing of his broken leg. He messed everything up. Always. He couldn't even manage to get a taco order right.

At least he had left his crutches beside the couch this time. Anita had offered him his usual spot on the bed, but it was too difficult to scale the mattress. So here he was. Burning up from the inside out in this hell of rainbow-colored throw pillows.

Using one crutch under his arm, he heaved himself onto his good foot. He would just get some water and antacids. Five, ten minutes, and then he would be good as new and maybe get a decent night's sleep.

He had half-filled the glass when lights curved into the apartment through the open curtain. Blinking rapidly in the sudden brightness, he checked the wall clock above the stove. Two thirty in the morning? Who would be out in the parking lot at two thirty in the morning?

Wincing as he accidentally put too much weight on his injured leg, he hobbled to the edge of the galley kitchen to peer out the window. His perspective from that angle wasn't the best, but at least he was shielded somewhat.

He could just make out the outline of a vehicle, large enough to be a van, but now that the lights were off, he couldn't see more detail. It was parked in front of the antiques store. Tomorrow, he would call the city to have that damned broken streetlight fixed. It was messing with his snooping.

A soft, warm arm encircled his middle. He leapt into the air as high as his crutch would allow.

Anita arched her eyebrow. "What are you doing?"

"Shhh!" He held up his finger in front of his mouth, and she rolled her eyes. "Be quiet. I think those vans are back."

Anita peered out the window, then back at him, a skeptical, concerned look on her face. "So Mrs. DeVeaux has another delivery. People get deliveries all the time."

"Not at two thirty in the morning. Don't you think it's odd?"

She pursed her lips together, silently assessing. His hand was going numb, he clutched the handle of his crutch so tightly.

"I suppose so. I don't know anything about antiques stores. Maybe they have to take deliveries at all hours, if they're coming from a ways away. Or shipments. You had asked about shipping stuff."

"You've never seen this kind of thing before? You've lived here for years."

"No, but I'm never in my living room at two thirty in the morning, either." She bit her bottom lip, the small flesh swelling under the pressure. Patrick suddenly realized he was holding his breath. "We should go to bed."

"Anita—"

She patted his arm and smiled, reassuring. "It's okay. I'll call Mrs. DeVeaux tomorrow and make sure she's all right. Don't worry."

"I just think it's all weird."

"It isn't the usual, but things are always changing. We'll figure it out." She leaned in and kissed his cheek. "Come to bed. The lights won't bother you in the other room."

He nodded but the reflux in his stomach would not subside. He popped open the tube of antacids he had found and slipped one into his mouth.

Anita knelt on the couch and pulled the curtains shut. But Patrick could not be entirely, completely, one hundred percent certain that there hadn't been a silhouette in the parking lot, watching them through the window.

Chapter Nine

Patrick concentrated as hard as he could, his brow furrowed so deep he could feel the valley of skin boring into his forehead. "Almost there." He folded another teensy piece of the fragile paper, hope welling inside of him. This one was going to work. This one was—

He ripped the tiny origami boat in two. Sighing loudly, he tossed it into the growing pile of rejects beside him.

"Patrick, should I regret I asked you to help me make these wedding favors?" John Flaherty completed yet another perfect origami boat with tight perfect creases and added it to his overflowing basket.

Patrick sighed and took a new sheet. Maybe paper folding was some skill John had picked up in the Navy, which was why his boats were so flawless. Or maybe Patrick was just shit at this, like he was shit at everything lately.

"Is this something people really do? Give out handicrafts as wedding favors?" This next one was going to be better. He could feel it.

John chuckled, his laugh deep and resonant. "Katie saw these in a wedding magazine and thought it would be perfect since she's doing a whole ship-to-shore theme. She was all, 'It will be so easy and such a good bonding experience with your groomsmen.' " He rolled his deep brown eyes, but there was a glimmer of contentment behind them that Patrick wished he could have. "Be grateful I talked her out of the personalized handwritten messages in bottles."

Patrick groaned and inspected his latest handiwork. Not an entire train wreck. Serviceable, even. He added it with a soupçon of pride to the other two in his basket. "Do you remember Marty Stevens's wedding? Those little containers of coffee beans they brought back from their first trip together to Costa Rica?"

John narrowed his eyes. "You mean, illegally transported from Costa Rica."

"It isn't like they smuggled the coffee beans. They bought them, right? It's not illegal to bring in coffee."

The massive deputy leaned forward, his posture conspiratorial. "It's illegal if you're hiding pot in the bags of coffee beans."

Patrick's cheeks flushed. He was an idiot. No wonder Marty Stevens always looked like he had allergies. He wasn't naïve, he just didn't like prying into other people's business. "People do that?"

John shrugged. "Katie's brother, Declan? He works customs at the airport. He says you would not believe the stuff people try to hide. And those are just the ones who get caught. You're on social media. Don't you follow the TSA feed? It's *wild*."

He didn't, but he added it to his mental to-do list in case he never wanted to fly again. "That's crazy. Who would have thought you could hide drugs in coffee beans?"

John added another perfect origami boat to his overflowing basket. "Really, Patrick? You can hide drugs anywhere. Furniture, false shoe bottoms, taxidermy animals, emptied candy boxes. You have to hand it to people. They're creative when they're breaking the law."

Patrick shifted in his seat to try and relieve the ache in his leg. Waiting six hours between doses of ibuprofen seemed like torture at times. There was always the tiny bottle of hydrocodone his orthopedist had prescribed, but Patrick wouldn't touch it. He never touched anything stronger than whiskey. He liked his faculties about him.

He focused instead on the minute details of folding the paper boats. The next one was going surprisingly well. He would probably mess it up by the end.

"How's the investigation?" Patrick asked, sipping his coffee so he could crack his aching knuckles.

John sighed. "Suffice it to say, it completely sucks. I can't really say more." John arched an eyebrow at him. "These boats aren't going to fold themselves, Groomsman Extraordinaire."

Patrick grunted and set to the task before him. A true crime podcast played in the background, but it was one he'd heard already. It didn't quite offer enough distraction.

"So, how are things with Anita?" John raised both his eyebrows. "Does helping with all my wedding stuff make you think about anything?"

Damn it, another one ripped.

In his mind, he visualized the little black ring box in one of the two drawers he had at Anita's apartment. He shouldn't have left it there. What if she found it? No, Anita would never snoop. But what if someone broke into the house? Had he remembered to buy insurance for the diamond?

Blackness crept into the edges of his vision, but he

deepened his breath and focused on the task at hand. Folding origami boats out of brightly-colored squares of paper. It was supposed to be soothing, after all.

Baloney.

"Patrick?"

He looked up, saw the concern in John's face, the curious narrowing of his dark brown eyes. How much time had he lost? "Sorry. Everything's going great."

John did not relax back into his chair. He maintained his watchful posture. "Okay. Is she looking forward to the wedding?"

"Yeah, of course." He focused on the lines he created in the paper, the symmetry of them. It was quite pretty when he wasn't tearing everything to shreds.

"How's the leg?"

As if in answer, a lightning bolt shattered through his leg. Patrick bit his tongue to hold back the scream. "It's fine," he said through clenched teeth. The spasm gradually subsided. "I have an appointment with the doctor this Friday. Hopefully I'll be up and back to my old self in no time."

John made some noncommittal noise, and they both set to the task Patrick was fairly certain awaited him in the fifth circle of hell.

He managed two more, though both paled in comparison to John's.

"You know," John said softly, placing a delicate, navy-blue-and-white-striped boat into his basket. "Anita loves you no matter what your insecurities are."

All the air in the room went out of it. Patrick rubbed at the center of his chest, whether to stimulate his circulation or push all the despair back in, he wasn't sure.

He swallowed and picked up another piece of origami paper. He was fine. Absolutely fine. Nothing to see here. Nothing wrong. Nope. "Yeah, you're right. I know you're right."

****

Anita clapped. "Lovely, Nina. You've really improved your timing in that fleckerl."

Her associate dance instructor Rodrigo spun Nina Rabinova out, and she made an exaggerated curtsy. Today she wore a scarlet leotard with fire-orange marabou dripping from the sleeves. "*Spasibo*, Anita." Nina pinched Rodrigo's cheek when she straightened. "My Rodrigo is such a good teacher. But when is Patrick returning? He always gives me the best compliments."

Rodrigo, Anita's only other instructor at the moment, rolled his eyes good-naturedly. He had often voiced how grateful he was to have Patrick back in the studio, since it took some of the pressure off him. Anita's ex Mikhail had never been interested in pulling his weight.

"Hopefully soon." If he could get his head out of his ass. Anita sipped the green tea in her Rumba Walk Away mug and flipped idly through the *Lewis Gazette*, a weekly local news publication. This week's edition was all about the high school kids and why it seemed to be taking the police so long to figure out what had happened to them.

She closed the newspaper with an unsatisfactory shushing sound.

Nina draped herself into the folding chairs and removed her bejeweled practice shoes. "How is he doing, Anita? Dear Patrick. Not being able to dance or run must be such a trial for a man such as he."

"He's all right. You know Patrick. He'll bounce back in no time."

Rodrigo flicked his gaze toward her and kept his voice low. "What about the winter comps?"

Something leaden twisted deep inside her gut, but she sipped her tea instead of frowning. "We'll postpone. It should be okay. We have more of a rainy-day fund after this past summer than we had last year. We'll still attend with the students."

Rodrigo arched one perfectly-maintained eyebrow. "Is that enough? It will affect your standings for next year, not to mention the financial hit."

As if she needed the reminder. "It will be fine. We can either rent out the small studio space or Patrick suggested I start doing online tutorial videos. He says there's a huge market for things like that."

"Tutorials?" Nina sashayed over to them. She had exchanged her enormous flouncy yellow tulle skirt for a pair of neon-green and blue tweed bell trousers. "Anita, darling. That would be fantastic." She batted her three-inch-long, neon-blue eyelashes. "Allow me to offer my service for makeup tutorials? I am very good, as you can see."

Rodrigo tilted his head and nodded slightly at Anita. "She has a point."

Who was she to turn down free help? Her experience making videos was limited to grainy images that reeked of *The Blair Witch Project.* Professional help would be fabulous. "That would be fantastic, Nina. Thanks. Comp makeup tutorials, all you."

The older woman beamed, literally beamed, which reversed her aging process by about twenty years. She scooped up her vintage trench with the thick mink collar and flounced out the door.

Rodrigo sat down and removed his dance shoes. "That was good of you, to include her."

Anita picked up the broom and pushed it across the studio floor. "It's one less thing for me to do. Plus, she'll do a fantastic job."

Rodrigo yawned and slipped on his loafers. "I can always dance with you, if you need."

"No, thanks." She had tried it once, and the pair of them just didn't click. The moves worked, but there hadn't been any pizzazz. "Everything will be all right."

He shrugged and waved. "I'm out for a coffee at Amore. Be back soon."

She didn't stop her sweeping.

A few minutes later, the bell over the door clanged again. "Rodrigo? I thought your next lesson didn't start for another hour."

"I am not here for lessons, Ms. Goodman."

Anita turned slowly, already etching the smile across her face. "Mrs. DeVeaux. What a pleasure."

Today, the antiquarian wore a tailored jacket of emerald-green crushed velvet and high-waisted, light-gray trousers. Wasn't that color green once associated with arsenic poisoning? Patrick had definitely held her hostage on a road trip once and forced her to listen to a podcast about it.

The woman sneered. "Is there a reason you and your paramour cannot mind your own business?"

Was there a reason her neighbor couldn't learn to use a phone? Maybe crossing the parking lot was her daily exercise. "Is something bothering you, Mrs. DeVeaux? As I promised, we kept the parking spaces open as you had requested." Shit, she had meant to call her and ask about the deliveries. "By the way, we saw some vans outside your shop early in the morning. Is everything all right?" She did her best to feign sincerity.

For a flash of an instant, Mrs. DeVeaux paled beneath her expertly-applied contouring. When she spoke, she overenunciated each word. "Mind your business, and I'll mind mine. Good day."

She spared Anita the trouble of reply by storming out and slamming the door behind her. The bells rattled fervently.

Well, that was weird. Mrs. DeVeaux realized she had gotten deliveries at two thirty in the morning, didn't she?

Anita sighed deeply. It really was none of her business.

If ever there were a time when a girl needed some Journey, this was it.

Chapter Ten

Neither hell nor high water could keep Patrick from his class with his high school ballroom dance students. Though his leg tried. It burned like the fiery chill of a thousand-year frost, and after several days of relative immobility, the hips and quads controlling his lower leg might as well have been made of stone.

He was still going to make it to the class.

Patrick pushed open the heavy doors of the Lewis High gym with his shoulder blades and stumbled through on his crutches. At least he had a spare bag of supplies in his friend Will's office. He couldn't haul his usual gear today.

As if thinking about him summoned the man himself, Will Forbes strode out of his office, humming a pop song. There were definite benefits to being the gym teacher. "Hey, Patrick! How's the leg? I wasn't sure you'd be in today."

"I couldn't leave the kids hanging just because I'm shit at paintball." Patrick winced and made his way to the bleachers, which suddenly seemed ten thousand miles away.

He felt a hand on his shoulder and turned. Will held out a folding chair, like the most princely offering of all time. "Stop making yourself miserable. Have a seat. I'll bring over the remote for the stereo system."

For the briefest of moments, Patrick debated

refusing, debated pushing himself onward and thrusting aside the pain and making it work. Then he wobbled on his crutches, decided for once to stifle all the ingrained patriarchal bullshit, and rested his tired ass on the cold metal of the folding chair.

"Thanks, Will."

"No problem." Will stood to his full six-foot-plus height and raked his hands through his shock of blond hair. "Mind if I stick around for your class? I don't necessarily see these kids a lot otherwise. I like making sure everyone is okay."

Patrick glanced up at him. Will's benignly schooled jaw seemed tinged with shadow, and the man had never been great at growing facial hair. "Everything all right, Will?"

Without looking at him, Will opened his mouth to speak, but he was interrupted by the obnoxious clanging of the school bell.

"Don't worry about it." Will disappeared back into his office.

Patrick watched him stalk away, unable to fathom why his shoulders were set so tightly. He didn't have a lot of time to ponder, as the gym rapidly filled with his students.

Lucy Knight and Daniel Riley sauntered in first, each resolutely not looking at the other. Lucy's river of straight black hair was up in a high ponytail, and she stood half a foot shorter than Daniel, who would never consent to be called Danny.

He didn't quite get the relationship, but who was he to judge? He had found the love of his life in a high school ballroom club, but that didn't mean everyone had the same experiences.

"Hi, Mr. O'Leary!" Lucy called, her voice resounding in the empty gym. "How are you feeling?"

"I'm doing fine, thanks."

Lucy and Daniel settled themselves on the bleachers, as far apart as humanly possible, and set to changing their dance shoes. Daniel sent her looks that would frost hell, but she didn't seem to care. Whoa. Things had changed since last week.

The sounds of the other teens entering the gym distracted him from his thoughts. He pasted a smile on his face and raised a hand in greeting, mentally checking off his list. Jess, Tim, Sophie P., Sarah with an H, Sara, Callum, Jack...

Sophie M.

He checked the clock above the basketball hoop. Five minutes into class, and everyone should be there. He gestured to the petite brunette with the commanding flare in her large brown eyes. "Hey, Jess? Where's Sophie M?"

Jess, the ballroom dance team captain and a member of Lewis High School's pep squad, paled considerably, and she wrapped her arms over her chest. If he wasn't mistaken, those were tears glistening. "Umm."

Will cleared his throat beside Patrick, and he handed him the stereo remote. "You don't know? I figured you had heard. Sophie MacAllister is in the hospital."

"What?" A thundering herd of buffalo rampaged through his brain, down his spine, and across his chest. He had the niggling sensation he was missing something. "What happened?"

Will extended his lips in a facsimile of a smile, but

it didn't reach his eyes. "It's not good. She was one of the kids who was hospitalized after that party at Lewis Creek."

Patrick looked out over the teenagers sprawling on the bleachers. They changed into their dance shoes, brushed their soles, laughed, talked, joked, showed one another photos. But even Patrick in all his self-absorption could tell that something was off. There was a brittleness in the air, like the onset of a lightning storm on a frigid beach. He should pay more attention to the news and less to his own minor problems. "John said he can't talk about it. Do you know anything?"

Will sniffed and looked at his hands. He sat rigid in his chair. "It's all terrible. We aren't sure what it is or where they're getting it from, since the kids involved so far haven't been able to tell us."

An icy thrill ran through his body, numbing his leg. "They're keeping it quiet?"

Will looked directly at him, the expression in his eyes world-weary and pained. "None of them can talk right now. They're still in intensive care."

The air abruptly left the gymnasium, and Patrick's chest tightened and seized. He pictured Sophie MacAllister, her icy blue eyes twinkling under the thick swaths of mascara that Anita had applied, cha cha-ing to Filly Bee. He couldn't quite conjure the image of the same girl, faded and pale, hooked up to tubes.

Patrick should watch the news more often. He wasn't sure how he had missed this connection. What else had he missed?

"None of the other kids have said anything, either." Will put a hand on his shoulder. "I know. It sucks."

Something his mom had said stuck in his head. "I

heard there have been more ODs lately. Is it like a designer drug?" Sophie hadn't seemed the type, but what did Patrick know? Everyone seemed to dabble in something nowadays, though his experimentation went the route of trying every holiday coffee concoction at Amore.

His friend sighed and ran his hands through his hair again. "Probably. Their health history is private, of course, but the public health department has been talking to the principal. And my mom's told me to be on the lookout for certain things."

Will's mother, Sheriff Forbes, was a Lewis legend. "You're a deputy by default?"

"Something like that. She figures I have an in, even though the principal doesn't really want me involved. Politics."

Thoughts and facts swirled through Patrick's mind, but he couldn't latch onto anything, couldn't tie anything down exactly where it needed to go.

His chest burned, and when he gazed across the gym toward the bleachers, he noted Lucy, staring intently at him, her lips pressed together. Maybe she had been friends with Sophie.

"Mr. O'Leary?" Jess had returned to her normal cheerful, perky self. "Is everything all right?"

Right. Teaching. He was supposed to be teaching.

"Let's get started and warm up." He hit the button on the stereo remote and queued his teaching playlist. Nothing like a waltz to limber everyone, and classic Strauss was the order of the day.

He would have to remember to talk to Anita about all this later.

Chapter Eleven

Patrick hobbled out of the backseat of Anita's little hatchback. At least he was finally learning to use the crutches, and the throbbing in his broken leg had receded to mosquito-level annoyance. He could do this.

"Poor Patrick!" Anita's mother Marina rushed to the car and took one of his crutches so he could maneuver the cast out. "You must be in so much pain!"

"I'm all right." He gritted his teeth as he spun slowly and took the crutch from her. "It's not as bad as it looks."

Anita wrapped an arm around his waist. "It's exactly as bad as it looks. Hi, Mom."

Marina kissed her daughter on the cheek. "Hello, love. Come inside, come inside. It's so chilly tonight! Winter comes earlier every year."

Anita supported him as he moved with the pace of a three-thousand-year-old tortoise to the front door. A mess. That's what this was. That's what he was. He should have stayed home with the blankets over his head. Except it wasn't his home, it was Anita's, and eventually she was going to—

"Is the pity party over?" Anita asked, helping him up the flagstone steps.

A wave of exhaustion and relief flooded through him, and his shoulders relaxed. "Sorry."

She walked him inside and closed the door. "Don't

worry about it. But don't believe for a second you're any different just because you broke your leg. You're still Patrick, and you're wonderful." She pecked his cheek. "Can I take your jacket?"

He shook his head. Trying to extricate himself from his pea coat was more than he was ready for at the moment. He did not deserve his girlfriend.

He followed Anita into her mother's kitchen. Marina had redecorated since the spring. She had painted the walls a comforting eggshell-white and upgraded her stainless-steel appliances. Everything gleamed with the patina of good and regular use.

Unlike his kitchen, where the most-used tool was his mini smoothie blender. Not that he'd used his kitchen much in the last few months.

Marina guided him to the kitchen table where she had set up a chair and ottoman. "Sit here, Patrick, darling. I'll take your crutches."

"You are the best, Marina." Patrick eased himself into the chair and managed to lift the heavy cast onto the ottoman. He sighed as he sank into the well-upholstered dining chair. He had spent the last few days balancing groomsman duties, blog, and studio work and trying not to bite his cuticles every time his leg burned. Not to mention leaving a message for Sophie M's parents, wishing her a speedy recovery. Wednesday night dinner at Anita's parents' house was exactly the balm he needed. Especially since Anita's father had a standing commitment and never showed. Dr. Bill Goodman was supposedly good at many things, but liking Patrick was not one of them.

Marina kissed the top of his head. "I made *pastitsio*. You sit. We will bring you everything you need."

Patrick closed his eyes and relaxed against the chair. The smells of meat and cheese and pasta, the lull of Anita and her mother's conversation, the soothing instrumental pop songs in the background. It was the best he had felt in ages.

The front door slammed. "It's freezing out there!" Dr. Goodman called from the foyer.

Patrick's eyes snapped open, and his spine went rigid. He sought out Anita, whose fingers had turned white around the stem of her wine glass.

"Bill!" Marina ran toward the man and embraced him. "I thought you were in Philadelphia this evening."

"Dr. Martin had to cancel. His son's team is vying for the championships. You have to show up for the family when they win, right?"

A thrill of rage blurred through Patrick. Bill Goodman rarely if ever showed up for Anita's competitions, and she was his only child. Shouldn't she rate more than a rare dinner appearance?

Bill shook his burly mane of dark blond hair. Either he had somehow defied the ravages of aging or it came from a bottle. Patrick wouldn't put the latter past the man.

Patrick used the edge of the table to bolster himself to a standing position. He held his wounded leg behind him as casually as he could muster without wincing. Bill Goodman was not a man who brooked weakness.

Anita hugged her father with one arm. "Hi, Dad."

"Anita. You brought Patrick?" Bill swept toward him in a cloud of pungent sandalwood aftershave. "Patrick!" He slapped him on the shoulder. "It's been quite a while."

And yet never long enough. "Hello, Dr. Goodman." The force of the man nearly knocked Patrick sideways. For an obstetrician, he would have expected a lighter touch. Patrick had always suspected Anita's dad was a doctor with a better bedside manner for his patients than his family. Then again, he was super biased.

"I heard you broke your leg. Painting?" There was a bite in his tone that was impossible to miss.

Patrick tried to find the expression he usually wore for Bill Goodman, the one of quiet interest and low-key enthusiasm, but it was impossible to muster when his leg was preparing to mutiny.

"Bill." Marina handed both her husband and Patrick glasses of red wine. "Paint*ball*. Even I know that."

Patrick found Anita across the kitchen. She was running one fingertip around the rim of her wine glass, listening to the crystal sing.

"Paintball, hmm? John Flaherty didn't want to go to Vegas?"

"Only if Vegas offers team-building, guerrilla-warfare experiences." He kept his voice soft, but Anita caught it and narrowed her eyes at him. *Shit.* Bill frowned at him as well, his watery blue eyes assessing, always assessing.

Patrick held up his hands. "Guess I'm not cut out for the paintball army, huh?"

It was a feeble joke but thawed the atmosphere at least temporarily.

Marina and Anita brought the huge platters of food and the bottle of wine to the table. Anita helped Patrick back into his chair, but he refused to put his leg up on the ottoman again.

Bill Goodman presided over this table, and Patrick was an unwelcome guest.

****

"I saw your mom at the hospital, Patrick." He phrased it as a question, though it reeked more of an afterthought than an honest inquiry. Marina stiffened beside him. That was odd. Normally she was one of the most genuine, friendly people Patrick had ever met.

Bill patted Marina's hand and gazed into her eyes, which seemed to settle her. It made Patrick want to squirm in his seat like he was eight years old. Anita's parents had always been affectionate, but Bill Goodman's attentions tonight were more obsequious than usual.

"That's great."

"She's staying busy, I imagine. A nurse's duty is a higher calling."

Patrick winced. He chanced a peek at Anita, who was rigidly examining the table scape.

"Bill." Marina's cheeks paled. She rose from the tablet and placed a protective hand on her daughter's shoulder. "You know how proud we are of Anita. And Patrick, too. They have built their own successful business, and they dance so beautifully. They've competed all over the world."

Patrick flushed, but Anita's smile remained anemic.

Bill blustered and polished off the last of his after-dinner cognac. "Tromping about in a leotard and high heels had a different name when I was a young man."

"Bill!" Marina's good-natured demeanor dissolved rapidly. "That is enough."

"I'm just saying, she could have done anything, anything with her life, and she decided to struggle as a mediocre dancer."

Patrick squirmed, sending flares of pain through his broken limb, but he pushed through it. "Dr. Goodman—"

Anita stood abruptly, her expression tight. "That's enough, everyone. Mom, thank you for dinner. Dad, I'll see you later."

She moved around the side of the table and helped him to his feet.

"Look at that." Bill's voice was leaden and slurred. "Picks a man who can't even pick himself up."

"That's super ableist of him," Patrick muttered, earning himself a murderous look from his girlfriend's sperm donor.

Patrick heard Marina slap his shoulder. "You are drunk, Bill. Let it go. Patrick is the best man for our Anita."

"Two of them will be poor as church mice."

Patrick managed to get onto his crutches and swung toward Bill, keeping a jocular, easy expression on his face. Even if it hurt like a bitch to do it. "Rats know all about mice, don't they, Dr. Goodman?"

Anita squeezed his upper arm, tears brimming behind her expressive blue eyes, and together they hobbled out of the house.

****

"Anita! Patrick!" Marina ran from the house, pulling a brightly colored wool scarf around her neck.

Anita finished helping Patrick into the back seat. He cut his gaze at her, and she nodded very slightly. At least she still had Patrick and could work some of his regard into her own strength.

She turned back toward her mother, who immediately enveloped her in an enormous bear hug. "I am so sorry, sweetheart. So sorry. He didn't mean it."

Anita blinked back tears but leaned into the embrace. "Didn't he? He's never liked that I didn't go to medical school."

"It's not that." Marina leaned backward and tucked an errant strand of hair behind Anita's ear. "Your father, he has not been himself lately."

Anita pulled away, lamenting the loss of her mother's warmth. She crossed her arms over her chest instead. "What do you mean? The drinking? He's always had a glass or two if he's not on call."

Marina chewed on her lip, and the hardness in Anita's heart softened. Her mother had never looked this concerned. "More than that." She kept her voice low, and her gaze flicked back and forth to the front door. "He—" Her breath hitched. "He isn't the same man I married."

Her blood felt cold, frosty. It would make sense. Her dad had never been effusive over her career choices, but he had never insulted her before. "What are you talking about?"

Marina opened her mouth and closed it again, then shook her head and pasted on a filmy sort of smile. "It's nothing. Do not worry about it, my darling. You take Patrick home and get him comfortable. I am so sorry about tonight."

Anita shifted from foot to foot, arms wrapped more tightly around herself in the sudden chill. Her father, the great Dr. Goodman. The one who never missed a call, never dropped a baby, never let a patient down, never let his wife down. His daughter was another story. "Mom? Are you sure you're okay?"

"Of course, my love." Marina kissed Anita's cheek, and her daughter could taste the salt of her lie the entire drive back to her apartment.

Chapter Twelve

Patrick flicked his gaze to Anita and then back down at his hands. She was pretending to read and playing Cyndi Lauper's *Greatest Hits* on the apartment stereo, her comfort equivalent of a giant tub of mint chocolate ice cream.

Patrick shifted on the couch from amidst his rainbow quagmire of throw pillows. "Do you want to talk about it?"

She sighed and re-read the same page she had been holding for the past ten minutes. "Not really."

Patrick tapped on the keyboard of his laptop. If only there were a manual on what to say in these circumstances. He turned the screen of his computer away from Anita's peripheral vision and did a quick internet search.

The internet was full of trolls.

He understood. Really, he did. His mother never approved of his life choices, either. Though she usually veiled her barbs in such thick layers of passive aggression, she may as well use weighted blankets.

A person, of course, could not know everything that happened in someone's home, but Patrick thought he knew enough. Anita and Dr. Goodman's relationship had been better before she refused to apply for medical schools. There had always been an undercurrent of tension, but never such outright hostility. It did not match what he knew of Dr. Goodman's reputation. Brusque but fair, generous. He volunteered at downtown Philly women's health clinics. Where some of his good ol' boy club colleagues had been caught in the web of scandals, Bill Goodman never had a word said against him. Marina wouldn't have stayed with her husband if he was as brutish in the past as he had been that evening.

Patrick deleted the telltale search history from his internet browser bar and sighed. Cyndi sang "Hat Full of Stars" over the stereo. He had tried once to get Anita a Bluetooth speaker, but she purportedly couldn't get it to work. A smile played across his lips.

"Reading something good?" she asked.

He glanced up and found her looking at him. Her lovely, sharp blue eyes were rimmed with red, even though no tears fell.

Covering her hand with his, he smiled, a real one this time. "I love you, Anita."

The tear hovering in the corner of her eye dripped with impossible slowness down the side of her nose. He used the pad of his thumb to wipe it away, then let it linger there on the curve of her jaw.

She sniffed and settled her face into his hand. "I love you, too."

His heart leapt and fluttered. This wasn't the moment, was it? She was still so sad after what her father had said. He couldn't propose when she was so upset.

"Anita—"

But she silenced him by sliding onto his lap, wrapping her arms around his neck, bracketing his hips with her thighs. She bent her face toward him, enveloping him in a cloud of her intoxicating scent, and pressed her soft lips to his. He leaned into it, into the sensation, the comfort of her body. This had not been what he intended, but he could roll with it.

She responded by aligning herself against him, rubbing the angle between her legs over the hard length of him. He groaned into her mouth, and she swallowed the sound, sweeping her tongue between his lips.

"I don't want to talk," she whispered. She moved her mouth from his and turned her ministrations to the soft skin of his earlobe, licking the tiny hollow behind it, pulling the cartilage softly between her teeth.

He groaned again and ground his hips against hers. "Anita—"

She pulled slightly away again, her gaze fixed on his. "I don't want to talk."

As she unbuttoned his shirt, pressing kisses against the skin of his chest as she laid it bare, he rapidly forgot exactly what it was he had wanted to say.

Chapter Thirteen

John Flaherty's phone buzzed with wedding reminders from Katie, but he couldn't focus on that now. Thank goodness Katie understood, or at least he hoped she did. He tossed back two ibuprofen and chased it with a swig of coffee.

"Six kids," Curtis muttered. "Six now. The doctors said there's fentanyl, PCP, ketamine? Who does that? Who sells that to kids?"

John paced in front of the whiteboard in the briefing room, thinking. Six students from Lewis High were now hospitalized, comatose from drug ingestion. Their faces were etched on his brain, and their names haunted him at night. He was getting married in a matter of days, and he couldn't focus any of his attention on that. Not when something like this was going on.

Photos of the students dominated the majority of the whiteboard space, but there was a small box in the lower left corner with three smaller photos. Two were beefy ex-Special Forces types, Jack Colby and Ray Pinter, and the third was a buxom, bottle-blonde real estate agent, Rita Forest. Back in May, John and Sheriff Forbes had apprehended them for smuggling drugs through a house staging company.

Sheriff Forbes joined him and tapped the tip of her glasses against the photos. "I think you were right about the connection. Drug smuggling is a hydra, right? We cut off one head, more grow to take its place."

Curtis didn't move from his seat. "Walk me through it?"

John crossed his arms over his chest, and his mouth twisted as he thought. Curtis had been on vacation in Cleveland that weekend.

"There were two civilians, Dennis Rayner and Tabitha Valby. They arrived at a supposed open house, but ended up victims of a home invasion. Colby, Pinter, and Forest were storing drugs at empty homes for sale, using a staging company as cover. Bad luck Rayner and Valby showed up before Forest could close down the open house."

"Why didn't she just cancel it?" Curtis asked.

John rolled his eyes. "She still maintains she didn't want to cancel it in case her boss found out and fired her. Anyway, we sent off samples of the product they were smuggling to the DEA and hospital for testing."

Sheriff Forbes nodded. "They call it Disco Balls. Marijuana laced with fentanyl and PCP. Some ketamine, too. But the composition of the drugs we found from the staging company must be different from what the high school students took. One of the earlier samples was so packed with fentanyl, the DEA says whoever took it would be dead within seconds. We should ensure the high school and local library are carrying Narcan."

There was a long pause while he digested that information. Until it was broken by Curtis ripping open a bag of potato chips.

"Baltimore and Philly P.D. haven't had any confirmed cases yet, though PCP intoxications have risen in local emergency rooms. Philly P.D. says they're getting a lot of calls to investigate people with psychotic symptoms."

John tilted his head, examining the clues on the whiteboard. "What if it's being tested, manufactured, and stored around here first, before they move it up and down the Eastern seaboard? Lewis is in a prime location between Baltimore, Philly, and New York. Maybe back in May, the staging company was an initial storage phase?"

"You think they're perfecting the formula?" Sheriff Forbes exhaled, her salt-and-pepper bob shifting with the movement. "We need to figure this out and shut it down before anyone else gets hurt. We've interviewed multiple students and teachers at Lewis High, but no one is talking."

"I don't know why the kids won't talk to us." Curtis munched loudly on his chips. "Wouldn't they want to make sure no one else gets the Disco Balls, or whatever?"

John sighed the sigh of the heavy soul. "There's a lot of distrust in the police force right now. They're probably scared, amped up, and spending too much time on social media."

"I thought public image was the reason we can't carry guns any longer?" Curtis rustled the potato chip bag.

Sheriff Forbes arched an eyebrow. "We moved to Tasers and improving access to social work and mental health care instead of militarizing the township force because of public safety. And you absolutely do not use your Taser unless strictly necessary. It's not about optics, it's about people's lives. But it takes time to change opinions. We'd be ostriches with our heads in the sand if we ignored that."

John knew that all too well. Sheriff Forbes had seen him as her son's friend, and she had helped turn him around. Every kid needed a chance like that. Every person deserved that, to be seen for their potential.

"We need an in. Someone the kids like, someone they trust." Someone who wasn't a definite authority figure. John had two such people who fit the bill perfectly. "I have an idea."

Chapter Fourteen

For someone who had only ever taken a passing interest in his life, except for the times she could commandeer so she could bask in the credit, Patrick's mom was suddenly everywhere. She stopped by the studio, she invited herself up to Anita's apartment, she was waiting at Amore with a honey matcha latte for him.

He preferred Americanos.

Will Forbes, who had driven Patrick to the coffee shop, sat across from them, sipping his skinny cappuccino with a dash of cinnamon. Will's usually quite expressive features were drawn, tense. Even his corn silk hair was shadowed and annoyed.

"Drink the latte, sweetheart," his mother said, her voice nearly as cloying and unpalatable as the beverage she kept foisting upon him. "It's so good for you. The honey helps with healing, and the matcha does wonders for inflammation." She turned to Will, her dark brown ponytail swinging. That was a new addition, too, the hair dye. As long as he had known her, his mom railed against societal dictums for women's hair. "Will, how is your mom? It's been so long since I've seen her. I'm sure she's so busy, keeping our town safe from rabid raccoons and sprinkler mishaps." She laughed at her own joke. Neither Patrick nor Will joined her.

Will sipped at his cappuccino, and small flecks of

foam caught in his short-cropped beard. He wiped them away with the back of his hand, earning a grimace from Patrick's mom. "She's fine. Lewis keeps her really busy, but she has excellent help. She led an initiative to change the officers from carrying firearms to Tasers, and has recruited more social workers and addiction specialists for the township."

"Really?" Diane rolled her eyes. "Seems short-sighted."

Patrick actually thought it was rather brilliant and progressive, but he was not about to jump into that foxhole.

Will cleared his throat. "It's an incredible accomplishment. It will save lives. Now she's trying to convince John to run for sheriff next year."

"Oh?" She nudged the matcha latte closer to Patrick. "She wouldn't run again? She's been sheriff for years."

"She'd like to retire, if she can wrap up her cases. She's always wanted to write or consult for TV or something. Patrick recommended she try podcasting."

Patrick didn't know why his friend bothered. His mom wouldn't ask about any of his accomplishments.

"Is she working on something now?" Patrick's mom asked. "I hear all about those kids in the hospital. Terrible, what the youth of today get up to."

Only decades of training in dealing with his mom prevented Patrick from rolling his eyes.

Will paled, his gaze flicking to Patrick then back to his coffee. "She isn't really at liberty to talk to me about her open cases."

Diane made a noncommittal sound of disappointment. "Patrick, you really should drink your honey matcha."

He couldn't avoid it forever. Patrick sipped obligingly at the latte. It tasted like someone had spilled infant cough syrup into hot, steamed swamp grass. He stifled his gag, another benefit of decades of self-delusion practice.

Diane beamed. "Isn't it delicious? You'll be all healed in no time at all."

Right. Bones healed in six to eight weeks. One non-potable drink was not going to change that. When she turned around, he could spit it out in the planter.

The conversation stalled again. Patrick wished desperately his mother would take the cue and leave, but it had never worked with her before.

"Did you hear?" She leaned conspiratorially toward them. "Christina Blake's trial is due to start in two weeks. Can you believe it? I don't know why these court delays take so long."

Patrick's lungs clenched and wouldn't open, wouldn't admit any oxygen. His vision narrowed and blackened around the edges, like he was looking at a faded photo from the 1800s.

When Will spoke, his voice sounded as though he were speaking through a wall of water. "Patrick? You okay, man?"

No, no he was not okay. He was dying. He was having a heart attack.

He had to pull it together. Anita, he wanted Anita. He also did not want her to see him like this.

He closed his eyes and focused on his breathing. That's what Anita always did. Two-three-cha-cha-cha.

Slowly the darkness receded, and his lungs filled. The ache in his chest remained but had lessened to enough of a degree that he could finally breathe like a human being.

Will hovered over him, his features etched with concern. His mom sat in her chair, lips pursed, tapping one finger on the table like the world's most passive aggressive metronome.

"Patrick, are you okay?" Will repeated, his hand on Patrick's shoulder. It was warm, strong, reassuring.

Patrick forced a smile. "Yeah, totally. Sorry about that."

His mom swung into action, simpering and cooing, pushing Will out of the way. "Sweetheart, you poor thing. Hearing about the trial is just so awful, but it will be over soon. Maybe you should come and stay with me until it's all over. I'll hide you from the publicity. Sometimes you need a good home-cooked meal."

The healthy part of Patrick's brain registered that none of those things sounded helpful or wise. Will's neon presence beside him radiated, "don't do that, fool."

He was saved from the need to respond by the arrival of John Flaherty. He was in his off-duty attire today, a black leather jacket over a white long-sleeved Henley, and jeans, and he held a to-go cup of coffee in his hands. He wasn't smiling.

"Will, Patrick, just the two I wanted to see."

Diane curved in her seat to look up at John. "Oh my goodness, little John Flaherty, all grown up!"

John smiled tightly at her. Patrick may have told him more about his mom than he should have. "Good morning, Ms. O'Leary."

Patrick knew he would hear later about how John had not said it was good to see her.

Diane ruffled and pushed her hands through her hair. "I must be going." She leaned over and pressed a kiss to the top of Patrick's head before ruffling his hair. He stifled his eye roll. "Patrick, honey, drink your matcha latte, and I'll talk to you tomorrow about coming to stay with me. Bye, boys." She scooped up her oversized handbag and marched down the street toward her car.

The air around their table cooled and crisped into the perfect October day it was.

John folded himself into the chair she had just vacated. He sipped his coffee and raised an eyebrow at Patrick. "I can tell my interruption was unwanted."

Will rolled his eyes, and he relaxed into the seat beside Patrick. "You have no idea. Patrick, are you sure you're okay?"

"I'm fine." Yup, totally, completely... "Fine." Repeat it enough times and it could be true.

John tilted his bald head to one side, the sunlight reflecting off his dark brown pate. "What happened?"

Patrick didn't respond, just stared into the cup of revolting liquid. It was solidifying now, which was probably not a good sign.

Will moved the honey matcha latte out of his line of sight. "Patrick had a panic attack when his mom brought up Christina Blake's upcoming trial."

Indignation rose up his spine, though it felt more like stabs of pain in his injured leg. "Hey, that's not—"

"She did what?" John asked. It was like Patrick wasn't even there anymore. He sat back sullenly, crossing his arms over his chest. "Why would she bring that up?"

Will rolled his eyes. "Because she's a sociopath?"

Patrick felt some long-dormant filial responsibility prompt him to action. "She's not—"

Will stopped him with a cutting look. Must be the one he inherited from his mother. "She totally is, Patrick. She's manipulative and passive-aggressive. How long have you been having panic attacks?"

"I'm not having panic attacks." Though now that Will mentioned it, it did not sound entirely unfamiliar.

The weight of their stares hung like anvils around his neck.

He flung his hands into the air. "I'm fine. Everything is fine. I don't want to talk about my mom or my leg or panic attacks or Christina Blake." He realized, dimly, that as he spoke, he was gesticulating like a trained sea lion and drawing far too much attention to himself at his sidewalk café table.

Patrick paused, sucking his lips in between his teeth and shrinking into his wire-framed chair.

Both Will and John regarded him with eyebrows raised. As did half the population of Lewis. He would definitely appreciate a Patrick-sized wormhole at this moment, to transport him to the moments before he broke his leg and fucked up his life so royally.

"Okay," Will said at last, drawing out the vowel sounds until the word was nearly as long as the Magna Carta. Without saying anything further, he scooped up the matcha latte from the table, winged it over his head, and made the full three-point shot into the trashcan. "No more matcha for you, Patrick."

He sighed, a bit in relief, a bit out of self-pity, but his friends didn't need to know that. He needed to get control of this conversation. The revolting drink no longer in his presence, he relaxed for the first time since he and Will had arrived at Amore and found its pleasant, soothing ambiance completely destroyed by his mother's presence.

"So, John," he said, keeping his voice deliberately calm and decidedly unaffected. "Why are you here? Aren't you swamped with wedding prep and your actual job?"

John's handsome features creased into a deep frown. "That's why I'm here."

"Are you trying to get your errant groomsman to help you fold more twee origami?" Will yawned, and Patrick felt a definite kinship for his fellow hater-of-crafts.

The faintest smile relaxed the valley in the middle of John's forehead. Poor guy. He must be swamped. "We finished those, thankfully. Her mother and her bridesmaids are wrapping the Mason jars with sailcloth and rope, so we are exempt from those activities."

Will and Patrick exchanged a high five under the table.

"Where I do need your help..." John trailed off, casting his glance at the other patrons of the café. It wasn't a busy afternoon at Amore, but their table had already drawn its share of attention thanks entirely to Patrick. "On second thought, can we go to someone's house? It might be better to talk somewhere a little more private."

Apprehension coiled in Patrick's stomach, but he would not freak out, not again, not here. Whatever John had to say, it couldn't be that bad.

He followed Will to his car, limping along on his crutches, telling himself over and over, that everything was going to be all right.

Even if he didn't believe it for a second.

Chapter Fifteen

In the comfort of her tiny office, Anita bopped her head and sang under her breath to her friend Toni's Zumba playlist. The group today sounded particularly boisterous, with lots of whooping and whistling and pounding of the floorboards. It didn't hurt that Toni had picked songs that primarily boasted bass and percussion.

It was more difficult than she had expected to find a time to call Mrs. DeVeaux. Between her own lessons and Toni's particularly exuberant day of Zumba, she had not had a quiet moment. She certainly did not want to invoke the antiquarian's wrath by calling her while Pitbull was thumping in the background. She had a feeling Mrs. DeVeaux was an easy listening fan.

She approved Rodrigo's timecard and sent the week's files to her bookkeeper just as the cool down was finishing.

"Hey," Toni said, her breath even despite the sheen of sweat on her brow and chest. She tossed her ponytail of braids over her shoulder and chugged at her two-liter water bottle. "I haven't seen you in a while."

Anita relaxed into the chair and smiled. "You've been busy. How's the boyfriend?"

Toni rolled her hazel eyes. "Honey, I dumped him last week. Not worth my time or bother."

Toni had a history of serial dating. She liked to say

it was because no one was good enough for her, but Anita always wondered if it was because she kept men at a distance. Anita could relate.

"Relationships are complicated," she said.

"Tell me about it." Toni leaned against the doorjamb, her toned muscles visible beneath her tie-dyed neon-pink, green, and yellow bodysuit. "We can't all date the sexy cinnamon roll of our dreams. Besides, I don't have time for dating."

"I hear that." Anita's computer screen drew her attention. Her balance sheets would definitely drop over the winter. Maybe she needed more weekend special events to draw in crowds and buffer the studio since she and Patrick couldn't compete.

Toni's features softened. "So how is the cinnamon roll?"

Anita's heart clenched. He was not himself. He was in pain and irritable as a honey badger. "He's okay. It's a lot for him."

Toni raised an eyebrow. "In what way? The leg?'

Anita sighed. Holding it all in was exhausting. "I think it's the upcoming Christina Blake trial. I've never been so grateful that I have no idea how to set news alerts."

Toni's understanding eyes deepened. "I know that's hard for Patrick. But what about you? You were there, too."

Anita's entire body frowned. "I'm fine. Really."

Even she could tell Toni didn't buy her bullshit but she glossed over it. For now. "Does he have to testify?"

"The lawyers have said neither of us has to testify, since she is primarily on trial for murder and not kidnapping Patrick. But who knows?"

"They could always change their minds and subpoena you." Toni and Patrick shared a deep love of true crime podcasts, so they were up on their legal and judicial jargon.

"I really hope not." Anita tightened her ponytail. There was something she was supposed to be doing, and it had completely slipped her mind now that her thoughts were full of Christina Blake.

Toni straightened and finished off the remainder of her water. "I'm here if you need me. See you tomorrow."

Anita waved goodbye and slumped in her desk chair. She rotated it slowly three hundred and sixty degrees, thinking. Was Patrick acting like a dipshit because of his accident or because of Christina Blake? Or was it something else entirely? Was it because of Anita?

She checked the digital time on the bottom of her desktop computer. Two thirty p.m. Way too early for a glass of wine. Rats.

****

"You guys are here!" Katie exclaimed, clapping her hands and bouncing on her toes like a pixie trampolinist. "John, why didn't you say they were coming? I can order pizza. Or snacks?" She launched herself into John's open arms and kissed him soundly. "I'll make some coffee. And my mom brought over cheesecake bars. Will, have you had my mom's cheesecake bars? Patrick?"

Will and Patrick had not even made it through the door of John's tidy, forest-green ranch home. The deputy and his exuberant fiancée took up the entire entryway and did not seem to be super interested in moving, as John was currently taking advantage of Katie's proximity and nuzzling her neck.

"Don't you know you're supposed to wait for such abhorrent PDA until your honeymoon?" Will said, a crooked smile on his face. He glanced at Patrick and jerked a thumb at the happy couple. "I like hanging out with you and Anita better. You two don't spoon in the doorway when I could be having cheesecake bars."

Katie laughed and pulled John deeper into the house, allowing Patrick and Will entry. Patrick's smile felt frozen and forced. He and Anita were not exactly physically expressive in company. What did that mean?

This was not the time for such wallowy self-reflection.

Will elbowed him in the ribs, which set Patrick careening to the right side of the hallway and smack into John's bright-orange hunting vest, hanging on an S-hook along the wall. "What was that for?"

"Get your head out of your ass," Will said. "What's going on with you?"

"Nothing." Everything. He rubbed at the ache in his ribs with one palm, but it didn't help, and earned him a scoff from his friend.

"There's a reason people go to therapy, Patrick."

If he had the time or money… He hobbled after Will into the cozy kitchen of John's house.

"Katie, you don't have to serve us," John said.

"Nonsense!" Katie bustled about, undeterred by John's protective arm at her waist, fetching coffee cups and plates and a glass tray of what had to be cherry cheesecake bars. Patrick's stomach rumbled. He and Anita had made avocado toast and scrambled eggs for breakfast, but he'd skipped lunch, thinking he would eat at Amore. He hadn't counted on his mom ruining his appetite.

"Sit! Sit!" Katie pulled chairs at the table out and placed little white plates in front of each of them. Patrick collapsed into the one at the head of the table, the one easiest to extricate himself from.

Katie's delicate features contorted with apparent concern. "Patrick? Do you need some ice? Ibuprofen?"

"I'm okay." If agony was okay. He had walked a lot more today than he had previously attempted. He had thought he could take it. He was an idiot, but that didn't surprise him.

Katie's grin did not leave her face. She leaned against the back of John's chair, one hand perched on her hip. "Are you guys looking forward to the wedding?"

"Definitely," Will said, serving himself a cheesecake bar. Patrick nodded his thanks when his friend served him one as well. "Bobby is really looking forward to seeing me in a suit."

"If you ever wore anything besides a track suit," John said, smiling. He turned to his fiancée. "Katie, you don't have to wait on us. You have a million things to do."

She kissed the bare top of his head. Patrick squirmed a little. It reminded him so much of him and Anita, of the warmth and comfort they used to have.

Wait. Used to have? They still had it, didn't they? They'd had sex the night before, so they must still have it. But it was possible the sex wasn't that good, or she had just needed something familiar after what her father had said to her. Maybe she didn't feel the same way he did. Maybe—

"Earth to Patrick." Will waved both of his hands directly in front of Patrick's face. "Jeez, man, you are on Neptune today. Taking the strong pills, huh?"

"No." He couldn't think of anything else to say. Maybe he was a little out of it lately. "Of course not. Ice and ibuprofen for me."

He noticed the tension emanating from John's chair. Katie had left, taking her bubbly warmth with her. The deputy stared at the coffee in his cup as though it held the secrets of life.

"What's going on with you, John?" Patrick asked. He bit into the cherry cheesecake bar and had to restrain himself physically from moaning. It was one of the best things he had ever tasted, creamy and sweet with the tart bite of the cherries.

Will seemed to share his opinion, as he had scarfed down one bar and was now serving himself two more.

John tapped pensively at the rim of his coffee cup. "I need your guys' help. You've heard about the students at Lewis High?" He addressed this primarily to Will, but at least Patrick felt included in this posse.

Will's features fell, and when he swallowed the bite of cheesecake bar in his mouth, it looked like it was dry and unpalatable. "There's six of them now," he said, his voice so soft and restrained Patrick wondered if it belonged to someone else. Older than him, Will had always been a mentor, on the soccer field and off. It was rare to see him discomfited.

Also, Patrick had not realized there were more teenagers who had gotten sick. His desire for the bake-off worthy cheesecake bars had substantially waned.

John nodded, his features drawn and grim. "I need your help. The students at the high school aren't talking to police."

Will scoffed. "Shocker. High school kids don't talk to anyone except themselves." There was a beat, and Will blanched. "Oh. I see."

"I don't." Normally Patrick wasn't so slow, and he didn't like it. Will opened his mouth to clarify, but then the pieces of the puzzle clicked together, and Patrick exhaled. "Oh wait. You want us to spy for you?"

"Not spy, definitely not spy. There's no *21 Jump Street* sting planned." John clearly was attempting and failing at levity.

Will tilted his head to one side. "I don't know. There are people who have told me I look like Richard Grieco."

"On what planet?" Patrick asked. The only resemblance blond-haired Will shared with the actor was the shape of his chin. Maybe the swagger.

"Don't hate because I'm prettier than you." Will took another cheesecake bar and stuffed the entire thing into his mouth.

John rolled his eyes. "Honestly, if there were anyone else I could ask, I would."

"Thanks for the vote of confidence, Deputy." Patrick sank lower in the kitchen chair. He knew perfectly well his history was not the most reliable. He had been stalked for weeks before he did anything about it, and even then he had missed all the signs about the identity of his perpetrator.

A familiar swirl of darkness threatened him at that thought, and he shoved it all aside. He didn't want to fall apart in front of his friends again. He didn't need that, didn't need their pity, their scrutiny.

John sighed and pointed at Will. "You have been

voted the most popular teacher at Lewis High the last three years. And you—" he shifted the direction of his speech toward Patrick "—teach one of the most popular clubs at the school. The kids trust you guys. Sophie MacAllister? She was in the ballroom club. You think she didn't talk to her friends about where she was going that night she got sick? Some of them were probably there. Anything, even a small clue, could help us figure out who is behind this so we can stop it."

Patrick ran his finger around the edge of his plate, thinking about that intense look Lucy Knight had leveled at him. At least the plate was soothingly bland. Anita liked a mismatched mélange of thrifted dishware, so he never quite knew whether he'd get the one with pink flowers or the one with the painted circus bear. "The kids wouldn't do something stupid, like try and stop the dealers themselves? Would they?"

Will crossed his arms over his chest. "You've met them. I wouldn't put it past any one of them. Lucy Knight, in particular, has seen *Veronica Mars* one too many times."

Patrick looked at John, hoping for help and guidance. The deputy did not disappoint. "I can handle some teenage armchair detectives. I need to get a foot in the door, which is where you two come in."

Will shrugged and pushed his plate away from him. He leaned backward in his chair. "I should have worn sweatpants instead of jeans. Your future mother-in-law is one hell of a baker. I'm in."

"Me, too," Patrick said. There was a solemn pit deep in his stomach, like an anchor dragging him down through the floor of the cozy ranch house.

"Great." John exhaled, as though he had been

holding the weight of the world on his shoulders. He probably was, given that he was getting married soon and managing a difficult case with very little support. The Drug Enforcement Agency did not exactly have an outpost in Lewis, and prior to the high schoolers getting sick, the only drug investigations they ran involved a twenty-year-old D.A.R.E. kit. Patrick felt for the guy, and worse about himself. John was his friend. He needed to step up, regardless of his own bullshit.

Patrick nodded. "We're here for you, buddy. Whatever you need."

"Did I hear you guys are willing to help?" Katie popped her pretty, petite head out from behind the kitchen door. "Thank goodness! My co-teacher just called and said she can't come over to do the Mason jars. Her son is sick with something. I'd love some extra sets of hands!"

Patrick managed to stifle the groan that threatened to escape at the idea of more DIY wedding planning. Will did not.

Chapter Sixteen

Anita stood at the check-in desk with her pen in hand, tapping down the list of students who had RSVPed for the evening beginner waltz class. Six today. Not too bad. Hopefully there would be a few walk-ins.

The bell over the studio door clanged. Anita's automatic welcoming smile quickly faded when she saw who it was. She cast her gaze on the check-in desk and picked with one fingernail at a divot in the wood. She really should paint the furniture or something. It was bland and unappealing.

"You cannot avoid me forever," her mother said. She held her bright-yellow leather hobo bag in one hand and a reusable coffee cup in the other.

Anita sighed and forced a smile that she knew didn't reach her eyes. "I'm not avoiding you. I've been busy."

Marina frowned at her, her typically expressive mouth overdrawn into a cartoonish grimace. "Anita. Please. You think I don't know?"

Anita softened. Her mother never had anything but her best interests at heart. Unlike her father. Even if he had never been so directly cruel, and she had protected him, it didn't mean her mom wasn't—

Without warning, Marina rushed toward her and enveloped her in her arms. Anita sniffed into the wet shoulder of her mother's cashmere sweater. Damn it, she was crying, and now she would she owe her mom for the dry cleaning. Her mom whispered soothing sounds into her ear as she stroked her back, just as she had when she was little and upset over some playground bully.

"I've never heard him like that," Anita said through the thick veil of tears clogging the back of her throat. "Is that really what he thinks?"

"No, of course not," Marina replied immediately. It did not reassure Anita. She was probably planning what to say the whole drive over here. "Of course he doesn't think that. He loves you. He is so proud of what you have built."

A black pit chasmed in her stomach. Proud? He had never once said anything vaguely resembling pride in her, not since she had told him definitively that she would not be taking the MCATs her senior year at Villanova.

Her mother always saw the best in people, particularly Bill Goodman.

Anita pulled away and wiped at her eyes with the hem of her long, black, slouchy cardigan. "What's going on with him then? You said he hasn't been himself."

Marina froze, her large eyes flicking around the studio, as if to check if anyone else was there. "Can we sit and talk? Somewhere private? I could use a glass of wine."

So could Anita. Maybe two. She checked the time on her fitness tracker.

"Sure. Let's go upstairs."

****

111

Three minutes later, Anita and Marina perched on the couch and overstuffed armchair, respectively, in her apartment. Two generous pours of viognier sat before them on the table.

Her mom picked hers up first and sipped it. She closed her eyes. "This is good. This is better."

Anita picked up her glass, as well, but twirled it between her fingers, watching the straw-yellow liquid paint the insides of the globe. Why had her mom wanted such privacy?

"Are you going to tell me what's wrong with Dad?" She steeled her spine, prepared for anything.

Marina sighed and set her glass back down on the table with an echoing clink. "I don't know. Not really. He isn't himself lately. It isn't all the time, rarely if he's been home all day. Usually it happens after he's been meeting friends in the city or after a long shift at work." Her mom paused.

Anita ruminated on all of the possibilities. If they were having this conversation, she might as well go for her worst fear. "What happens? Does he hurt you?"

"No!" Marina laughed, but it was a startled, awkward sound, not her usual rich cadence. "No, of course not. He would never hurt me, not physically. He's forgetful. Irritable. That night at dinner was the worst he's been."

Anita let the knowledge seep into her skin. She would let it marinate there while she pondered what to do with it. He had never hurt her physically? What about emotionally?

"Is it dementia?" she asked. She had other thoughts, too, ones that teased at the back of her mind, but she did not want to give them voice. Her father was barely sixty, a "silver fox," as Nina Rabinova had dubbed him. There was plenty of trouble he could be getting into.

Marina shrugged and took a deep draught of her wine. "I don't know. I am not a doctor. I hope it is nothing serious. Maybe a midlife crisis, or what have you." She gesticulated with one hand rolling in the air, a gesture that always reminded Anita of her and her alone and made her desperately want to visit her mother's homeland of Cyprus.

Anita sipped her wine, letting the flavors run over her tongue and taste buds. Yes, there was plenty of trouble her father could find. Plenty her mother would not want to admit to herself. She had fallen head over heels for Bill Goodman the day they'd met and had moved from England to Philadelphia with nary a second thought.

But relationships could change.

For some reason, the image of Patrick floated across her brain. He had not been himself lately, either. Maybe it was something in the water.

Marina drained the last of her wine and wiped the bottom of her eyes with the pad of her thumb. She had been crying. All this time, and Anita hadn't noticed. She was a terrible daughter.

Her mom stood and pressed a kiss to her daughter's head. "I have to go. Don't worry, my love. Everything will be all right."

Anita was way past beginning to wonder if that was true.

Chapter Seventeen

When Patrick shuffled into the studio ten minutes before her group beginner waltz class was due to start, Anita could tell he was not in the mood to talk. Even if she was desperate to get his opinion on what could be going on with her dad. He looked beyond tired or fatigued. He had become quite adept at using the crutches over the days since his injury, but he moved now like he had broken something anew.

He gave her a tired smile and nodded to the assembled students, who were putting on their dance shoes, chatting, or warming up. "I'm going to go upstairs." He rested his armpits on the brace of his crutches, but he winced when he uncurled his fingers.

"Are you okay?" She wanted to kiss his cheek, feel the reassuring stubble, press his body into his, and curl around him. She wanted him to ground her after the discussion with her mom.

He did not look like he needed her drama right now.

"I'm all right. Way too much wedding DIY." He yawned and winced again. "I'm going to head upstairs." He even sounded completely exhausted, world-weary. She ached to ease some of his pain.

"Sure, sounds good." She watched him go, eager to follow him as he slogged across the studio floor.

But she couldn't. She had a job to do. The doorbell

to the entry tolled again, announcing the arrival of some walk-ins. Anita pasted a smile on her face. Just a few more hours, then she could go to him. Just a few more hours.

****

It took longer than a few more hours. After the beginner and subsequent intermediate waltz class, Rodrigo canceled on his private lesson, so she stepped in to teach the wedding dance couple.

The couple, who were new to the studio, had brought along a rambunctious coterie of friends, who had all clearly been pre-gaming. These friends proceeded to whoop, holler, catcall, jeer, and were completely resistant to any of Anita's redirection or silencing tactics. The bride and groom had chosen Olivia Newton-John's "I Honestly Love You" for their first dance, which was some sort of omen.

She counted the minutes, no, the seconds, until the lesson was over. The groom was a reasonable dancer, but the bride was a mess. She could barely stand up, which Anita suspected was more due to the approximate gallon of vodka she had consumed rather than any deficient natural talent.

She finally called it with twenty-five minutes left in their hour, right at the time when the groom spun his blushing bride and she kept spinning until she collapsed in a puddle of synthetic fabrics on the floor. "That's enough for today," Anita said through clenched teeth. "Next time try this without the entourage." Seriously, even her ponytail was frizzled and irritated. She leaned over and helped the bride to stand. Her groom was with his friends, already laughing and pulling from a silver flask he had not kept hidden in his waistband during the lesson.

The bride stumbled on her three-inch heels but managed not to fall. Anita kept one hand under the woman's arm for balance as she led her back to the changing area. Just a few more minutes. A few more minutes, and they would be gone. She would lock up, sweep, lock up again, and then head upstairs to check on Patrick. A few more minutes and she could blast all the Aerosmith she wanted through her studio speakers.

That was the exact moment that all hell broke loose. Instead of landing in the chair Anita was practically shoving underneath her, the bride slipped, stabbing her three-inch heels into her groom's leg. He yelped, cursed repeatedly, and jumped away from his bride's unintentional footwear weapon. Which had him colliding with one of his friends, the one with the two-liter, reusable water bottle. The friend windmilled his arms, but to no avail. Anita watched in fatigued despair as the water bottle launched into the air, arcing over her beautiful, polished, hardwood dance floor, spilling two liters of vodka in a flood that would have discomposed Noah himself.

The room fell eerily quiet, tension dropping like a curtain after the final act of a performance. Anita heard a snicker and silenced it with her own murderous glare. The offender clapped his mouth shut so quickly it sounded like a door slamming closed.

She clenched her fists at her sides. Thank goodness they had paid ahead online. She wasn't sure she would be able to find the credit card machine through her red veil of rage.

"Um," the groom said needlessly, his blurry gaze fixed on the mess they'd made of her beautiful floor.

"Get. Out." She pulled each word from the depths of her very being, as if she were playing tug-of-war with her ability to speak.

With very little resistance and a suddenly sober demeanor, the group vacated within seconds.

Anita was not the most imposing person normally, but at times like this, when she was so pissed off she could not even see straight, she embraced her inner street fighter and let her roar.

That said, the minute the door clanged shut, the adrenaline rapidly ebbed, leaving her cold. And tired. Unbelievably, extraordinarily tired.

The group had left a small tornado of debris behind them: empty packets of chips, half-filled plastic water bottles, crumbs from what she presumed were brownies because they had better not be ants or she was going to charge them an extra cleaning fee. Besides the vodka on her floor, which needed to be mopped urgently before it warped the wood, there was at least thirty more minutes of cleaning.

She sighed as she slumped to the supply closet to fetch her mop. This was not the time for Aerosmith. This was a job for Springsteen, and only Springsteen would do.

****

Patrick heard the final strains of "Dancing in the Dark" wafting up the stairwell from the studio. She must be having a terrible night.

He would pace if his leg didn't feel encased in an igloo of pain.

He hefted his leg cast onto the coffee table, and desperately wished he had thought to get a hanger from the closet because the cast was itching like a

MOTHER—

As light as a kitten padding, footsteps sounded on the stairs.

Patrick pulled himself upright, which was more difficult than it ought to have been, due to the multitude of throw pillows messing with his balance. He launched himself into a sitting position just as the door opened.

"Hey," he said.

"Hey."

She looked tired, pissed off, and as though she should finally cave and buy that punching bag she kept eyeing for the small practice studio.

Unable to move, as he was perched in tenuous balance amidst the throw pillows, he gestured with his chin at the snacks and drinks he had laid out on the coffee table. "You look like you could use that."

"Thanks." She picked up a glass of wine and sank into the neighboring armchair, her eyes closed.

Her ponytail was askew, and her cardigan hung limply off one shoulder. He could not recall ever having seen her so disheveled.

Now was probably not the time to bring up that he needed to coerce a group of teenagers into confessing their knowledge of local Lewis drug culture.

"Looks like you've had a night," he said at last.

She sighed and drank half her glass of Malbec in one go. "Why do people feel they need to invite chaos and friends into their pre-marital preparations?"

Patrick stalled, his mind wrapped up in one tiny, black, felt-covered jewelry box that was taking up space underneath his gym socks.

She polished off the rest of the glass, opened her eyes, and stood, presumably for a refill.

He opted for levity. "I know what you mean. I activated my carpal tunnel decorating Mason jars at John's house today."

She glided into the galley kitchen and made a fatigued, noncommittal sound that left him wishing he had a mute button.

He watched as her long fingers pulled the cork from the bottle of wine, then tilted it into her glass. It was rare for her to have more than one, a full solar eclipse-style event if she had more than two.

He wished she would tell him what was wrong. They were friends first, weren't they? Friends who confided in one another, even if it had taken them over a decade to confide their true feelings.

"Do you—do you want to talk about what happened?" He attempted to sit up straighter but ended up sliding deeper into the morass of her couch. Would he ever feel comfortable moving them to the floor? Probably not. This was her space, and he didn't want to impose on her.

She held her wine glass in both hands and reclined against the partition to the living room. "It was all just a mess. A long night, and then a literal mess. The last couple brought their rambunctious wedding party who did everything but literally shit on the floor." She sipped her wine, then shook her head. "I'm sorry. I'm tired."

"That sounds awful." A thousand phrases ran through his brain, ones telling him to offer to help, to offer support. With his stupid fucking leg, though, they would all be empty promises, and she would know it, too. She would give him a tight, pitying, emasculating grin, and then she would manage all of it.

"It will be okay." She closed her eyes again and held the wine to her nose, inhaling deeply. "How's John? Are they getting ready for the wedding?"

"It seems for every box Katie checks off her to-do list, four more appear. Like there's an evil magic wedding gnome delighting in creating havoc." If only he could blame a similar gnome for his recent personal chaos. "They'll be all right. They have a lot of support."

Anita sniffed, and it could almost have been the start of a laugh, but he knew her laugh too well for that. "I doubt her brothers are chipping in, but I'm sure her mom loves all of this."

"Yeah. I imagine there will be copious buckets of tears on the big day." For the briefest moment, Patrick wondered what his own mother would say if he told her he was getting married. He had not even considered it. Diane did not relish Patrick sharing his affections with anyone other than his mother. Eloping was probably preferable to having her show up and ruin everything.

Anita was looking at him strangely, and his brain snapped back to attention. Had she said something and he had completely missed it? He could not exactly divulge what it was he had been thinking about.

"Patrick." Her voice was soft. He freaking loved the way she said his name, like he was one in a million and not one of the most popular Irish boy names of all time.

"What's wrong?"

"Nothing." Her eyes had a misty veil over them. Was she crying? Patrick picked up one of the napkins and handed it to her. She took it and crushed it against the stem of her wine glass. "Patrick, how are we doing?"

For the first time all evening, his leg stopped hurting. Not because he was healed, but because the blood all rushed toward his brain, swelling the vessels, and making his head thump like he was a drum in an 80s hair metal band.

"What?" he finally managed, coaxing the words from his desiccated, raw lips. His vision was hazy, like he was staring through a toilet paper tube after imbibing a quart of alcohol.

Her beautiful mouth curved downward into a disappointed arch. "Never mind. I'm going to go to bed. Good night."

She had closed the bedroom door before he could unstick his foot from his mouth.

This was not going to plan.

Chapter Eighteen

Shadows twisted and danced in the bedroom. Patrick would critique their dance frame if he wasn't so goddamned tired that his eyeballs felt like they had been permanently glued open.

First it was too cold in the room, then too hot. The sheets were bunched up in one singularly irritating space, then were too tight against his skin. No matter which way he rolled or turned, his broken leg stuck out its tongue and blew raspberries at him.

Patrick glanced over at Anita, her back to him. He had slept beside her enough at this point—thank his lucky stars and don't forget it—to know she was in her soundest period of sleep. Good. He didn't want to mess up her day any more than he already feared he had.

As quietly as he could, which was with all of the grace and poise of a water buffalo, Patrick clambered out of bed. Swinging his crutches gently to minimize the sound, he made his way into the living room.

He eyed his laptop but quickly ruled out work. If he started that at this witching hour, he would never get any rest tonight. Blue light was a bastard.

He could read. That wouldn't wake up Anita. He balanced on his good leg and perused her bookshelves. She had quite the collection of paperback romance novels, as well as a large selection of contemporary and historical books. He was more of a mystery/thriller fan, but at this point, he was not going to be choosy.

He selected a novel with a man's chest on the cover and lumbered toward the couch.

The throw pillows mocked him with their fluffy rainbow attitudes.

He huffed. Anita was asleep. Throw pillows be damned.

In a cleansing motion, he swept them all to the floor, clearing the space on the couch. Blissful relief settled into his muscles as he folded himself onto the cushions. At this rate, he would be asleep within minutes.

He had just cracked the spine on the novel to read the inscription—always his favorite part—when a bright light flashed across the living room windows, casting shadows over the furniture.

What was going on now?

He wrenched himself around, remembering to stay below the window ledge, and peered into the night.

That damn light at the corner of the parking lot was still out. Patrick shook his head. Idiot. He should have remembered to call the city to get it fixed. Too much on his mind lately.

One of the white vans was back, parked across both spaces in front of the antiques store. The rear doors were wide open, but Patrick couldn't see anybody moving.

Lights went on in the downstairs of the antiques store, but there was an old armoire blocking most of the action. From his vantage point, all he could see were shadows and suggestions of movement.

Where was his phone? Maybe he should be recording this or something. No, that was ridiculous.

Then again, he had thought the cyberstalking was ridiculous, routine internet troll shit, until it wasn't.

Patrick glanced away from the scene outside the window to look for his phone. Damn it, he had left it in the bedroom.

Anita had security cameras now, though, that were motion operated. They typically recorded stray cats pawing through the dumpster, but they would catch this.

His phone was too far away for his stupid injury, and it would take him far too long to get it. He'd have to rely on the security cameras.

He peered above the windowsill through the curtains again, trying to keep his head down and his body shielded behind the wall.

Two men, dressed all in black, carried large pieces of furniture on dollies from the store to the back of the van. He couldn't tell exactly what they were, but it looked like two antique dressers.

Patrick deflated slightly. He would smack his forehead, but he already had the beginnings of a migraine. They were just moving furniture. Out of an antique furniture store. At two in the morning.

What did he know? Who was he to judge? He was getting worked up over nothing.

He was seeing things where he shouldn't. Maybe he needed to talk to someone.

He was about to slink away and go back to sleep when he heard a high-pitched sound. It wasn't a cry of terror, more one of annoyance and frustration. It almost sounded like his mother had when she had caught him doing something he wasn't supposed to, like breathing too loudly or interrupting her very important phone call to tell her he had lacerated his forehead and needed to go to the ER for stitches.

But no, there was zero chance this was his mother. She had always called antiques "other people's junk." Who was it? Mrs. DeVeaux?

The two goons in black, for they were both tall and broad like they had been mail ordered from a goon catalog, exchanged a loaded look. They finished unloading the furniture into the van and went back inside the store.

Patrick wished he had some sort of music cue to tell him what to feel. Was he being an idiot? Was he hallucinating? Or was some really bad shit about to go down?

Any way the wind blew, his heart raced so fast he was worried it wouldn't be able to keep up. He let the beads of sweat run down his forehead rather than move and possibly draw attention to himself.

Through the window of the antiques store, he saw a petite frame move in and out of focus behind the armoire. It was replaced by one of the goon's shadows, hulking and menacing. Patrick held his breath. Something was happening. They were arguing.

There was a bright spark of light from behind the armoire in the window, like a firework that didn't fully explode. He couldn't hear anything this far away except for the sound of his breath catching in his throat.

He gripped the edge of the windowsill with white fingertips.

The two goons went back outside and collected one of the dollies from the back of the van. One went inside while the other moved around to the front driver's side door. He leaned his back against it, propping one foot against the metal, and puffed on an e-cigarette. Or was it a vape pen?

Damn it, Patrick didn't care. He had wanted the flare from a lighter to illuminate the guy's face.

The other goon came back outside a few moments later, now with a long wooden box balanced on the dolly. The henchman by the driver door put his vape pen down by his side and went around the back. Patrick watched as they hefted the wooden box into the rear of the van.

They didn't speak, or at least not loudly enough that he could hear from his second-floor window. Anita's security cameras didn't record sound, either.

The goon squad—if two really constituted a squad, Patrick wasn't completely clear on the vernacular—finished loading the wooden box into the van. The one with the vape puffed on it again as he went back into the antiques store, shutting off the lights and closing the door. The other got into the van on the passenger side.

Patrick felt his heartbeat returning to a slightly more normal, manageable pace. This was fine. Everything was fine.

The goon tossed his presumably empty vape onto the ground, climbed into the van, and slowly drove out of the parking lot with the lights off.

For several moments, Patrick couldn't move. Partially this was due to his leg, which had seized up due to the adrenaline and odd positioning on the couch. Mostly it was his unquiet mind.

What had he seen? What was going on in the antiques store? Why the fuck had he not brought his phone with him?

He stared across the way, trying to see into the

windows of the antiques store. All the lights were off, even in the upstairs where he knew Mrs. DeVeaux lived. Why wouldn't she have woken up when the delivery was being made? What was that flash of light?

He had no idea, but as soon as his leg stopped burning like the fire of a thousand wasp stings, he was going to go out and find that vape pen.

****

Anita awoke to clanging and swearing, coming from the kitchen.

She opened her eyes, still groggy with sleep, and reached across the bed. No familiar warmth. No Patrick.

"Patrick?" She slid out of bed and wrapped a rainbow-patterned shawl around the shoulders of her pretzel-print pajamas. "Patrick, is that you?

He didn't respond. She padded to the kitchen and halted abruptly at the door, her eyes wide.

Patrick was on the floor in front of her pantry, surrounded by jars of peanut butter, a flurry of plastic storage bags, kitchen utensils, and a spilled bag of pasta.

"What are you doing?" Anita asked, amazed she managed to keep her composure.

He glanced up at her, his eyes dark and wild with some fury she hadn't seen before. "I have to go outside and get it." He scooped pasta from the floor with his hands and poured it back into the bag. His bad leg jutted from underneath him like a broken mast.

This was very bad. She knelt beside him and took his hands in hers. They were shaking, so tremulous she was shocked he wasn't spilling the tiny grains of elbow pasta. "Get what? Patrick, what's going on?"

Patrick glanced rapidly between her and the window. "Next door. Something bad's happened. We need to get to the bottom of it. We have to go outside and get it."

"Get what? Honey, you're not making any sense." Shit, had he taken some of the hydrocodone the orthopedist had provided him? She knew people had all sorts of reactions to medications.

He pulled his hands from hers and started organizing the mess on the floor, piling plastic storage bags into their ripped cardboard container. "We need to get out there before they come back. Will you help me?"

Tears rose in her eyes. "Of course. I want to help you. I will always help you, but I don't know what's going on. Patrick, it's barely three in the morning, and you're not telling me what's going on."

"I think they killed her."

His eyes were fierce, so dark she couldn't see the blue in them she loved so much, the blue that soothed and calmed her.

He was so far away from her. She just wanted him back, wanted to feel the connective thread between them again.

She cupped his face in her hands, pulling his gaze to hers, trying to breathe calm into him. "Killed who?"

He was panting, whether from pain or anxiety, she couldn't tell. "Mrs. DeVeaux."

Okay, Patrick had lost his mind. "Patrick, I'm sure Mrs. DeVeaux is fine. I'll call her in the morning."

"Call her now."

"It's three in the morning. She'll call the police if I disturb her." She would, too. Anita wouldn't put it past her.

A frantic smile crossed Patrick's lips but never reached his eyes. "Good! Good. Let's call the police. Let's call John. He wanted me to talk to the high school kids, but this is more important."

What was he talking about? "John's getting married in less than a week. If we wake them up, Katie will murder me."

"You don't understand." Patrick sat on the floor, screwing and unscrewing the lid of the fallen peanut butter jar. "The lights weren't on, and there was this spark. Like a gunshot."

"Honey, how do you know it was a gunshot? The only guns you've seen are in movies. Did you hear something? Maybe it was a car backfiring."

Patrick pulled away from her, his entire body vibrating. "We have to go outside!!!" His cry rattled the walls of the apartment. As if realizing he was overreacting, he slumped against her, the air deflated from his body. Anita wrapped her arms around him. If only she could take this pain from him. "Please," he whispered, his voice small and so un-Patrick-like that it stabbed her through the heart. "Please help."

She tightened her hold on him. "Of course. Of course, I'll help you."

****

She texted John while Patrick went to put a sweater over his bare chest. She hoped for John's sake that he left the *do not disturb* on his phone overnight.

They cleaned up the pantry items, donned cleaning gloves, and went outside, toting a plastic storage bag and a pair of kitchen tongs between them. Patrick still wouldn't tell her what they were looking for, or why.

He kept muttering to himself about the proper collective term for goons and whether throwing a vape pen on the ground was considered an environmental disaster.

She had to keep her own head. Patrick needed her, if not some antipsychotics, but she did not want to think about that.

As she walked beside him across the parking lot, her phone flashlight in one hand, she sniffed him surreptitiously. He didn't smell like he had been drinking. Maybe there really was something in the Lewis water supply that turned the men around her into bizarro world versions of themselves. If she had a better relationship with her father or Patrick's mom, she would ask them.

Patrick inspected the ground like a bloodhound on the trail.

Anita wrapped her shawl more tightly around her shoulders. "Are you going to tell me what we're looking for?"

"The vape, the vape!"

It was more than a little disconcerting, watching him refuse help as he maneuvered around the edge of the parking lot on his crutches. He was going to fall, if he kept walking bent in half like that.

"Patrick—"

"Shit." He stopped at a nondescript pile of gravel and grass and stared into it like it held the mysteries of a lost treasure canyon.

"What's wrong?" If it was literally a pile of shit, she was calling the doctor stat. Anita stepped beside him and followed his gaze. "Ew. Don't these things have lithium batteries? This is a natural disaster waiting to happen." There was a cluster of cigarettes and used vape pens strewn around the weeds along the side of the concrete.

Patrick shook his head repeatedly from side to side. "We have to take them all."

"Why? It's garbage. Likely radioactive, leaky garbage that can explode if the battery is exposed. Tell me what's going on."

"I told you." He leaned over with the tongs, but his balance was too precarious. She snatched the tongs and plastic bag from his hands. "Give that back! I don't need your help."

Tears rose again in her eyes. "You *asked* for my help. I'm not letting you get hurt. I just want to know what's going on with you."

"I told you, they—"

A police cruiser pulled into the parking lot, its headlights chasing the shadows. Anita held a hand over her eyes to protect them from the sudden glare.

Beside her, Patrick relaxed, his entire body shifting. "John! Thank God, John is here."

Anita stifled the disappointed cry in her throat. She wasn't enough for him. He was her everything, and she wasn't enough on this, his worst day.

John Flaherty stepped from the cruiser. He was dressed in jeans and a navy-blue pea coat, and he tucked his wide hands into the pockets of his coat. "What's going on?" He addressed it to Anita, but before she could answer, Patrick started rambling.

"John!" He rushed toward him on his crutches, gesticulating wildly. "I got up, and I noticed that white van was back at the antiques store. So I watched them, but I was really careful. I didn't want anyone to see me. So I hid beneath the windowsill, and there were these two guys, or goons, or henchmen, or whatever. All in black. They went into the antiques store, and I thought about getting my phone, but then I remembered, the security cameras! Then they came back out, with these huge dressers, and I thought, never mind, they're just moving furniture, even though this is not really time to move furniture. So I was going to go back to bed, but then there was this sound, like a scream, and there were these shadows, and a light—" He gestured here with a finger gun and a POP. "—and they carried her out in a wooden box. So we need to find the vape pen because we can get the DNA."

Anita couldn't watch Patrick, couldn't listen to his incomprehensible derailed train of thought, so she focused on John Flaherty. On his impassive expression, the blank set of his jaw, his arms crossed over his chest.

He waited for Patrick to finish, which he did with a flourish of plastic storage bag, gesticulating toward the pile of lithium garbage.

Anita's heart sank.

"Okay," John said, his voice even and unhurried. "So you believe you witnessed a murder? Of the lady who owns the antiques store?"

"Yes. Mrs. DeVeaux, yes."

"Because you saw some shadows and a light that you think was a gunshot?"

"Yes." The muscles of Patrick's forehead relaxed, as though he were relieved someone finally understood. Someone who was not his girlfriend.

"And you want us to find this supposed murderer by DNA testing a vape pen?"

"Exactly!" Patrick looked at her, as if to say, *why didn't you get it?*

She still didn't.

John paused, a muscle twitching along his carved jaw. "Which one?"

"What?" Patrick's eyes widened and his mouth went slack.

"Which vape?" John leaned over and looked at the garbage pile. "There's at least five here. Which probably should be illegal, to leave that on the ground. Not to mention the cigarette butts." He glanced around the parking lot. "There's probably a few more dump sites around here. How do you know which pen we should test?"

Patrick's jaw opened, and he closed his mouth. Anita saw the fatigue etch itself into his skin. "I don't know. All of them."

John nodded slowly. "You want us, the Lewis police department, who shares an overworked lab with the major metropolitan city of Philadelphia, to test numerous vape pens for DNA?"

Patrick slumped against his crutches, all the fight having gone out of him. "I don't know." Anita slid an arm around his waist, but he didn't seem to see her.

John softened. "Let's knock and see if Mrs. DeVeaux is home. She'll yell at us for waking her up, then everyone can get back to bed. We could all use some more sleep."

"Sure. Sure."

Anita held onto Patrick as they walked toward the door to the antiques store. It really was creepy in the middle of the night, all long shadows and blown fuses in the torchlights.

John knocked, and they waited. Anita could hear her heart beating in her throat. What if something really had happened to Mrs. DeVeaux? She should believe Patrick. She loved him. If he needed her help, she would offer it.

After what felt like a thousand hours but was probably only minutes, lights went on in the upstairs apartment. Anita let out her breath, unaware she had been holding it.

Patrick deflated further beside her, like a hermit crab pulling itself inside its shell.

She heard the turning of door locks, then it creaked open.

Instead of Mrs. DeVeaux's irritated petite frame, there was a tall, lean man wearing twill pajama bottoms and nothing else. A man she recognized. Her stomach churned with acid.

His gaze found her, and Steve Barnes reclined against the doorjamb, arms crossed over his muscular chest. "Well, hello."

Patrick tensed beside her, and she squeezed his waist, trying to reassure him. Of course it would be Barnes. Was nothing going to go right tonight?

"I'm sorry to bother you at this late hour," John said in what Anita considered his cop voice. "Mister—"

"Barnes. Steve Barnes." He shook John's hand but kept his gaze on Anita and Patrick, his eyes flicking between them. She wanted to smack him four ways to Sunday.

"Mr. Barnes, we're looking for Mrs. DeVeaux, who lives here and runs the antique shop. Do you know where she is?"

"Of course." Steve Barnes offered what seemed to Anita an attempt at a disarming smile. "She went down to Rehoboth Beach. She needed a vacation." He looked at John. "She's my aunt. I told her I'd help out while she's out of town."

Something prickled at the base of Anita's spine. Mrs. DeVeaux never mentioned any family, not that she and Anita had the type of relationship that involved sharing personal details. And in the years since she had opened the studio, Mrs. DeVeaux had *never* taken a vacation. The antiques store opened and closed every day at the exact same time. Anita had set her watch by it one day, purely for her own entertainment.

She couldn't read John's expression. "Okay. Anything unusual going on tonight, Mr. Barnes?" he asked.

"Nothing." Steve Barnes's face was all innocence. "It's been a quiet night. I've been asleep."

John arched an eyebrow. "No deliveries?"

Barnes laughed, a harsh, caustic sound that bit more than the October chill. "At this time of night? Hardly."

Anita glanced at Patrick, but she couldn't read his expression, either. He was either going to fall asleep or fly into a martial arts rage.

Barnes yawned theatrically, and his gaze laser-focused on her again. Perfect. Just what she needed. "I need to get back to bed. I have a busy day tomorrow."

John shook his hand and took down his cell phone number. Barnes nodded to her as a means of farewell, but she didn't respond. The prickle along her spine had intensified into a full-blown throbbing.

Barnes closed the door, and it was the three of them again, illuminated in the headlights from the cruiser.

John turned to Patrick, and his expression changed,

softened. He held his arms wide in a "trust me" gesture. "See? Mrs. DeVeaux's fine. She's in Rehoboth. We can all go get some sleep."

Patrick's jaw was tense. Anita rubbed his back, but it only seemed to make it worse. "I don't believe him." His voice was flat and raw. "Mrs. DeVeaux didn't have family. She's not in Rehoboth."

John sighed and ran a hand over his bald pate. "Look, Patrick, I can't question someone when there is no evidence of a crime." He held up a hand as Patrick opened his mouth. "A discarded e-cigarette is not evidence of a crime. You know this."

"What about the security cameras? We should check the security cameras."

Anita wasn't certain that would be helpful. Since she had installed them, the only thing they captured were kids joyriding down Main Street late at night and feral cats.

John hung his head. When he spoke, he sounded resigned and so tired that Anita almost offered to drive him home. "Patrick, I'm sorry. But it's late. And you said you'd reach out to the dance students in the morning. Get some sleep. We can check them tomorrow." He caught Anita's glance, and she stilled. If ever there were an expression that said *let's talk in private*, this was it.

"Patrick, go upstairs," she said. "It will be okay after we get some rest. We'll talk in the morning."

"But what about the—"

Anita took the plastic bag and tongs from him, keeping her smile soft, reassuring. The complete opposite of how she felt internally. "I'll collect them. All of them. I promise." She would search online tomorrow for one of those e-waste recycling plants.

Patrick's shoulders slumped. "Okay. G'night, John."

She didn't get a good night. Perfect.

John waited until Patrick was already back inside the studio before he turned to Anita, his eyes frowning. "Is he on something?"

"No! At least, I don't think so. He hasn't been himself." Her breath caught in her chest. Her father wasn't himself, either. What if there was something going around? Some sort of brain-altering virus? She needed to stop watching Patrick's dark Scandinavian mysteries before bed. "His doctor gave him some hydrocodone, but I don't think he'd take it. He never does anything except drink alcohol."

"Something's up with him." John shook his head slowly. "Will and I were talking about it earlier. Did he tell you he had a panic attack this morning at Amore?"

"No." Not that it surprised her. She should have asked more about his day. If she hadn't been so wrapped up in her own family drama, she would have.

"It was bad, Anita. Has he ever talked to anyone about what happened with Christina Blake?"

"No." She pulled the shawl around her shoulders. If only she weren't standing out here in her salty pretzel pajamas. She should have opted for fleece. It was slightly more respectable. "I've tried talking to him about it, and I found the names of some counselors, but he says he doesn't need them."

John ran his hand over the hard curve of his jaw. "He needs something. Keep an eye on him, okay?"

"I will." She forced a smile. "Are you all right? You look stressed. With the wedding and all, I did not expect you to come out tonight."

He softened slightly. "I'll be fine. I can't sleep much anyway, with the high school case." He exhaled loudly. "It's nothing I can't handle. I was glad to come."

"Thanks."

She watched as John stepped back into his cruiser and drove from the parking lot, leaving her alone.

Though it was far too early in the morning and she had gotten far too little sleep, she was wide awake. The high school kids being drugged at a creek party. Her father acting like an actual monster. That creep Barnes showing up. Patrick's fading grip on his mental health.

Something was wrong in Lewis. Very wrong. And she didn't know what to do to stop it.

She cast a narrow glance at the upstairs windows of the antiques store. The lights were off, and the curtains were still, but how did she know that smarmy asshole wasn't watching her?

If he was, he could watch her be a dutiful girlfriend. Fuck him.

She sighed, knelt on the ground, and used the tongs to pick up the used vape pens. Patrick had better appreciate this.

Chapter Nineteen

Patrick flipped through page after page of search results on his phone. *Single use e-cigarettes versus ones that use cartridges. What drugs can be vaped? Labs that do DNA testing. How to test objects for DNA at home.* Why were the turnaround times so long? And there was no way for a civilian to cross-reference that DNA sample with other people's samples?

Why wasn't there a website for armchair detectives who wanted to solve backyard mysteries using twenty-first century techniques?

He heard the door shut in the studio below and the beep as Anita reset the alarm.

At least she believed him. He knew John didn't, knew from the moment John gave him the cop voice.

Anita wouldn't have bought the bullshit that dickhead Barnes slung. She was too smart for that, too savvy. Shiny, stupid posh guy.

She walked into the apartment as though she were weighed down with four-hundred-pound iron chains. While he did not personally mind some light bondage, Anita didn't seem to be enjoying herself with her plastic bag full of vapes.

"Thank you," he said. He stood and leaned on one crutch. "I've been researching private labs, and I think—"

She held up a single hand in front of his face.

"Stop. We need to talk."

"Okay. Absolutely."

She sank onto the couch beside him, and he folded his good leg to sit beside her.

She swallowed, set the plastic bag on the coffee table, and took his hand in hers. "Patrick, what's going on?"

He frowned. How could she not see it? "I told you. Someone murdered Mrs. DeVeaux. We have to find out who did it."

She dropped his hand and sighed. "Did you take something tonight? For the pain?"

"What do you mean?"

"I mean the hydrocodone that your orthopedist gave you. Did you take some?"

"No. I don't like it. I only took ibuprofen."

Tears welled in her eyes. He leaned toward her to brush them away. She pressed her cheek into his palm.

"Patrick, you need to talk to someone."

"I am." He cradled her face between both of his hands. "I'm talking to you."

"No." She shook her head, and he lost his grip on her. "I mean a professional. Patrick, I'm not the only one who's worried."

"Worried?" No, she couldn't mean that. He didn't worry her. He helped her. That was his mission. "Why are you worried?"

Anita swallowed and folded her hands in her lap. "You've been having panic attacks. John told me all about it, too. You're not yourself. I think you have PTSD."

He stood up, but he reached for his crutch too late and smacked his ass against the arm of the couch as he fell back onto the couch. "I don't have PTSD."

"I think you do. After what happened with Christina—"

"This has nothing to do with Christina Blake."

"Patrick, please. I was there. I know what she did to you, to us. And with her trial coming up—"

"It has NOTHING to do with Christina Blake. Why don't you believe me?"

She picked up the plastic bag on the table and dropped it, the empty vape pens rattling like bones. "You had me calling our friend in the middle of the night to impart meaning to trash. Then I had to pick up said radioactive trash. Not to mention you had John wake up a stranger to accuse him of murdering his aunt!" Her voice quieted and slowed to the tone one might use for a recalcitrant child. "How do you not see this is a problem?"

Oh, he saw the problem all right. His blood ran thick, and he edged his words with ice. "So this is about him. That smarmy, sleek, rich guy. Steve." He deliberately accentuated the long *E* sound until it hummed like the world's most irritating white noise machine.

She rolled her eyes. "This has *nothing* to do with him. I'm worried about you."

This was ridiculous. He didn't need to listen to this, to her excuses and accusations. He was fine. He had some minor heart palpitations, but he was an athlete. He could manage this on his own. He would figure this out on his own.

He stood with the crutch under one arm and picked up the bag of vape pens from the table. He shook it in her face, hating himself the entire time he did it. "If you don't believe me, I'm not staying here. I'll call my mother."

She arched an eyebrow. "You're upset, so you're going to call *your* mother?"

Okay, no, he would much rather call Marina, but that was not an option at this moment, when he was busy lighting his life on fire. "Yes. I don't need your permission."

She deflated a bit, reaching her arms for him. "Patrick, please. We can talk about this. We can figure it out. I just want to help you."

"I don't need your help." He punctuated his statement with a hard thump of his crutch against the floor, which was a terrible idea, as it radiated through the bundle of nerves in his armpit and nearly made his entire arm go numb.

With the most dignity he could manage, which was very little given that he was about eighty-nine percent self-loathing at this point, he left the apartment.

Chapter Twenty

Calling his mother at four in the morning to pick him up was an enormous mistake. He would have been better off walking the three miles than hearing her rant at him over the din of her easy listening saxophone music.

"It's not that I mind picking you up," his mom said, turning up the air conditioning in the car, even though it was only fifty degrees outside and he had neglected to bring a jacket when he rage-walked away from Anita. "I never mind helping you out. It's just that I got home from the hospital so late. Of course, I don't really need much sleep. Other people might, but you're lucky I'm not as lazy as they are. I don't think we have coffee at the house. Oh, and the extra sheets are still in the washing machine. You don't mind sleeping on the couch, do you?"

Did he mind sleeping on the couch that still smelled of the cat she had allowed Patrick for exactly one month before giving it back to the animal shelter? "No, Mom. I don't mind." She had supposedly developed allergies, but he had a feeling it was because he had given the cat his attention rather than her.

Who could blame him? At least the cat had been direct when it showed its claws.

His mom glanced at the plastic storage bag gripped in his hands. "What are you doing with that? Don't tell me you started smoking. It's those Europeans you hang out with. They give people these terrible ideas and habits." She said *Europeans* like it was a four-letter word. Patrick well knew it was code for "people who are not me."

"It's a project." Shit, she was not going to accept that. "For the ballroom dance club. Drugs are…bad. Et cetera."

"Hmpf." She pursed her lips. "I don't know why you spend so much time with those kids. Teenagers nowadays get into so much trouble. You would not believe what I see at work, all the time. It's terrible, just terrible. You were always such a good boy."

"It is terrible, what those poor kids are going through after that creek party." The moment the words left his mouth, he regretted them. He wasn't supposed to talk back.

Her eyes narrowed into slits, and her mouth twitched at one side. "No one is completely innocent."

Super.

Patrick stared out the window, his stomach sinking, as his childhood home came into view, a single story filled with fraught memories and a work shed out back he'd never been allowed to see. What was terrible was the way he had treated Anita. She had attempted to help him, and he had shut her down. What was terrible was thinking that his mom was in any way preferable to his girlfriend, even if they were fighting.

He should text her and apologize for being an idiot.

"Here we are! Home again!" His mother's singing voice grated on his ears.

She parked in front of her split-level home with the brown siding and fading red roof. Diane tsked. "I know, it really needs a paint job. I was going to have it repainted over the summer, but I was so busy, and I didn't have any help at all." She sighed, her entire body following her exhalation. "It will have to wait until next spring. You'll be healed by then, won't you, Patrick?"

Patrick grimaced as he stepped from the car. So she was still angry about the time he had spent with Anita this summer. Should he really feel guilty for spending time with the one person who liked him for who he was?

Besides, she had clearly hired someone to expand the shed out back. It was at least twice the size he remembered, with tan walls and a green vinyl roof. Where had she gotten the money?

Money. Home. *Shit*. He had left the ring box in the drawer when he had stupidly stormed out of the house.

He yawned. He'd get it tomorrow afternoon. He needed some sleep, that was all. A few hours of sleep, and he would be right as rain.

****

John stopped tossing and turning and got out of bed at five in the morning. Katie would not appreciate more sleeplessness this close to the wedding. She had a half-week of work at the elementary school before next weekend's party blitz. She had enough stress as it was.

Hell, he should be getting more sleep, too.

He pulled on his running leggings and a thin, long-sleeved shirt. A run would ease his mind, especially in the brisk October air.

He stretched outside the door to their house then headed down the road past the high school.

That Steve Barnes was...something. John had recognized him from Home Squared, the home shopping channel, ubiquitous viewing at the assisted living where John's grandmother resided. Even on TV, Barnes had always struck him as too smarmy. Dead eyes, that's what his grandmother said. Up close, they were not so much dead as slick and dank, like an oil spill in a hell dimension.

John's breath crystallized in the early morning dark as he puffed. The cool air burned his lungs, but he was getting used to it as his body warmed.

He raised a hand in greeting to a pair of early morning joggers in matching fleece and fanny packs, but there weren't many out this early on a cold day.

Steve Barnes. Patrick's wild-eyed conviction. Mrs. DeVeaux. The Lewis high school kids in the ICU. Too many happenings in small town Lewis.

Footsteps pounded against the pavement behind him. Someone was pushing themselves this morning.

He glanced over his shoulder mid-stride but didn't see anyone. Not unexpected, as the trees lining the street grew thick. Still, his spine tingled, and his nerves stood alert. He never ignored his gut.

He paused along the side of the road under the pretense of needing to stretch and examined his surroundings.

A few geese honked overhead as they made their way south for the winter. The trees around him rustled in the slight breeze.

In the distance, he heard a buzzing sound that sent another chill up his spine, one that had nothing to do with the ambient temperature. Was it a drone? A motorcycle?

Was someone chasing him?

Adrenaline pulsed in his veins. After his stint in the

Navy, he knew he could handle himself. But he was alone out here.

His house was a forty-minute run in one direction, town was twenty minutes. He was somewhere between cow pastures and Route 322, which was nowhere helpful if he was being chased. Was he being chased? It wouldn't be wise to dally if that were the case.

He weighed the options in the span of time it took him to exhale. He braced himself for the sprint, bent his massive frame against the wind, and took off down the road toward town.

He pumped his arms, schooling his breath to give him the most oxygen while he pushed harder. His muscles burned, but he was well-trained enough to love it.

He turned the hidden curve, moving so fast everything in his peripheral vision was a blur of brown and evergreen and orange. His body tensed, ready for the fight, ready for the battle, pure adrenaline flooding his body.

But there was nothing there.

He skidded to a stop, panting, breath heaving hot crystals of air. There was no one here. No one following him.

How had he gotten that so wrong?

His phone rang, startling him so badly in the stillness that he leapt four feet in the air.

The caller ID said *Deputy CW*. He wiped the sweat from his face with his palm and accepted the call. "Curtis? What's up?"

"You need to get down to the hospital. There's been an accident on the road to Lewis Creek."

Chapter Twenty-One

Patrick woke after far too short a time to the insistent trilling of his cell phone.

He reached over to the coffee table, sending a lightning strike of pain from his neck down his arm. Sleeping on a couch was nowhere near as comfortable as sleeping with Anita.

He fumbled for the phone, suddenly convinced in his half-awake daze that it was, indeed, her. He could apologize. He could tell her he was wrong. He could tell her whatever it took to fix this.

When he looked at the display screen, he frowned. Not Anita. Bobby? Why was Will's boyfriend calling him?

He slid the bar to accept the call. "Bobby?" Shit, his voice sounded like he had been up all night at a rager instead of driving everyone around him to the brink of sanity.

"Patrick, hey."

Bobby's typically casual, easygoing voice was filled with palpable tension.

"Is everything okay? Is Will okay?" Patrick propped himself on one elbow and rubbed the sleep from his eyes with his knuckles.

"Will's fine. I'm sorry to call."

"No, it's fine."

"It's just, Will could really use somebody right

now. I'm here, but I have this teleconference I can't miss."

"What's going on?" Patrick forced himself to a sitting position, which was not easy to do as the couch was almost as old as he was and had the butt divots to prove it. "What happened?"

"It's bad, man." Bobby sucked his teeth over the phone. Patrick could picture him cleaning his black-framed glasses. "It's his mom. She was on patrol this morning, out by Lewis Creek, and she got attacked in her car. She's in the hospital."

Patrick's stomach roiled, and acid rose up his throat. "Oh fuck. Is she going to be okay?"

Bobby sighed. "I don't know. Is there any way you can come to the hospital? I don't know if they'll let us in or whatever, but it's worth a try. Will's really upset."

"Yes, yes, absolutely."

"Thank you. I'll pick you up at Anita's in twenty minutes?"

Patrick glanced around his mother's living room. "Um, I'm not at Anita's. I'm at my mom's house."

The line went silent for a long moment.

"Bobby?"

"Why are you at your mom's house?" Bobby clipped the words.

Patrick's heart tossed in his chest, as if it were admonishing him for his mistakes and idiocy as well. He hadn't realized Bobby and Will had discussed his mom. Why would that even come up in a conversation? "I-It-It's a lot to go into right now."

Bobby's silence was so loud that Patrick could practically feel his breath against his ear. "Fine. I'll be there in half an hour."

Patrick put the phone down on the coffee table amidst the careful arrangement of magazines and covered his face with his hands.

"Oh, you're awake."

He looked up to see his mom, dressed in blue scrubs and holding her purse. "Good morning, Mom."

She jiggled her keys in her hand. "I didn't know you'd be awake. I didn't make breakfast. I suppose I could be late for work and make something."

He was starving but knew this script well. "No, Mom. I don't need anything."

"Good. There's medicine in the cabinet if your leg hurts, and food in the fridge. Dinner will be at six sharp."

She shut the door behind her with the finality of one who does not expect a reply.

Patrick's tired, aching body collapsed into the divot on the couch. It would take him six hundred years to climb out of this hole he had dug for himself.

****

Anita poured her attention into her tax forms, which may have been the worst possible way to distract herself.

If she had poured sand directly into her eyeballs, it would be easier to keep them open.

She had watched the footage from her security cameras overnight, but either someone had deactivated them, someone had erased the footage, or their antics from last night hadn't triggered the motion sensors. She was too exhausted and weirded out to investigate more right now.

She checked her phone for messages, but she had no notifications. Out in the ballroom, Toni had her

Zumba students in a high-intensity routine that was literally shaking the thin walls of her office. It was like a drum beating directly into her brain and rattling it around.

Fuck it. She was an adult, and this wasn't 1982. She could reach out to Patrick. She sent him a quick text, which she deleted and edited about seven times.

—Can we talk? Please.—

Maybe it needed a gif, like a cat with prayer hands. No, too much.

She waited for a few moments as her computer screen flipped to the screensaver, which was a collage of photos of her and Patrick. One from the day trip to the Jersey Shore over the summer, laughing with John and Katie and Will and Bobby. One from a date to the Franklin Institute. One from the Keystone Star Ball, Patrick's bruises covered in a thick layer of concealer.

Her heart clenched. *Patrick needed help.*

She checked her phone again. No reply yet.

Toni knocked at the doorjamb. "Hey, Anita."

Anita looked up and rested her chin in her hand. Toni looked gorgeous as always, in a burnt orange jumpsuit with her long braids coiled on her head. "Hey. Sounds like class went well."

"Mostly the regulars today, the ones who like the high intensity." When she was tired, Toni's Georgia accent thickened. She took the seat opposite Anita and chugged from her two-liter water bottle. "How are you?"

"Finances." Anita grimaced. "Not even worth talking about." Nor did she want to discuss Patrick, though she knew Toni would bring him up if she let the conversation lag. Toni was one of Patrick's biggest supporters.

"I wanted to tell you, I love Nina Rabinova's makeup tutorials on the studio channel. She's totally rocking it. She even has her own hashtag, BallroomDivaBabe."

The ghost of a smile flitted across Anita's face. "Good. I'm glad she loves it."

"It's getting a ton of exposure, too. There are all these comments in Russian." Toni showed her one of the video pages, with line after line in Cyrillic.

"I wish I could read Russian better." She spoke a little, enough to count and find a bathroom, the crucial parts of any language.

"Me, too." Toni stuck her phone into the pocket along the side of her thigh. "I could run it through the translation app, but I always get weird results when I do that."

Anita didn't want her friend to leave. She didn't want to be left alone again to her own fevered machinations. "How's the nonprofit?"

Toni rolled her dark brown eyes. "I started it thinking I was going to help kids have access to good nutrition, dance, and fitness. Then the pesky bureaucracy steps in and muddies everything. Do you have any idea how much capital it takes to get something off the ground?" She sighed, her trademark exuberance tamer than usual. "I've exhausted the Philly donors."

"So, more in New York?"

"Yup. I've got a ton of meetings coming up before December." Toni shrugged her toned shoulders. "Anita, I've got to cut down on my classes. There's no way I can teach and make these meetings, even if I schedule them all together."

A pit opened in Anita's stomach, but Toni didn't need to know that. She forced a smile. "Not a problem. We'll be fine. The nonprofit is what matters. You're doing a great thing."

"I know, but with Patrick out…"

Anita waved her hand. "Don't worry about it. Really. You've always been such an immense help to us. We want to help you. If I had any extra money, I would very happily invest."

Toni's smile creased her cheeks. "I know you would, and that means a lot. Once this first stage is out of the way, hopefully it will get a lot more fun."

"Absolutely." Though Anita knew from experience that making your hobby or passion your full-time job did not automatically make it fun. It often blurred the lines between work life and personal life. She had only crawled out of the overworked and overtired hole when Patrick had come back and reminded her why she loved what she did.

As if reading her thoughts, Toni asked, "So how's Patrick?"

"Ugh." Anita dropped her forehead to her desk.

Toni laughed lightly. "Honey, everyone has problems, right?"

"I know." Anita dragged herself to a sitting position. "I wish he would talk to me. Something is going on with him, and he won't get help."

"Men are idiots. You don't need me to tell you that. Do what I do when life is getting me down. Drink half a bottle of wine and watch *A Star is Born*."

The smile took Anita by surprise, but she was grateful for it. "Which one?"

"Is there one without Bradley Cooper? I can't believe you even had to ask."

Her phone buzzed, and she jumped on it as if it were a fly and she a frog.

Toni chuckled. "I'll let you talk to Patrick. See you later, Anita."

"Bye, Toni."

As soon as the other woman left, Anita tapped the code on her phone screen and pulled up her messages.

Her stomach fell. It was from her dad.

—Your mother wants me to talk to you. Lunch?—

What an inviting request.

She could say no in about eight languages, which was seven more than her father, not that he saw it that way.

She should go. He was her father.

Yet she couldn't move her fingers to type the *Y,E,S.* His words that night reverberated in her ears, louder than all of the other self-positivity statements she had been telling herself to counteract the years of paternal disappointment.

Her phone buzzed again, and this time, the ache inside of her kindled to flames of anger.

—Noon, Stella Luna.—

She hated Stella Luna. It was overpriced, and the food was greasy. He only liked it because he had delivered the owner's kids twenty years before, and they always seated him at a window table and gave him free wine. She would have to put on a dress and makeup and sit and simper, listening to his self-congratulatory speeches while choking down over-sauced linguini.

No. She didn't have to put up with this. She was a

grown, independent woman. One who would much rather watch Bradley Cooper crooning to Lady Gaga.

She typed out a quick reply and hit send before she could reconsider.

—*I can't, I have other plans.*—

Three dots popped up on her screen, but then no further words appeared.

Anita flipped the screen of her phone so it faced the table and stared blindly at her screensaver. If only Patrick were here. He loved *A Star is Born.*

****

Patrick hopped out of Bobby's black SUV and followed him across the hospital parking lot. He hadn't expected to be back here so soon after his own accident.

"Is John here?" Patrick asked as they waited in the line of visitors at the hospital reception area.

Bobby's forehead furrowed. "He and Curtis are at the station. Hopefully they got her a room by now. When she was in the emergency room, they only allow one visitor."

Patrick sighed. "Poor Will."

Bobby's gray eyes flashed. "He's not the best at handling things like this. What if he—"

"He wouldn't do anything stupid." He would, but Bobby probably wouldn't appreciate the reminder at that moment. They'd been going out for over two years now, so there was no way Bobby had missed Will's hair-trigger temper. He was the best of guys in good times, but if he was overwhelmed, things could go south fast. It was one of the best things about their relationship, that Bobby smoothed out Will's razor edges.

Bobby cut a glance at him, as though he knew

exactly what Patrick had been thinking about. Last fall, Will had heard about a teacher at Lewis High abusing one of the students. He had broken the teacher's nose, arm, and several ribs before John had pulled him off.

"Name?"

They reached the front of the reception line, and a woman, her gray-brown curls pulled back from her face with a knitted headband, tapped at her computer screen.

"Name?" she repeated.

"We're visiting Allison Forbes. We're friends of the family," Bobby said, tugging at the loose tie around his collar.

The woman, whose ID badge said her name was Kathy, scrolled through a list on her screen. "I'm sorry, but she is not permitted visitors right now."

Bobby exhaled through his teeth. "Please. She's my boyfriend's mom. He's with her, and he needs some support."

Her eyes softened. "I really am sorry, but it's hospital policy. Maybe he could meet you down in the lobby?"

"Come on, Bobby, it's okay." Patrick led him away from the reception area and toward an empty bench.

Bobby collapsed onto the seat and ran his hands over his face. "Shit, Patrick. Who would do this to Will's mom? Everyone loves her."

"I don't know." Though he had his suspicions, starting with Steve Barnes and the antiques shop. He was seventy percent sure his suspicion of Steve Barnes had nothing to do with his slick charm or obvious interest in Anita. "Are you sure she was attacked?"

Bobby nodded. "That's what Will said. Someone ran her car off the road, and then she was assaulted."

Patrick shivered. "That's awful. You said it happened by the creek? What was she doing there?"

"I don't know. She takes patrol sometimes, though Will's tried to talk her out of it. Maybe she was looking for something? Something about the high schoolers?"

"Maybe." The bench he sat on was cold and sterile. "There's something big going on."

Bobby leaned against the wall. "What do you mean?"

He shouldn't have said anything. Bobby was a lawyer. He could probably smell the stink of paranoia wafting from him. But when he looked at him, Bobby's expression wasn't one of disbelief.

It gave him a bit of courage. "I don't know. There was that home invasion and drug bust back in May. The kids at the high school getting sick. All the streetlights that are burned out, like someone moving in the dark doesn't want to be seen. Sheriff Forbes getting attacked. There's something weird going on at the antiques store next to the studio. It's a bunch of coincidences that don't make any sense. Lewis used to be such a quiet town."

Bobby removed his glasses and cleaned them. "They closed that drug case. The cartel used a phony house staging company."

Patrick couldn't stop himself, though he knew he should. "But where would a staging company get their supplies? An antiques store. One in a small town with a pliable little old lady in charge." He slammed his hand against the bench, and the resounding pain settled his fervor. "I'm probably being stupid. Mrs. DeVeaux wasn't a pushover."

"It's not stupid. There's a lot going on. Not to

mention John's getting married on Saturday."

A flush of shame reddened his neck. He should have remembered that. He should have called John and offered to unload some of the wedding preparations. Instead, he was spinning conspiracy theories to Bobby, who he didn't know very well and who was preoccupied with his own troubles. Patrick needed to keep his shit to himself.

"Bobby?" Will's voice echoed in the marble lobby, accompanied by the percussion of footsteps.

Bobby jumped from the bench and ran straight into Will's arms. Will shook with tears. Patrick had a feeling he should turn away, but he couldn't. They melded so well, Bobby's arms around him, supporting him.

It reminded him of Anita, whom he had left last night in a fatigue-fueled hissy fit.

He was a total megawatt idiot.

He pulled his phone out of his pocket and cursed. Dead. He hadn't been able to charge it at his mom's house. It must have turned off after Bobby had called.

He looked over at his friends. Bobby cupped Will's head in his palms, speaking softly, likely soothing him. Patrick would be a third wheel.

He needed a mission. There had to be a gift shop in the hospital. Undoubtedly they had phone chargers.

Patrick followed the signage to the gift shop, deftly avoiding doctors whose attention was glued to their electronic devices rather than the people in their path.

The small gift shop had an enormous selection of grinning teddy bears, as well as candy and snack foods. "Excuse me," he asked the volunteer manning the register. "Do you sell phone chargers?"

The volunteer knelt behind the counter and pulled out a box. "Here you go. How many do you need?"

"Hopefully just the one." He pulled his credit card from his wallet as the volunteer rang up the sale on an ancient POS machine.

"Mr. O'Leary?" a small feminine voice said behind him.

He turned and forced enthusiasm into his posture. "Lucy! What are you doing here?"

Lucy Knight stood behind him with a bottle of grape soda in one hand and a bag of chocolate candies in the other. "I was visiting Sophie M."

"Oh. Right." He hadn't entirely forgotten that Sophie M. was one of the high school kids who had gotten sick, nor had he entirely remembered. It was one of those facts floating around the back of his mind that didn't have a proper berth. "Here. Let me get that stuff for you."

"Thanks." She loaded her snacks onto the checkout desk and the volunteer added them to his sale.

"How are you doing?" Patrick asked, unsure of the etiquette when a teacher met a student outside of the classroom. Even if it was in a neutral hospital gift shop.

"I'm okay." Her tone belied her true feelings. She gathered up her snacks. "Bye, Mr. O'Leary."

She exited the gift shop.

What was going on? Lucy wasn't the type to be reticent, and she looked visibly shaken.

Patrick stood, paralyzed for a split second, before picking up his new charging cable and going after her. "Lucy?"

Lucy paused, and he could see the tears glimmering in her light brown eyes.

"Do you want to talk?" He pointed to a bench, and Lucy collapsed on it before covering her face with her hands.

He sat down beside her and waited, giving her space to cry. He should have bought a pack of tissues in the gift shop.

At length, she wiped the tears from her eyes and looked at him through her fall of straight black hair. "I'm sorry. It's all a lot, and I really want to know what's going on."

"Do you want to talk about it?"

She sniffed and arched an eyebrow at him. "Are you sure you wouldn't mind? I broke up with Daniel, which doesn't matter because he thinks I'm some sort of conspiracy nut, but like, six kids have gotten sick at our school. That isn't a coincidence. It could totally be a conspiracy."

John should be here. Patrick had no idea what he was doing, but if he were honest with himself, he was glad someone else saw it, too.

"What kinds of things have you seen?"

She pulled a notebook from her heavily decaled messenger bag. Most of the patches were either ballroom related or from true crime podcasts he also enjoyed. He pointed at a prominent logo, his personal favorite podcast, but it was pretty NC-17. "Your parents let you listen to that?"

She rolled her eyes. "As long as I get good grades and don't complain about the number of extracurriculars they sign me up for, they don't care what I listen to in my free time." She pointed at the notebook. "Okay, no one is talking much, but I've kept my ear to the ground. I think—"

"Patrick?" Bobby called. He and Will approached them, hand in hand.

"Lucy?" Will asked.

Lucy's cheeks reddened, and she stuffed her notebook back into her messenger bag. "Oh, wow. Hi, Mr. Forbes. I've got to go. See you at ballroom club." With that, she dashed from the hospital like her sneakers were on fire.

Will looked terrible. His face was blotchy with grief. "What was that about?" he asked.

Patrick shifted his weight, considering. John had asked the both of them to look into the mysterious illness of the kids. Will, though, did not appear to be in any shape at the moment to participate in such an interrogation.

"We bumped into each other at the gift shop," Patrick said. "I needed to get a phone charger."

Will crumpled, and Bobby slipped an arm around his shoulders. "My mom's phone. I don't know where it is. She'll need it when she, when she—"

He heaved a few times then caught his breath. It probably helped that Bobby was there, literally holding him up.

"It's okay. We'll get her phone," Patrick said. "I'll call John and see if they have it."

"Okay."

"Come on. Let's get you some food," Bobby said. Patrick followed them toward the cafeteria. Bobby installed Will at a small table and went to get coffee.

Patrick sat opposite his friend, who kept clenching and unclenching his fists. "Do you want to talk about it?"

"I'm going to kill the guy who did this." His voice

was low, broken, menacing. "How could they hurt my mom? She's the best."

Patrick couldn't deny that. She certainly beat Diane, no matter the volume of "Best Mom" merchandise she had insisted he buy for her over the years.

Will shook his head, terse and too quick. "She was just doing her job, out on a late-night patrol. I keep telling her, she should let Curtis or one of the other deputies do the graveyard shift, but she won't. She won't listen." His shoulders heaved twice, then he bit his lip and pulled his breath back into himself. "I don't know. I have to call the school and find a sub for today. Do you know this hospital only allows one visitor at a time?" Tears sprang to his eyes. "What am I going to do, Patrick?"

Patrick had a feeling this wasn't the time for a fist bump or funny memes. He put a hand on his friend's shoulder. "This sucks, Will. I'm really sorry."

Bobby returned bearing a tray with three cups of coffee, a breakfast burrito, and a bowl of fruit. "What did I miss? Do you want something besides coffee, Patrick?" He unloaded the food in front of Will, coaxing a fork into his hand.

"I'm fine, thanks."

He liked watching Will and Bobby together, the way they leaned into each other even when the other person wasn't there. It was as though they had a sixth sense for their partner.

He took his coffee and sipped it black. Did he and Anita really have that, or had he imagined it? The first time he had ever seen her, she had been part of a volunteer group picking up trash in the parking lot.

Only Anita picked up trash while practicing her rumba walks. For him, it had been love at first sight.

His heart warmed inside of him, a sensation that had nothing to do with the terrible hospital coffee. He needed to talk to her. He needed to apologize. He needed to propose.

He needed to charge his phone or else he wouldn't be able to do any of those things.

Will picked at his breakfast burrito, scraping the fork through the eggs and tortilla. Bobby scrolled through his phone, probably searching for things to say to your partner whose parent is ill. That's what Patrick would be doing.

"Thanks for coming, Patrick. It means a lot."

"Bobby and I can switch off, if you want. So you have someone here for moral support."

Bobby's phone rang. He gave them an apologetic frown then moved away, ear glued to his phone.

Will watched him leave, his gaze empty. "I want my mom to be okay."

"She will be. I'm sure she will be."

Will picked up his fork again but instead of eating his food, he twirled the utensil between his fingers. "You don't know that."

Patrick opened his mouth, about to reply, when a nurse with familiar curly hair passed their table and then stopped, turning slowly. Patrick's stomach sank.

His mother straightened, her too-bright smile fading from her face. "Patrick. You're supposed to be at home."

Patrick's gaze flicked between her and the man she was with. His pulse beat so quickly he wasn't sure he would be able to form words. What were they doing here together? "Hi, Mom. Hi, Dr. Goodman." He hadn't known they were friendly, and before they had noticed Patrick, they had been standing so close together their hips were practically touching. Potential ew.

Anita's father flared his nostrils. "Patrick. Will." His white coat was pristine, like it had recently been bleached. "I'll talk to you later, Diane." He nodded brusquely to Patrick's mom, his eyes flicking around like he was a nervous iguana, and stalked from the cafeteria, the tails of his white coat swishing in his wake.

Patrick could not ignore Will's arched eyebrow but kept his gaze on his mom. This was an interesting day. Who knew the hospital was such a good place to run into random people.

He could practically see the fumes rising off her.

"You should go home," she said, her tone curt. "Hospitals are full of germs."

"Mom—"

"I have to go. Six sharp for dinner." She wheeled on the squeaky heel of her work sneakers and departed without another word.

Will looked brighter than he had before the interruption. He sipped at his coffee, frowned, and added another half of a sugar packet. "What in the ever-living-fuck was that about?"

Patrick sank back into his uncomfortable chair. "I have no idea."

"Do they work together? Your mom and Anita's dad?"

"I don't think so." Intrusive thoughts churned in his brain like chum in the waves. He would be very happy to sink all of those thoughts into a deep, deep chasm.

"My mom works the medical/surgical floors. I don't think she'd be caught dead on the labor and delivery floors."

She was also fond of remarking on how the maternity nurses were the worst ones in the hospital. "They only take care of well women and babies. How hard can that be? Do they know what it's like to deal with a crashing post-CABG patient?"

Not that she had made that speech so many times that Patrick had memorized it or anything. He could barely imagine caring for himself, let alone a newborn or a woman who had brought life into the world.

Will tucked into the breakfast burrito, shoveling food into his mouth, his shoulders a little lighter.

The corners of Patrick's mouth twitched. "I'm so glad the intrigue of my mom and Dr. Goodman has distracted you from your own troubles."

Will grinned through a mouthful of food. "I need distractions. Give me another one. What were you and Lucy Knight talking about?"

"Sophie MacAllister. Lucy says she has a notebook with clues that she's been collecting."

Will dabbed at the corners of his mouth. "Shit, man. I know John asked us to talk to the kids, but there's no way I can help until my mom is better."

"It's fine. I'll take care of it." He had no idea how, but Patrick would swing something. Maybe Anita would have some ideas. Once she was speaking to him again.

Bobby slipped back into the other chair and chuckled. "Thinking about Anita again?"

Patrick colored. "What do you mean?"

Will made moon eyes and pursed his lips as if for a

kiss. "Whenever you think about her, you get all doe-like and full of wonderment."

Patrick tossed an empty sugar packet at him, a terrible projectile as it splatted uselessly against his forearm. "I liked it better when you were moody and about to rampage."

Will pushed his empty plate away from him and sipped his coffee. "Trust me. When I find out who hurt my mom, the rampage will roar."

"Oh, Will." Bobby frowned and kissed the side of his head. "That was a terrible metaphor, honey."

The three of them laughed, the pent-up anxiety and grief and stress leaching into the cafeteria air.

****

Patrick stayed with Will for another hour while Bobby finished several work calls. At least he found an outlet and could charge his phone.

At Will's behest, he texted John first, but he did not reply. Likely because he was extra busy investigating the crime scene.

Then he texted Anita. He wrote, edited, and deleted several texts before settling on

—*Hey. I'm so sorry, phone dead. Talk today???*—

It didn't sound super desperate, so he hit send.

Will must have heard the whoosh from his position on the bench, where he sat with his head against the wall and his eyes closed. "You need to lock that down, man. Anita is awesome, and perfect for you."

Patrick stared down at his broken leg, the ugly heavy cast. "What if she turns me down?"

"Why would she do that? She loves you."

"I don't know."

Will sighed and leaned forward. "Did your mom

really fuck you up that badly that you don't think you and Anita are perfect for each other?"

"This has nothing to do with my mom. She was a single mom. She had to make sacrifices." Even Patrick knew his voice sounded hollow, echoes of mantras drilled into his head that he had never fully believed.

"It has nothing to do with being a single mom. My mom raised me on her own after my dad died. She is always there for me." Will's voice caught in his throat, and his swallow echoed in the hospital hallway. "When I told her I wanted to be a gym teacher, she offered to help any way she could. When I told her about Bobby, she said, 'Treat him well, and be happy.' " Tears pooled along the sides of his aquiline nose. "Has your mom ever said anything like that to you?"

Nope, not even remotely close. At least he had stopped expecting it after two decades.

Patrick placed what he hoped was a soothing arm around Will's shoulders.

"My mom loves Bobby," Will said softly. "She jokes around that he's too good for me, and she's probably right."

"He loves you, too. Maybe you should lock that down."

"I'd like to." Will's features softened.

Footsteps echoed along the corridor. Bobby returned from his work call, his smile apologetic, hands stuck in the pockets of his light gray trousers.

"Everything okay?" he asked, pressing a soft kiss to Will's temple.

Will found Bobby's hand and squeezed it. "Yeah. Everything is going to be okay."

Patrick couldn't look away from their conjoined

hands. His heart ached and burned. "I'm sorry, guys, I have to go home."

They said their goodbyes, and Patrick called a ride share from the app on his phone. He needed, more than anything, to talk to Anita.

Chapter Twenty-Two

Anita slogged through more studio financials until her eyes glazed over, and if she drank any more green tea, she was going to turn into a lightning bug.

Patrick had finally texted, and the muscle-melting relief had made her practically useless for the last hour. At least he had reached out. Maybe they could find their rhythm again.

The bell over the main studio door chimed. "Hello?" She stood from her office and walked out onto the dance floor, wrapping her long black cardigan around her body.

Steve Barnes stood in the changing area, dark hair swept to one side and hands tucked into the pockets of his sharp-creased pinstripe trousers. If she looked up the definition of "rake" in the dictionary, she would find his picture. Maybe "smarmy rake."

Her stomach plummeted as the hairs on her arms and neck stood to attention, a distinctly unpleasant sensation. "Hello, Mr. Barnes." She hadn't forgotten how he had introduced himself that first night. Just driving through, huh? If he were really Mrs. DeVeaux's relative—

"Steve, please. I hope I'm not late," he said.

Late for what? An impending court order?

She tightened her ponytail. There was no use escalating a situation. "Did we have a lesson?" She didn't need this. Not after last night.

His brow furrowed. "Sorry, if this isn't a good time..."

She went to the check-in desk and fiddled with the appointment roster. What was the worst that could happen? John had said he wasn't a cold-blooded killer of fashionable, grouchy *grande dames*. She'd already had three cancellations that day, which ate into her bottom line. It would be seventy-five dollars for an hour of her time. After a day of mind-numbingly boring finances, she well understood how those hours added up. And if he was an asshole, she had a wicked roundhouse kick. Maybe she could somehow wrangle his lies from him, not that she was any sort of hard-bitten interrogator. "Did you bring dance shoes?"

He winced, the expression creasing his features like he was ironing in wrinkles. "Sorry. I haven't had a break long enough to buy them." He paused, then added, "With my aunt in Rehoboth, it's been challenging. Balancing the store and Home Squared."

She tilted her head, keeping her own expression neutral. It wasn't like anyone could click a button on the computer and have something shipped. "Have you heard from her? Your aunt?"

He barely blinked. "Of course. She texted earlier today. Enjoying the crowd-free beaches."

Anita doubted that. "When should we expect her back? Your aunt, I mean."

He scratched his freshly shaved chin. "I'm not sure. She seems to be enjoying herself."

Patrick should be there. People opened up to him more. She needed to move this along. "Your current shoes should suffice, unless you would prefer to pay extra for rentals again. Feel free to hang up your coat. We'll get started in just a moment."

She moved toward the sound system where she kept her coffee mug, currently full of chilled water, and flipped through the playlist on her phone.

The descent of a miasma of sandalwood and cedar aftershave stilled her movements, and a shadow fell across her light. She coughed against the fumes and spun in place.

He wasn't pinning her, not necessarily. He was just…leaning. Leaning too close for comfort, a half tilt to his full lips, almost like a sneer.

She ducked under his arm and popped up on the other side as she hit the "play" button on her remote. A lively quickstep belted from the speakers, as if the big band were right there in the studio itself.

Steve stuck his hands into his pockets and arched an eyebrow. Ew, that was definitely his "I'm a hit with the ladies" expression. Anita shuddered and hid behind her cardigan.

"Everything all right, Anita?" he asked.

"Are you sure you wouldn't rather reschedule your lesson?" When was Rodrigo due? She checked the clock. Thirty minutes. She could break Barnes's arm and incapacitate him in five.

"I'd rather do it now. It was a late night. It's not every night the police wake me up for an impromptu interrogation. I could use some exercise."

Her blood transported ice to her vital organs. "Mr. Barnes, this is a dance studio. If you're not here to dance, get out."

His body contorted with apology. She supposed his lack of subtlety was the reason his acting career extended to the home shopping channel and not Hollywood.

"I want to learn to dance. That's all. I'm by myself, with my aunt out of town. I'd like to surprise her when she gets back."

She searched the words for subtext and examined his body language. She would stay on guard. Maybe she could learn something that would help Patrick.

"Fine." Her voice was too sharp, her tone too brittle, but she wouldn't soften for him. "Today we will work mostly on your positioning, so we won't do any partner work. Show me your frame."

In a manner both obliging and infuriatingly juvenile, he extended his arms to the sides in a ballroom dance frame. She circled him, keeping her focus more on the music than the way he was eyeing her like she was some damned prize heifer at a farm show. She made gentle corrections to his posture.

"I suppose it will do for now. Now follow me." She stood at an angle to him, her back facing him, but she could see everything he was doing in the mirror. Not that she wanted to see everything he was doing. "Mr. Barnes, keep your eyes up. Your feet go where your eyes do."

"It's not my feet that want to go somewhere," she thought she heard him mumble, not lifting his gaze from her ass.

Ugh. Fine. She had dealt with misogynistic, entitled douchebags before, in spades if she were honest.

She cleared her throat, loudly, which finally caught his attention, and he met her gaze in the mirror. "Mr. Barnes, if you are not serious about ballroom dancing, I have many other better things to do with my time."

He wasn't chastised, a privileged golden boy like him wouldn't be and she didn't expect it, but at least he focused on her steps instead of her body.

****

The hour-long lesson lasted at least seventy-two thousand minutes. By the end, her forehead ached from perma-frowning, her cheeks burned with the fire of a thousand hell demons, and she had never wanted a wooden ruler so badly to smack someone's hands.

Where the hell was Rodrigo? He had been due at the studio ages ago.

"Mr. Barnes, for your next lesson, I would like to schedule you with our other instructor, Rodrigo."

He stuck his hands in his pockets again, clearly an affectation. "Really? Is something wrong, *Ms.* Goodman?"

She bit the inside of her cheek to keep from screaming at him in eight languages. "With all of our new clients, we find it is extremely beneficial to get multiple perspectives. And particularly with same sex instructors. I do it with all of the female-identifying students, as well."

He looked away and mumbled, just loud enough so she definitely heard it, "I bet that's not all you do with the female students."

All right, fuck him. "Get out." She crossed her arms over her chest, pressing the angry fists into her armpits. She hadn't hit anyone since Christina Blake and she wouldn't mind the practice.

That seemed to shock him out of his affability. "I beg your pardon?"

"Get out. Get out of this studio, or I will make you

get out."

He advanced on her, his movements slow, not menacing exactly, but not in friendship. It reminded her of a cat stalking a sparrow. Poor little cat didn't realize this sparrow had talons the size of an eagle's. "I'd like to see you try."

He was inches from her, mere inches, and the only thing that shocked her was that the waves of revulsion flowing off of her were not enough to repel him.

He lifted a hand, whether to brush back a tendril of her hair or strangle her, she never found out, because she just as quickly grabbed the upraised wrist and twisted it behind his back.

At that exact inconvenient moment, the bell over the studio door chimed. "Anita?" Patrick thumped into the entryway, his crutches making a dull thudding sound on the polished floor. "I'm so sorry, I—"

She saw the exact moment he registered what was going on. Saw the recognition in his eyes, the anger, the frustration. Patrick always did have very expressive eyes.

She released Steve Barnes, who, rather than look pissed like a normal sociopath, rubbed the wrist she had grabbed and headed out the door. As if she hadn't nearly broken his arm. She had felt it just there, beneath his skin, the bone straining. Here he was now, brushing it all off like nothing had happened. "Bye, Anita. See you soon."

The sound of the bell jangling again muffled Anita's frustrated scream. She made some unintelligible sound. "Asshole! What a goddamned, entitled—"

That's when she noticed that Patrick hadn't moved. She had to pull herself together. Patrick didn't need messy, not right now. He needed her tidy, organized, capable of helping him in his hour of need.

She inhaled deeply, unable to take her eyes off of Patrick's immobile frame, how he was still staring at the closed door. "Hi, Patrick. I'm so glad you're home." She smoothed back the tendrils of hair that had fallen from her ponytail, streamlining her hair along her temples.

"Was he hurting you?" he said.

If she hadn't seen his mouth actually move, she would not have believed that the voice belonged to Patrick. It was so listless, so dark.

"No, of course not. He was being a dick. I handled it."

Patrick's grip on his crutches was so tight Anita could swear she heard the tendons popping. "You shouldn't have let him in here."

A tickle ran up Anita's spine, and she crossed her arms over her chest. "John said he did nothing wrong. Am I supposed to background check every single student who comes in?"

He whirled on her, his normally placid and warm features contorted into a mask of anguish. "You're supposed to know better."

"You're being ridiculous. This has happened before. I handled it. Let it go." She stalked toward the check-in desk and needlessly rifled through papers. Anything to avoid looking at Patrick.

"You're supposed to call me."

"Really? And what exactly would you do?"

She knew it was the wrong thing to say as soon as the words left her mouth.

The mask of rage melted until he looked like a sad,

lost little puppy, propped on a wayward branch in the middle of a seething river.

She melted. "Patrick, I'm so sorry, I—"

"It's fine." His eyes flicked here, there, everywhere but at her. "I need to go."

"No, please." How in the world would he get home? Not that it was a far walk, but she could tell from the set of his muscular shoulders, the shaking of his good leg, that he was nearly done for the day. "Please. Stay. We'll order pizza or something. We need to talk."

His gaze flicked again toward the door, and he took one step on his crutches. It was impossible to miss the wince of pain across his face, even as he rebuilt his handsome placidity inch by painstaking inch.

"All right. Pizza. Pizza sounds great."

Anita exhaled deeply, not realizing that she had been holding her breath the entire time. She rushed forward and looped her arm around his waist, anchoring herself to his solidity, molding him to her. She pressed a kiss to his temple, which was beaded with cool sweat. "Come on. I'll help you up the stairs."

****

John shut the door on his cruiser and sighed, exhaling all of the stress and bullshit of the day. Katie was going to kill him. Sure, it was the job, but they were getting married in less than a week, and he had been gone since before dawn.

Curtis Wyczenczak knocked on the window, his wide, eager face lined with concern. John steeled his spine before rolling down the window. "Hey, Curtis."

"Are you heading out?"

John nodded. "I have to get home. We're done with

the final survey. I'll work on the paperwork tonight from home."

"Okay." Curtis stared at the wreckage left behind from the sheriff's cruiser, and the detritus of the crime scene they had been processing all day. The tow truck had taken the broken, twisted hulk of the car to the crime lab, but there were bits and pieces strewn around the road, still cordoned off with yellow tape. "Who would have done this, John? Everyone loves the sheriff."

"Not the people who want her nose out of their business."

"You don't have any leads?"

"I don't know. It's best to keep an open mind until we have all the data." He needed data, but his sixth sense tingled. This was all connected. The drugs, the kids, the sheriff's investigation, the drug bust back in May. Someone had taken over that drug ring and tested the new product. But who?

Too many questions, and not nearly enough answers.

His phone buzzed beside him, and he felt Curtis's eyes on him as he checked the screen.

"Katie?" Curtis asked.

"Yeah." John's furrowed brow softened into a smile. "I do not deserve her."

"She did agree to marry you. That makes me question her sanity."

John's fingers flew over the screen, typing out his reply before hitting send.

Curtis rapped twice on the hood of the car and stepped away. "See you tomorrow, John."

John nodded, but his attention was elsewhere. With

the messaging screen open, John hovered over Will's name before hitting the call button.

"John?" Will answered after half a ring. "What did you find out? Did you find the pricks who did this?"

"Hi, Will." John squeezed his eyes shut, as though the discomfort would mitigate what he had to say. "We have a few leads, nothing concrete right now."

"What leads? What's going on?"

John could picture Will with tense fists, his face going red. He couldn't tell him they didn't have much. Some paint flecks from a black car embedded in the cruiser's ruined bumper, tire treads. He had been combing the ground for hours. His back hurt, his head hurt, and he didn't have enough data. "I'll let you know as soon as I know anything. How's your mom?"

He could hear Will's sniffles over the phone. "She's doing a little better." His voice was low, hoarse, probably from a day of grief. "The doctor says she's more stable. I'm hoping she'll wake up tomorrow morning."

John made a mental note to check in at the hospital before heading to the station in the morning. "Is Bobby there?"

"Yeah." A wistfulness crept into Will's voice. "He's been amazing today."

"He's a good guy." John pictured Katie, her long chestnut hair against his skin, her laugh bubbling through his body. Will had found that, too.

There was a rustle of papers over the line. "I've got to go, John. The night nurse is here, and I want to ask some questions."

"Sounds good. Let me know if you need anything."

John pressed the button to end the call and turned

on the ignition to start the car. He had less than a week before his wedding and his honeymoon. He had less than a week to solve this case.

He'd done harder things.

****

In his mind's eye, Patrick could picture exactly where he had stashed the ring box. He had nestled it between his gym socks and his Tokyo cat café T-shirt, figuring all the black would meld together and camouflage the box's true identity.

Patrick knew instinctively, though, that now was not the time to propose.

They were only through a quarter of the pizza and a half hour of *Romancing the Stone*, and she was still pissed at him.

Or maybe not pissed. *Concerned*. Which in many ways was worse. At least he had stashed the bag of vape pens beneath a pile of throw pillows. Out of sight, out of mind, hopefully.

"Is the pizza okay?" she asked.

"Yeah." Hmm, a little lackluster. Maybe he should be more effusive?

"Oh, hey, does your dad know my mom?" Shit, that had come out of nowhere, too, but he hadn't been able to shake the image of his mom and Dr. Goodman all day. It had lurked in the back of his mind like a virus.

She shrugged. "They've worked at the same hospital for a while, so they've probably known each other for years. I doubt they're close. They work on different floors. Why?"

"Oh. Um, I just, I saw them at the hospital today. Talking." Together, like they did it frequently, but he didn't want to worry Anita.

"You were at the hospital?" Anita was suddenly on high alert, tucking both of her feet underneath her on the couch. "What happened? Are you okay? Is it your leg?"

"Me?" Shit, he had neglected to tell her about Sheriff Forbes. He really was losing it. "I'm fine. Totally fine. Bobby called me. Sheriff Forbes was attacked."

Her jaw dropped open, even as her pretty brow frowned. "Seriously? How did you not tell me?"

He felt his ears turn pink. "I'm sorry, my phone died, and there was a lot going on, and Bobby asked me to be there with Will while he had some work calls to manage. I'm sorry."

"You don't need to apologize. You didn't do anything wrong. I feel bad I didn't know. Is she going to be okay?"

"I hope so. They wouldn't let me in the room, since I'm not family."

"Poor Will." She chewed on the inside of her cheek. "Poor John. He has this investigation the week of his wedding? I'll text Katie and see if she needs anything."

She picked up her phone and swore.

"My lessons are waiting downstairs. I'll be a few hours. Are you going to be all right?" Her eyes were dark with worry.

Anita stood from the couch and stretched, the hem of her tunic rising just enough to show a sliver of her stomach.

His body responded immediately, but his mind filled him with shame. He should not be thinking about sex when they had bigger issues between them. Having sex was not always an effective coping mechanism.

"I'll be fine. No worries." He folded his hands in his lap. He would behave. No wild accusations of their neighbors. No midnight trash hauls.

"Okay." She smiled from one side of her mouth, but it didn't reach her eyes. Patrick's heart sank. "See you later."

And then he was alone.

He stared at the rapidly congealing pizza and flipped off the movie that he couldn't follow right now. He needed to exercise his demons away. It had always cleared his head in the past, but he couldn't run or anything. He searched on his phone for some therapy exercises to do while recovering from a broken leg. Upper body it was.

He found Anita's five- and ten-pound dumbbells in her closet. They were tie-dyed blue and green and pink, but they would get the job done.

His phone chimed, angry as an inanimate object could be, as he walked back to the living room. He set the ten-pound dumbbells on the coffee table and stared at the screen.

It was his mom.

—*Where R U???????*—

Had he?—shit. Yes. He had completely forgotten about dinner with his mom. But it was only six thirty.

Before he could sit down to text out his reply, three more messages rapid fired across his screen.

—*You were supposed to be here.*—

—*I made you dinner.*—

—*It's cold. This is so insensitive*—

Patrick arched an eyebrow. Was it his imagination,

or was this a huge overreaction on his mom's part? He waited for further vitriol, but there weren't even three waiting dots.

—Sorry, Mom. With Anita.—

She'd be pissed if he mentioned the pizza. Dealing with his mother on top of everything else going on right now was as overwhelming as contemplating the ramifications of climate change.

—Fine. I made your favorite, even though you know I don't like meat—

—I'll just have to throw it in the bin—

He knew what she wanted. He always knew. It would be easier to give in, to eat the meatloaf even if it settled in his stomach like a lodestone. Damned waste of meatloaf.

—That sounds great. I'm sorry I'm late. I'll be there in twenty minutes—

It was easier to lie via text.

He called a ride share through his phone app before going into the bedroom. No use in forgetting the ring again. Maybe he should keep it on him at all times, to surprise her.

He opened the box, and the ring inside glinted, light refracting from the facets of the sweetheart setting. A rose gold band, because the color reminded him of her hair in the light of a sunset.

His phone pinged. His ride share was two minutes away, and here he was, fawning over a piece of jewelry. Even if it was the most important piece he had ever bought.

He walked downstairs and paused at the edge of the dance floor.

Anita   stood   in   the   center   of   the   floor, demonstrating the proper technique for a New York to her beginner cha cha class. Students of varying heights, all dressed in comfortable clothes, watched her every movement. Meanwhile, Rodrigo practiced a tango with his student, Lydia Swann, a septuagenarian whose dance skills had markedly improved. "Evening, Patrick," Rodrigo said as he led Lydia through the silver rumba curriculum.

Patrick held up his hand in greeting and waited for them to pass before crossing the dance floor.

Anita paused, her eyes bright as they often were when she was teaching. "Hey."

"Hey. I'm sorry, I have to go to my mom's for a bit. I'll see you later?"

"Sure." She pressed a quick kiss to his cheek, a soft peck that pricked like razor burn. He wanted to grab her in the middle of the floor and kiss her until she forgot why she was mad at him. "Have fun." She turned directly back to her class, correcting posture and positions, demonstrating how to weave the step into choreography.

Patrick could have watched her all night. He would rather have done that than spend any more time with his mother, but rather inconveniently, his ride share had arrived and would not be kept waiting.

He left the warmth of the dance studio and stepped out into the cold, windy October night.

****

Giving in to his mother was always a mistake. Even if it got her off his back in the short term, she made him pay for his submissiveness.

"You've barely touched the meatloaf." Diane sat across the table from him, arms crossed over her chest, the storm cloud of her brow gathering for thunder snow.

Patrick forced a tight grin, picked up a forkful of meatloaf and mashed parsnips, and placed it on his tongue. He wouldn't gag, not this time. That hadn't gone well after his first bite.

She put too many odd spices and seasonings in her meatloaf. It had an acrid aftertaste today, like battery acid. How had she eaten this?

"It's delicious." He choked it down and followed with a large swig of too-sweet lemonade. "Thank you so much."

"Eat it all up." She tapped her foot repeatedly on the bottom rung of the plain brown kitchen chair. She had a large glass of iced white zinfandel in front of her. "You need your strength if you're going to heal."

His stomach groaned and churned in protest. He eyed his plate, piled with meatloaf, mashed parsnips, and green beans. There was no way he was going to be able to eat this without a desperate need to purge. He hadn't done that since he was eleven and his mother had forced him to eat an entire birthday cake, after he had dared to ask for chocolate instead of red velvet. Damned red velvet cake.

He pressed a fist over his sternum to ease the acid burning inside of him.

"What are you doing at Anita's?" his mother asked, sipping so loudly from her wine glass he could practically hear the pucker of her lips. "I thought you two were fighting. Probably for the best. She isn't good enough for you. Better to break up before you do something stupid, like knock her up or ask her to marry you."

The ring weighed down his pocket, anchoring him

to the chair. He tried another bite of food mixed with lemonade. "Anita's not like that."

His mother scoffed, which echoed in his ears like gunshots. All sounds seemed too loud, too invasive. Even his own swallowing was deafening. Patrick glanced down at his hand. The blue of his veins pulsed beneath his skin like strobe lights. "I know her type. She'll ruin your life."

"But I love her," Patrick thought he had said, but it sounded like he spoke underwater at an aquarium. He wasn't sure of anything at the moment.

His mother's face across the kitchen table expanded like it was being stretched in a fun house mirror, then small black dots like thousands of gadflies exploded across his vision.

Patrick leapt backward in his chair so quickly the legs scraped against the floor, hard enough to make the linoleum bleed. He was convinced that if he looked down, he would see the oozing red rise from the scars he had made.

"Everything all right, Patrick?" The monster who had been his mother opened its gaping lip-less jaws, revealing millions of shard-like onyx teeth.

"Mom?" His voice sounded both a thousand miles away and right inside his brain, boring through the gray matter like a drill.

Darkness encroached on his vision, like a fog machine on a stage, rolling in wisps.

"No!" he shouted. Christina Blake stood before him in her yellow sundress with the little flowers on the shoulders. She loomed over his tiny body, her bottle-blonde hair drowning him in her scents of musk and too-sweet lemonade.

"Patrick," she whispered, only it wasn't Christina's voice, but that of a thousand chainsaws chewing their way through his bones. She crawled over him, settling into his lap, her weight stifling.

"No," he whispered, but his lips were numb and raw. This couldn't be real. She was in prison. Her trial started next week.

The monstrous Christina leaned over him, covering his mouth and nose with the empty hole where her face had been. "No one will ever love you like I will."

The all-encompassing darkness swallowed his terrified screams.

Chapter Twenty-Three

Anita couldn't find her rhythm. She ran through her usual list of tactics when her mind was distracted: changing the music, altering the routine, foregoing all of it and kickboxing. None of it helped.

She walked toward the stereo in her practice heels and flipped the music to Bon Jovi.

She chewed on her bottom lip and checked her phone for the ten thousandth time that morning. It was only seven a.m.

Patrick hadn't come home last night.

She fetched the glass cleaner and a microfiber cloth from the utility closet and worked on the mirrored wall. Smudges. She could erase smudges.

Patrick hadn't come home and now was not responding to any of her texts.

She knew Diane well enough to know she did not appreciate phone calls before nine. But she couldn't calm the racing of her mind. Maybe this one time Diane wouldn't mind…but of course, she would.

Bon Jovi was not helping today. Maybe Roxanne would do it.

Moving toward the stereo again, she set down the cleaning supplies on the bottom rung of the wooden storage tower. From the periphery of her vision, she saw a shadow cross in front of the studio windows, moving toward her studio door.

Frowning, Anita picked up the broom from its resting place against the wall and held the sturdy wooden end of it. Protection came in many forms.

Someone tried the door, and, after rattling it against the locks, knocked.

Anita walked cautiously to the door and peered through the glass top portion. Her body relaxed, and she set the broom aside before tackling the slightly complicated series of deadbolts.

"Lucy?"

Lucy Knight stood outside her door, a well-decorated messenger bag slung across her chest, and her hands tucked into the pockets of her navy-blue pea coat. "Hi, Ms. Goodman." Her pretty brown eyes darted around the parking lot and over Anita's shoulder. "I'm sorry to come by so early."

She didn't know Lucy terribly well but had coached her several times. Enough to realize something was wrong. "It's fine. Shouldn't you be at school?"

The teenager rolled her eyes. "It doesn't start until nine."

"Oh." When she had been at Lewis High, classes had started at seven forty-three on the dot. Times do change. "Is there something you need? Do you have a competition coming up or something?" Though Patrick hadn't mentioned anything. He only enrolled his club students in local competitions and usually added practices to her schedule. Never one this early in the morning.

"Is Mr. O'Leary here?" Lucy tucked a long strand of straight black hair behind her ear, which was studded with one hoop and two small gemstones in the upper part of her helix.

"No. Sorry. He's, um, not here right now." A gust of wind thrust itself past the flimsy barrier of the open door and straight through Anita's body. "Do you want to come inside?"

Lucy worried her bottom lip before nodding. "Only if you have a moment."

"Of course." Anita stepped aside to let Lucy pass, then sat beside her in the folding chairs in the entryway. Now that the girl was here, Anita had zero idea what to do with her. "Do you want something to drink? Water? Tea?"

Lucy shrugged off her messenger bag and it dropped on the ground with a thud of finality. "Um, maybe some water?" She lifted the flap of the bag and pulled out a black notebook.

Anita went to the water filtration unit and filled a spare mug with water. She handed it to the girl and folded herself into the seat again. "Is everything all right?"

Lucy crossed her legs at the ankles. She wore black leggings with a Gothic lace pattern, and Anita had the passing urge to ask her where she had gotten them. Probably not the right time or place. "I don't know. You heard about the kids? At my school?"

"Yes. Yes, of course. What does that have to do with Patrick?" It wouldn't have anything to do with him, would it? Patrick wouldn't hurt a fly. Once when they were driving home from a ballroom competition in college, they had found a turtle trying to cross the road. Patrick had pulled over and moved it out of harm's way.

Lucy rolled her notebook into a cylindrical shape. "I ran into him yesterday. At the hospital? I was visiting my friend, and he was there." Her cheeks colored. "I just want to find out what's happening. Mr. O'Leary said he wanted to help."

Anita put a gentle hand on Lucy's shoulder. "I get that."

Lucy tossed her head from side to side, not making eye contact. "I tried telling my parents, and the principal, but they won't listen to me. They say I'm just a kid, and I should leave it up to the police. But what do the police know? Besides, they're now targets, too. Did you hear what happened to Sheriff Forbes?"

Anita could do nothing but nod. This speech had a ring of familiarity.

Lucy slapped the front cover of her notebook. "Look, I was there, at the party, but I left before everyone got sick. I feel so utterly guilty, and it's eating me up. I need to talk to Mr. O'Leary. Please. It can't wait until ballroom club tomorrow. What if another kid gets sick?"

Anita nodded again, unable to speak through the thoughts swirling and coalescing in her brain.

Lucy's features fell in disappointment. "You don't believe me, either," she said softly, standing.

Anita shook her head to clear the jumble of thoughts spinning in her head. She needed to focus on what was right in front of her. "I believe you. I do."

Lucy searched her face. Anita had never been quite so scrutinized before, as if the girl were sifting from her features the truth of the world. If Lucy found out, hopefully she would share the info.

"Okay." Lucy sat back down in the chair. "Mr. O'Leary said he had some information that would be helpful, that we could pool our resources, and go to

Deputy Flaherty together."

That sounded like a very well-thought-out plan, particularly for a sixteen-year-old girl. What were they teaching in schools nowadays?

"But you were at the party. The police didn't question you?"

"My ex and I had just left the party. I didn't know anyone had gotten sick until the next morning when I saw my news alerts." She colored. "I didn't want to tell them I was there, since I didn't know anything. Not yet. So I did some digging on my own."

Lucy opened her notebook and showed Anita complicated graphs and lines connecting text boxes, different ones circled in different colors. "Do you see? Where's Mr. O'Leary? We need to show him." Words popped out in black curlicue script: *Disco Balls, Sophie.*

Anita knew she couldn't stall any longer. "I don't know where Patrick is."

Lucy's mouth curved into a perfect, round *O.* "What do you mean? Did he get kidnapped?"

"No, of course not. He went to his mom's house last night. He hasn't come back yet."

"So he's missing," Lucy said.

"He's not missing. He just... didn't come home." Anita squirmed under the intensity of Lucy's stare.

"And he hasn't responded to your texts? Did you call his mom?"

"Um, no. She doesn't like to be bothered until after nine." Or really at any time, if Anita was calling.

"But she's his mom. Surely she would want to know if there's a potential he's in trouble."

Anita scoffed and hid it behind a cough. "You haven't met Patrick's mom."

Lucy worried at the cuff of the long sleeve shirt she wore under her pea coat. "What about GPS on his phone?"

"I don't know." Anita frowned. "If he's fine, he might be mad I violated his privacy like that."

"Oh please. Have you not seen a single true crime show? It's not a violation of his privacy if he's missing and in trouble."

"We don't know that he's missing and in trouble. He just isn't here."

"Ms. Goodman." Lucy inhaled deeply, as though she were the adult in this conversation. She probably was, if Anita were being honest. "You are arguing semantics. If he allowed you to put his phone on your GPS tracking app, then he gave his tacit consent for you to use it to find him." She shrugged. "I suspect many a cheating bastard has been caught this way."

Anita sighed, warring with her internal mandates toward personal privacy and her deep-seated worry over Patrick. "Okay." She went over to the check-in desk and picked up her phone. Lucy followed, standing across from her and watching Anita's movements intently. Anita swiped past her lock screen, a photo of her in Patrick's arms as he twirled her, hair flying in the wind.

"Okay." She pulled up the GPS tracking app, tapped a few buttons, and waited, her heartbeat rising in her ears.

"This is so exciting!" Lucy squealed, eyes glued to the map on the screen where a tiny red circle pulsed over a grid. "So where is his phone?"

Anita frowned, the lines settling into her face as though they were going to stay awhile. "It's next door.

At the antiques shop."

Lucy raised her eyebrows and torqued her mouth into an expression of disbelief. "Why would Mr. O'Leary be at the antiques shop at seven in the morning?"

"I don't know." Anita bit her bottom lip, but spending time with this girl steeled her spine. It gave her a bravery she hadn't felt in, well, six months. Patrick had been in trouble then, and if he was in trouble now, she was damn sure going to do something about it. "I'm going to find out."

****

Lucy insisted on following her once Anita had changed her shoes. They argued the very short walk to the antiques shop. "You shouldn't come with me. You're a teenager."

"I'm a part of this, Ms. Goodman. There's no way you can make me stay behind."

"You have school soon."

"It can't take that long to search an antiques shop."

"Have you ever been in an antiques shop? It's bric-a-brac from here to Jupiter."

Lucy rolled her eyes. "Mr. O'Leary is hardly the size of a Revolutionary War-era door knocker, Ms. Goodman. It's not like he'll be hiding in a mid-century modern dresser."

Anita would be annoyed by the girl's sarcasm if she didn't secretly find it hilarious. She crossed her arms outside the entrance where she had stood with Patrick and John two nights before. "It's too dangerous. I don't know what's in there."

Lucy faced off, mimicking her posture and tone. "If you don't let me in the front door, I'll sneak in the window that's open in the back."

"That's breaking and entering."

"Not if you—"

"Enough." Anita held up a hand to silence the girl's gray morality and closed her eyes. "Fine. But stay with me."

"Sure. Whatever."

Anita could feel the exhilaration streaming from the girl as she stepped behind her. Anita straightened her spine, lifted her hand, and knocked on the door to the antiques store.

Lights went on in the stairwell, followed by sturdy footsteps. Her heartbeat matched the rapidity of Lucy's breathing. Anita wished she had thought to bring the broom with her.

She could see the shape of Steve Barnes in the small window at the top of the door, and she heard the locks opening.

"How many locks does he have?" Lucy asked.

"Don't judge how many locks people have." Anita's neck reddened.

The door opened, revealing Steve Barnes in nothing but a pair of black sweatpants that hung low on his hips. Did the man not own a damn shirt?

His mouth curled into a lascivious smile, and she stifled the urge to plant a right hook straight in the center of it. "Hello, Anita." His eyes grazed over her, taking in everything from her hair to her comfortable fur-lined boots. She pulled her sweater around her, hiding her body from his uninvited gaze. "It's good to see you. Especially since you told me to fuck off yesterday."

"I wouldn't be here if I didn't have to be," she

replied, biting the words between her teeth.

Lucy stepped from her shadow. "Who are you?"

He arched an eyebrow as he inspected the teenager. Anita not so subtly shifted her position to shield the girl. "Who are you?"

"I'm Lucy Knight."

"Okay."

To Anita's untrained eye, Lucy was mimicking the movements of a television teenaged detective. "Where's the lady who runs this shop? The one who looks like Jackie O?"

"My aunt's in Delaware." He leaned against the doorjamb, his muscles prickling in the early morning chill. Would it have killed him to put on a fucking sweater? Probably. It would have messed with his whole evil power vibe.

Lucy's eyes narrowed in apparent disbelief. "Your aunt? You look nothing alike. Delaware in October? Does she love hurricanes? She doesn't strike me as the type to make a random trip for tax-free outlet shopping."

This was getting out of hand. Anita needed to be an adult. "Lucy."

Steve Barnes yawned, making the cords in his neck stand out. Anita caught Lucy's sneer of disgust and stifled a laugh. "Look, as much as I like this whole Betty and Veronica thing you two have going, I have to get ready for work."

"That's gross," Lucy said. "Betty and Veronica were teenagers."

"So are you, Veronica."

Lucy made a retching noise and rolled her eyes.

Anita stepped in front of her. "We're sorry to

bother you, Mr. Barnes. Have you seen Patrick this morning?"

"Patrick?" He scratched at the stubble on his jaw.

"Yes. Patrick. My boyfriend." Speaking to this man was like speaking to a box of razor blades.

"I haven't seen him since he barged in here with that deputy and accused me of murdering my aunt." Steve affected a smug look, as if to say, *what are you going to do now?*

If only a swift roundhouse kick wouldn't count as assault in a court of law. Being an enormous asshole wasn't really grounds for self-defense.

"Did Mr. O'Leary really do that?" Lucy whispered, barely above the threshold for sound.

Anita sighed and ignored her. For the moment. Lucy wasn't one to let things go. "I'm sorry, again. But he didn't come home last night."

"Oh really?" He arched an eyebrow. "He didn't come home?"

She continued as if he had never spoken, as she really wished he would shut his stupid mouth so they could find Patrick and be out of there. "I checked the GPS, and it says his phone is here. Can we look?" He didn't answer as the smirk on his face widened. Anita gritted her teeth. "Please?"

He stepped away from the door, gesturing like the pompous ringleader he was. "Be my guest."

He allowed Lucy more space to pass than Anita, which made her skin crawl like he was covered with fire ants. He had the personality of a fire ant, if she were being totally honest.

"I have to get dressed. I'll be right down." He opened the door to the main showroom and turned for the stairs. "If you find Patrick stuck in an old refrigerator, tell him it's his own fault." He mercifully left them in peace for a few moments.

Anita shivered. "Ew."

"Ugh, he is the *worst*, Ms. Goodman," Lucy said.

"You have no idea." She pulled up the GPS app on the phone, and they both leaned over the glow to inspect it.

Lucy got her bearings first and pointed to a corner of the showroom floor. "It looks like the signal's coming from over there."

Anita's stomach dropped. There wasn't anything in that corner apart from a hodgepodge of furniture, including a Victorian-era vanity made of walnut and inlaid with mahogany and rosewood. While she wouldn't mind owning that if she suddenly won the lottery, there was nothing Patrick-sized.

Which, upon reflection, was probably a good thing.

Lucy glanced toward the door, presumably checking to make sure Steve Barnes was nowhere in sight, then wove her way through the displays to the corner.

Anita followed, listening carefully to the footsteps upstairs. She didn't want Lucy exposed to any more of that asshole's gross flirtations.

Lucy dug through the knickknacks, opening the drawers of a Shaker-style armoire, and moving aside candlesticks.

Anita joined in the search, focusing on the walnut and rosewood vanity. For detective purposes, of course, and not because she would really love something like that in her apartment.

Lucy, clearly a future criminologist, knelt on the

ground and tapped on the legs of the vanity. "They're hollow," she whispered with a hiss.

"Hollow? We'll have to check online to see if that's typical for this style." Why was she whispering? Steve Barnes was upstairs and had given his permission for them to be there. It still felt very covert.

Lucy nodded, biting her lip as she took her notebook from her messenger bag and jotted a quick note.

Anita pulled open the central drawer of the vanity and gasped. It was Patrick's phone, still enclosed in his PhillyProud-branded case.

Anita picked up the phone and scooped it into her pocket. Her heart was racing so fast she couldn't hear anything beyond its pulse in her ears. "Come on." She grabbed Lucy's hand and pulled her toward the door. "Let's get out of here."

They maneuvered quickly to the door, but just as her hand closed on the knob, she heard Steve's footsteps on the stairs. "Find what you were looking for?" She turned around and he smacked her in the face with that goddamn smirk. The one that radiated dishonesty and bullshittery. There was only one thing to do when faced with such an untrustworthy expression.

Lie.

"No. Nope. No phone. So sorry to waste your time."

She pushed Lucy out of the door, across the parking lot, into the studio, and then deadbolted the door behind them.

Lucy panted beside her. "What is it?"

"I found Patrick's phone."

"Why did you lie to that guy?"

"Because it was the right thing to do." Anita peered over the glass door, certain only the top of her head was visible, and gasped.

Steve Barnes stood directly across from her, arms over his chest, his lips pressed into a thin line. While she watched, he took out his phone, keeping his gaze on the studio the entire time, and brought it to his ear.

Shit. Anita knelt and took out her own phone. "I need to text John."

Lucy bent beside her. "Who's John?"

"Deputy Flaherty." She typed out a quick SOS text. She hated bothering him, but this did qualify as a police-level emergency.

That done, she peeked through the door again, but he was gone.

Anita heaved a sigh of relief and sat on the floor, her head resting against the comforting wood of the doorframe.

"Do you know Patrick's code?" Lucy asked, pointing at his cell phone.

She did, but when she tried turning it on, it had run out of battery. "I have a charging cable at the check-in desk." While she plugged it in, she called Diane O'Leary from the desk phone, but all it did was ring and ring. After the fifteenth unanswered ring, she hung up and started to pace. Pacing seemed wise. It was preferable to tearing her hair out.

Lucy dropped the messenger bag on the ground, drawing Anita's attention back to her. "Are you okay, Lucy?"

"I'm fine. I want to know what's going on." Lucy moved over to the check in desk and did a doubletake. "Um, Ms. Goodman, why do you have a bag of empty vape pens?"

Anita eyed the bag she had brought down that morning after finding it beneath a mountain of throw pillows. Patrick must have hidden it there the night before. "It's a long story. I was going to look for a recycling program this morning, but, obviously, I got distracted."

"This is perfect!"

"Um, hardly."

Lucy's eyes brightened. "So, I ordered this drug testing kit online, and I have it in my locker. Maybe we could try it out on some of those vapes?"

"Why do you have—" Anita shook her head. This was out of hand. "Lucy, no. You are a teenager. Those things might have nicotine or something else awful that can get on your skin and make you sick. You can't put yourself in danger, if we even are in danger. I shouldn't have let you come with me into that antiques store."

Lucy rolled her eyes. "Ms. Goodman, I'm not a child. I'm almost seventeen. I can make my own decisions."

"Your parents might have something to say about that."

"Please." Lucy's eyes filled with tears, which seemed genuine as Lucy did not appear to want to be crying. "Please let me help. These are my friends."

"Lucy—"

She never got to finish her sentence as they were interrupted by a knock on the studio door that echoed through the space, shaking the furniture.

Lucy's eyes widened, and she darted a glance between Anita and the door.

All right. Anita was the adult. She could do this. If

it was anyone besides a deputy, she would turn all the lights out, leave the deadbolts in place, and hide with Lucy under her desk like a rational human being.

She went to the door and peered over the glass. "It's all right," she told Lucy, beginning the laborious process of unlocking her door. "It's Deputy Flaherty."

Chapter Twenty-Four

John was having one hell of a morning. Katie had been up half the night stressed about the seating charts. She had moved tiny pieces of paper around a large poster board until she finally burst into tears and ripped the poster board in two. John had poured her a very large glass of red wine, put her to bed with a white noise machine, and spent another hour repairing the seating chart. Which was exactly what he had not wanted to do. Fiddly bits of paper were not a fun thing in his wingspan-sized hands, origami aside.

Then he had risen early and headed to the hospital for a status update on the sheriff, where he was told in no uncertain terms, "No change." Perfect. Will had been asleep on the tiny pull-out chair in the room, and John hadn't wanted to disturb what was probably the first rest the poor guy had had all night.

So now he was on his third cup of frou frou coffee, because he hadn't had time to make his own before he left his house, so he had to buy it from Amore, where he had to order his drink like he was booking a vacation. And it cost about the same.

Even his eyeballs and fingernails were throbbing with hot red pain from this shitty day, and it was barely eight thirty.

His phone chimed as he pulled up at the station, and he sighed. Here it came. The onslaught of phone calls that meant he wouldn't finish his paperwork or have time to actually investigate what had happened to Sheriff Forbes. Not to mention the time crunch he was under, as he was supposed to take off Thursday and Friday for wedding festivities.

He closed his eyes, counted to five, then checked his phone. Might as well prepare mentally.

He read the text twice before he reversed the car and headed in the direction of the studio.

—*Need help. Please come. Anita.*—

****

John knocked at the door again, and this time heard the answering thunks of deadbolts being unlocked. How many locks did one studio need? He shouldn't judge. If Katie had been a stalking victim, he probably would have screwed in as many locks as the door could take.

Anita pulled the door open, her pretty face lined with relief. "Please come in. I don't know if he's still out there."

He followed her inside, but his eye caught sight of a pretty Asian-American teenager in a navy-blue pea coat, patterned leggings, and black ankle boots. "Hello," John said, straightening his spine into his official deputy posture.

Her eyes widened, but her stance firmed. She was a fighter. He approved of that. He knew his appearance could be intimidating, particularly when he was in uniform.

"Hello," the girl replied.

Anita stepped between them, putting a soft arm around the girl, like they were friends. "Lucy, this is Deputy Flaherty. John, this is Lucy Knight, one of Patrick's students from the ballroom club at Lewis

High."

John nodded. "Hello."

Lucy examined him intently, then seemed to decide he was friend versus foe. "Hello."

This interrogation was not going to plan. If he didn't have a migraine, he would have come up with some better phrases. "Anita. Did you want to talk alone?"

"No. It's okay. Lucy knows a lot of it already. I was hoping, maybe you could drop her off at school? I don't want her walking by herself right now." Anita worried at the cuffs of her long sleeve cardigan.

John pursed his lips. He had not had enough sleep for this conversation. "Catch me up."

He took out his tiny spiral notebook and noticed Lucy mirroring him from the corner of his eye.

Anita could not stop pacing. "Patrick never came home. He went over to Diane's house last night for dinner, and I thought he would be back by the time I finished my lessons. I called and texted him, and I tried his mom's house, but we couldn't get through. Lucy came over, and she and I used the GPS tracker on his phone. It was in the antiques store."

"The antiques store?" That smarmy asshat with his bullshit "aunt" story. If John's migraine had not been practically volcano-level destruction, he would storm over there now and—

And nothing. He didn't have probable cause. Yet.

Anita picked up Patrick's phone, recognizable from the branded PhillyProud case. "We found this, in an antique vanity."

Lucy affected a disgusted expression. "That guy is awful, like Earth-eating-monster awful. He called us

Betty and Veronica."

Now that she mentioned it, John sort of saw the resemblance, but this wasn't the time. "The phone was in the vanity? Did—" He checked the name against the one he had written in his notebook. "—Mr. Barnes give an explanation for why it was in the vanity?"

"No." Anita exchanged a glance with Lucy. "We ran out of there. I had the weirdest vibe."

"Hmm." It was the most he could muster as he started to lose vision in his right eye. Fucking migraines. He hadn't had one in two years, but he couldn't cover his head and sleep it off as he preferred to do. "Anita, do you have any ibuprofen?"

"Sure." She went into the small office at the back of the studio and returned a moment later, holding two bottles with a frown puckering her features.

She handed the one with the generic printing to John and stared at the other bottle. It was a plain white color, as if someone had removed the label. "Something wrong, Anita?" He popped three of the ibuprofens and washed them down with water from the dispenser.

"It's so weird." She didn't sound like the Anita he knew. She sounded distant, unengaged, like she was floating in the stratosphere and talking to him on Earth. "I don't where this came from."

"The pill bottle?"

"Yeah. I don't remember this. I wouldn't have bought something without a label."

"Do you think Patrick bought it?"

She shook her head. "No. His medicines for his leg are all upstairs. I don't know what this bottle is. I haven't looked in that drawer in a couple of weeks, but it wasn't there before."

John took a plain plastic bag from the utility belt at his waist and held it open. Anita slid the bottle into the evidence bag.

Lucy pointed to it. "Let me get the drug testing kit from my locker, and we can figure out—"

"You have a drug testing kit in your locker?" John asked.

Lucy's face closed immediately. He recognized the look and admired it. "It's not illegal. How else are girls supposed to know if someone has roofied their drink?"

She had a point, not that he would concede it. "Regardless, you need to be in school, and we have a crime lab that tests things like this."

"Yeah, that probably has twenty thousand other cases with higher priority. So when will this get done? Two years from now?"

He did not have the time or mental capacity until his migraine subsided to deal with this. "Look, you need to be in school. The bell rings in fifteen minutes. I'll drive you there, I'll drop this bottle at the station for *official* testing, and I'll go to Patrick's mom's house to see if she knows where he is. Okay?" He held his hands open to the two women, and they both nodded. "Great."

"I just have to go to the bathroom," Lucy said, and darted toward the washroom at the rear of the studio.

"She's a spitfire," John said, yawning. Maybe Patrick's mom would have some non-terribly overpriced coffee, even if she did accompany it with a passive-aggressive lecture.

"We've barely scratched the surface of what she's capable of," Anita replied.

****

John waited outside in the cruiser while Lucy

finished up in the bathroom. Anita took the time to pace and finally decided to turn to her old friend, anxiety-sweeping.

She pushed the broom around the floor, muttering to herself like the crazy old lady she was rapidly becoming.

The door to the bathroom opened, and Lucy darted toward her. "Hey, Ms. Goodman."

"Hi. The deputy's waiting outside, to take you to school."

"Ms. Goodman, please." Everything about the girl's posture implored. "Please. I have a free period around lunchtime. Pick me up, and let's keep working on this."

"You can't leave school in the middle of the day."

"I'm on the honor roll. They let me leave for lunch and free periods."

School had changed substantially since Anita had graduated in 2012. "Lucy, what about your parents?"

"They don't care as long as I get good grades and keep up my extracurriculars for my college transcript." Lucy flipped the waterfall of black hair over her shoulder. "Think how awesome my Harvard application will look if I solve an actual mystery!"

"You're getting way ahead of yourself."

"Please, Ms. Goodman. They're my friends. I want to help. I can't stand aside and not do anything."

Anita chewed on her lip and examined the girl's face. She was smart, determined, and if Anita didn't help her, she would probably find another way. A potentially more dangerous way.

She relented and rolled her eyes. "Okay. Get permission from your parents, and I will pick you up."

Lucy squealed and leapt into the air, practically clicking her heels. "Thank you thank you thank you. I'll text them right now. Bye, Ms. Goodman!"

"Bye, Lucy." Once the teenager had left, though, the studio felt barren, empty, like it was waiting for someone to jump out at her. She shivered.

She would call Diane's house again and see if anyone answered. Nope, not even a tinny voice requesting for someone to leave a message.

How else could she find Patrick?

She picked up the broom again to continue her angry/anxious sweeping, when her cell phone chimed. Patrick. It had to be. Thank heavens.

She swiped *accept* before registering the caller ID. "Patrick?"

"Anita?" Her mother answered, but it didn't sound like her mom. Her voice was thick, wet, blurry.

"Mom? Mom, what is it?"

"Oh, honey. It is not good."

"Are you hurt?" Anita grabbed her purse and car keys from her office drawer and ran across the studio floor.

"No, I'm not hurt. It's-it's your dad."

Anita froze in the entryway. Her stomach clenched and a rainfall of dire inevitability washed over her. "What happened?"

"He—" Her mother's voice hitched and caught, then a sob erupted from her in a great heave. "Please, can you come home?"

Anita hovered on the edge of indecision. On the one hand, her father had never agreed with her major life choices. On the other hand, he was her dad. He had taken her to her first dance lessons. He had hugged her so tightly when she graduated from high school that she thought her heart might burst. He had made mistakes, particularly lately, but in his heart, she knew he loved her. Besides, her mom needed her.

"I'm on my way."

****

Thank goodness for ibuprofen. With his migraine finally in remission, John felt more up for small talk.

"Do you want to be a cop when you grow up?" he asked Lucy as they waited in the drop-off line.

"I'm already pretty grown-up, Deputy." Lucy tucked her hair behind her ear, exposing the line of studs in her helix. "I'm not sure yet. I listen to this awesome podcast, where the host, like, interviews retired FBI agents? That sounds so interesting."

"That's amazing. You know, sometimes we offer internships at the station."

"Really?" Her dark eyes lit up. "I mean, yeah, that sounds cool. I might apply to the Philadelphia FBI office, too, but, like, I'll keep it in mind."

John pushed away the beginnings of a smile. "Have a good day at school. Don't get in trouble."

She saluted him as she exited the cruiser. A group of her friends stood nearby, gawking with mouths wide enough to catch mosquitos.

John exited the high school parking lot and turned toward Diane O'Leary's house. He would stop there and see if she knew where Patrick was, then head to the station to see how they were faring with the crime lab results from yesterday.

He hummed along with the radio as he turned down the maple tree-lined street, the vibrant orange and red colors glowing like embers in the morning sunshine. It wasn't such a bad day. His migraine was almost gone. One decent cup of coffee and he would be ready to face anything the day had in store.

He pulled up outside the nondescript single-story house and parked along the street. A lot of people had left for work or errands already. There was only one other car, a flashy black coupe parked two houses down.

And, of course, Diane's car in the driveway. John tilted his head, the prickle of suspicion tickling along his spine. When had Diane O'Leary gotten a new car? This one was a white SUV with a flashy front grill and a vanity plate secured by a pink heart-covered license plate holder. As long as he had known Patrick and his mother, Diane O'Leary had driven different versions of the same beige sedan. Complaining about her lack of funds also featured prominently in her usual haranguing.

John noted the make, model, and plate number in his notebook.

The sunlight glinted off a structure in the backyard, and he peered around the edge of the house, catching sight of a shed that looked newly renovated.

Hmm.

John rapped on the door with the plain metal knocker.

There was a flurry of activity inside the house. John peered through the glass lining the door, but he couldn't see anything through the thick fabric lining the windows.

He took out his phone to text Katie, to tell her where he was in as innocuous a way as possible, when the door swung open. He shoved the phone in his pocket, text unsent.

Diane O'Leary stood before him in jeans and a long-sleeve shirt, like the kind worn underneath scrubs. "It's you."

He had to remember this was his friend's mother, not a suspect. Not yet, at least. Buying a new car wasn't a crime. "Good morning, Ms. O'Leary. Do you have a moment?"

She pushed her dark curls from the sides of her face then shrugged. "I suppose."

John waited, but she didn't move from her position. Irritation floated off her, curling like the lines of her hair. "May I come in?"

She bit the inside of her cheek then shrugged again. "What's the matter?"

"Hopefully nothing." He moved past her into the house. She favored a busy aesthetic, boxes from online shopping stacked along the walls, furniture and old magazines piled haphazardly.

The house smelled a little funny, too. An acrid under taste, oily, like car grease and bleach, mingled with the loamy scent of cannabis.

Diane followed him as he strode into the house and stood by the kitchen table. His senses tingled. Something was wrong here. He glanced down at a stack of paperwork on the table, but she noticed and hurriedly swept it into her arms. Interesting.

"What do you want?"

"Is Patrick here?"

"No." She shook her head once, twice, then stopped, as though on high alert. "Why?"

"Anita's worried. She said—"

Diane rolled her eyes. "That woman worries about

everything. She's terrible for him. Surely you know."

He personally thought Anita and Patrick were pretty perfect together. A little bad at communication, but that could be taught.

"Ms. O'Leary, she said he was here last night. Now he isn't answering his phone."

She clutched the stack of paperwork to her chest like it was a newborn baby. "How should I know where he is? He came over last night to have dinner with me. Then he left. I don't know where he went."

She was nervous. He might not be a seasoned detective, but it didn't take Sherlock Holmes to tell. She twitched her fingers against the papers she held, and she couldn't keep her feet still.

John stayed calm and kept his notebook in his pocket. He would give her some space. When the time was right, he would dive right in.

Suddenly, as if she had been injected with hospitality juice, her entire demeanor changed. She lengthened, relaxed her grip on the papers, and a grin spread across her face.

John's nerves tingled so loudly they practically buzzed in his ears.

"John. May I call you John? We've known each other so long. Where are my manners? Have a seat. Let's chat. Can I get you a cup of coffee?"

John smiled, reached into his pocket, and tapped the voice recording button on his phone. "That would be wonderful."

She beamed, fucking beamed like a sociopath supernova. "Wonderful. Sit, sit. Cream? Sugar?"

"Black, please." John folded himself into one of the kitchen chairs, careful not to move too much as to ruin the quality of the voice recording.

While she puttered in the kitchen, humming an old Karen Carpenter song to herself, John surveyed the house from his perch. Nothing outwardly wrong. Nothing obvious. A thousand little things, a thousand points of data, but no clear picture. Not yet.

John was determined to get the clear picture.

"Here you are." She bustled around the kitchen, now without her stack of papers, but holding a china teacup and matching saucer embossed with little pink and blue flowers. "It's nothing special, but I hope you like it."

John held the cup below his nose, sniffing as politely as he could. He didn't smell anything funny, but that didn't mean it wasn't there. He should have asked for bottled water.

He set the cup in the saucer. "Thank you, it smells delicious."

Her smile tightened. "Drink it."

"In a minute."

Her eyes narrowed. He should have his service weapon with him, but he had left it in the lockbox in his car. Maybe he could reach his Taser.

"Drink. It."

John stood up, schooling his heartbeat, taming his adrenaline. "Ms. O'Leary, what's going on here? Where's Patrick?"

Ms. O'Leary sighed dramatically, and a feline, predatory grin slid across her face.

Shit. Shit, fuck, he had to get out there.

He knocked the chair over and groped for the Taser, but a thick arm wrapped around his neck and a needle was shoved into his arm, the pain a sharp, burning bite followed by encroaching darkness. He fought it, struggled against the arm, the barriers, the darkness. He was losing. Fuck it, he was losing. He never lost.

He kicked wildly, but instead of striking flesh, his legs went out from under him, and he crashed backward onto the floor.

The darkness swallowed him, paralyzing his muscles, sticking its barbed nails into his brain.

Ms. O'Leary loomed over him, her eyes wide and unconcerned. "You should have just drunk the coffee."

John's vision faded to complete and utter black.

Chapter Twenty-Five

Anita parked in the driveway of her parents' Tudor-style manse. She jumped from the car and ran to the front door. "Mom?" She rapped so hard on the door that her knuckles ached. "Mom?"

Marina pulled the door open, and Anita went straight into her arms. Her mom looked terrible, her hair disheveled, her face drawn and eyes puffy from too many shed tears. "Oh, Anita, it's terrible," she whispered.

"What happened?"

Her father barged into the foyer, his feet in thick-soled shoes pounding against the flooring. "What's happened is there's a conspiracy! They're trying to take what's mine. None of this is right, none of it. I'll sue them all." He had a piece of paper in one hand that he kept slapping with the other, or shaking it like he was a fire and brimstone preacher.

Anita's eyes widened. What The Actual Hell.

Marina shrank against her side, and Anita tightened her hold on her mom. "Will someone tell me what's going on?"

Her father turned to her, his pupils dilated, his cheeks flushed. "They're fucking with my life!"

He clearly was not going to be helpful. "He-he had a random drug test at work," Marina said, whispering against Anita's ear. "He failed it. They suspended him."

The warring sensations of complete despair and bitter rage roared through her. "You failed a drug test? What are you taking?"

Her father's gaze narrowed on her, as though he was only just realizing she was there. "This is your fault. If you had only gone to medical school—"

Fuck this. "Absolutely not. This is in no way my fault. My not attending medical school did not drive you to do drugs."

"I don't do drugs!" The cords on his neck stood wide, like ropes anchoring a ship.

Anita crossed her arms over her chest and jutted her hip to the side. "You're acting like you do, Dad."

He didn't inflate so much as explode. He lunged for her. Marina tried to step in front of her, but there was no way Anita was going to let her mom get hurt. She neatly stepped around her mom and planted one single, rapid kick to the back of her father's knees. His legs went out from under him, and he landed on his ass in the foyer, panting. She hated to admit it, but it was oddly satisfying.

Marina covered her face with her hands. "Oh my God, what are we going to do?"

Anita took her hand and pulled her upstairs. "We're going to find what he's been taking."

They started in the master bedroom with attached bath. Downstairs, her father caterwauled, but Anita tuned it out.

She searched the bathroom cabinets and the drawers of her father's bedside table, knocking over paperback copies of thriller bestsellers and ancient business cards. It had to be somewhere. Whatever he was taking had to be somewhere. What had Marina said? *...after he's been down in the city or after a long shift at work.*

Marina searched the other side of the room, combing through his laundry.

"What have you found?" Anita asked, though a sense at the back of her skull said they wouldn't find anything here, not where her mom cleaned regularly. Marina handed her a basket full of bottles of routine household medications. "What about salves?"

"He has an anti-inflammatory cream, but it's a prescription." Marina went into the bathroom and returned with a tube bearing a prescription label.

Anita paused, considering. If she were going to hide drugs from her family—not that she ever had—where would she hide them? *In the city, or a long shift at work...*

"Where's his work bag?"

"In the study."

They hurried back downstairs, neatly avoiding her father, who had propped himself up against the staircase. "I need help!" he bellowed, attempting to stand and failing.

What a shame. She had zero sympathy. "Tell me about it." Anita and her mother reached her father's study simultaneously and proceeded to tear it apart. She doubted she had done any real damage to her dad, so it would be wise to hurry.

Marina found his work bag in a drawer. She pulled out notepads, his tablet, his badge, a spare bottle of water. "Nothing."

Anita walked over, took the top off the bottle, and sniffed. At least that was water, and not vodka. "Okay, let's keep looking."

She yanked at the drawers of his mahogany desk, all of which slid open with very little provocation and had nothing of interest inside of them.

A memory stilled her frantic movements. She had been eight years old, drawing underneath her father's desk while he charted and returned phone calls. She looked up at the underside of the desk, studying the framework for the systems of drawers. There was an extra one, behind the central door. An extra frame, extra wood. Her father said it wasn't anything, to go back to her drawing. *"Don't worry about it, sweetheart."*

She would bet anything there was a secret drawer.

She stood up, pulled open the central drawer, and stuck her hand in deep, feeling for a hidden panel, a latch, anything.

"What are you doing?" her mother asked, pausing from her position by the bookshelf, shifting books as though feeling for a lever to a secret door.

"I thought I remembered a hidden drawer in Dad's desk."

Marina joined her at her side, frowning at the drawer she held in her hands, at the spray of pens and tape and loose staples. "Let me try."

Anita stepped aside to give her mom room. Marina set her hands on either side of the drawer, lifted, and pulled it from its rolling track. She set it on the floor and shrugged. "If he wants it back, he can put it there himself." Marina stuck one arm into the empty space and felt around. Her eyes widened. "It's here!"

A thrill of triumph rushed up Anita's spine. She crouched beside her mother as she pulled out a small cigar box that had been stuck behind the drawer.

"Please God, let it not be heroin," Marina prayed,

and opened the box.

It was not heroin, at least not to Anita's untrained eye. Inside the box was a small, twist-top plastic jar and an unlabeled brown bottle of small white pills. There was one half of a joint, too, the leaves wrapped in brown paper and lined with white crystals. It must have been there a long time. It was almost innocuous.

Marina took out the plastic jar, untwisted it, and sniffed. "What do you think it is?"

Anita caught a whiff. "I don't know. I smell hemp. Maybe some kind of CBD?"

They took out the pills next, but they were so nondescript that Anita was certain there would be no way to identify them even after an exhaustive internet search. They were white, round, with absolutely no markings on them, not even a score line down the middle to make it easier to cut them in half. Anita had no idea what to make of the joint.

She didn't have time for her dad's shit. She had to pick up Lucy at noon.

"This is useless." She took the cigar box from her mother and marched back into the foyer.

Her father sat against the rails where they had left him. Beads of sweat pooled along his forehead, and he was breathing rapidly. His eyes brightened when he saw the box. "That's mine." He held out a tremulous hand for the box.

Hah. "Oh, is it? Is this the reason you were such an asshole to me? The reason why Mom is busy looking up dementia support groups? What have you been doing?"

"Give it to me." His voice was practically a growl.

"Absolutely not."

"I need it. It's for my arthritis."

Anita took the jar of salve from the box and held it just of his reach. "Why do you need unmarked drugs for arthritis? What's in them? Meth? Heroin?"

He scoffed, but it came out as a blubber through the thick shiver that ran through him. "I would never do those."

"Well, Dad, I've never gone to medical school, but even I know you shouldn't take drugs from strangers."

His face clouded, and the atmosphere in the room shifted perceptibly, with a temperature drop of at least fifteen degrees.

"Who gave you the drugs?" her mother asked.

Anita whirled. Not that she had forgotten her mom was there, but she had never heard her mom's voice like that before.

She looked quiet, but there was a seething undercurrent of rage that Anita hadn't known she possessed. "Who gave you the drugs?" It was less of a question than a threat.

His eyes cleared for the briefest of moments, and he shifted his gaze down and to the left. "Marina—"

"They're from *her*, aren't they?" Marina's hands clenched into fists at her sides. "You promised me, Bill. You promised me that you had stopped—"

Anita stepped away, eyes wide. Something much bigger than her father's drug problem was happening. Her? Which her?

"Marina, I swear—"

His mother stepped away, hands in front of her face. "Stop it, Bill. Just stop. I can't even look at you."

Anita knew enough to stay out of the way. She clutched the cigar box in her hand, needing it to ground her as her parents' relationship fractured right before her eyes.

Her dad stumbled to his feet, but he slipped and landed on his ass. "Marina, please, I need my pills. My arthritis—"

Marina slapped at the hands he outstretched. "I can't believe you, Bill. You said it was one time. Drugs? Another woman? Do you have any idea how much I have given up for you? I left my family, my friends. I've defended you and supported you. I've given up my career. All for you. And this is how you treat me?"

"Marina—"

"I am done, Bill!" She stepped around his flailing form and picked up her purse from the hallway closet. "I cannot do this anymore." She kissed Anita's cheek as she grabbed her keys. "I'm sorry, my love, I will call you later. I cannot be here another moment."

She slammed the door as she left, loudly enough to make the pictures quake in their frames.

Anita turned back to her father. His larger-than-life stature had appropriately diminished, but she could still see the dad who had taken her shopping to buy her first pair of dance shoes.

He stared at his hands, turning them over like they were something precious.

"What was she talking about?" Anita sat across from him, at a safe enough distance.

"I don't feel well," he grumbled. Another shiver wracked his body.

"You're in withdrawals, you idiot."

"It's safe."

"It doesn't seem like it. What was Mom talking

about? Who's the woman?"

"It's none of your business."

She didn't have the brain space for this. Anita checked her watch. She couldn't be late to pick up Lucy, not if she wanted to find out what had happened with Patrick. Maybe they could test her dad's stash, too. "Look, Dad, I don't have time. Get your shit together. Or you're going to lose everything. Including Mom."

"Not you?"

She wouldn't look at him, not at that puppy dog face that masked all the years of pain he had caused her.

"Oh, Dad. You are the one who pushed me away, a long time ago."

She kept the cigar box under one arm, wiped away the tears under her eyes, and left.

****

Anita tapped her fingers on the steering wheel. She could be forgiven for being a bit on edge after what had happened at her parents' house. Her dad had cheated on her mom? Oh, and her dad was also addicted to drugs, and had been suspended from his job. The one person Anita wanted to talk to about it all was MIA.

What a fucking day.

Lucy opened the door of the sedan and tossed her messenger bag in ahead of her. "Oh my gosh, you will not believe what I found on the field this morning during gym."

"Hi, Lucy. Did you get permission from your parents to leave campus with me?" It reassured Anita slightly to pretend like she had some authority. It was also an excellent distraction from her own personal troubles.

Lucy rolled her eyes and held up her text

messaging app. Apparently her parents had given her permission "for a school project."

Anita sighed and pointed at Lucy's seat belt, which the girl dutifully fastened. "Does this really count as a school project?"

"They're kids from my school. And I found *this* this morning." Lucy brandished a plastic sandwich bag filled with empty vapes. She rolled her eyes at what must be Anita's look of incredulity. "Please, I wore gloves. I'm not an idiot."

Oh dear, Patrick had started some sort of terrible trend. "What did you do?"

"I saw the ones on your desk, and it made me think, maybe that's how they're getting the kids to take the drugs. So I thought we could test some of these, and maybe some of the ones that you found, too."

"So, you think someone's adding illegal drugs to vape cartridges?" Was that even possible?

"I guess?" Lucy frowned at the bag. "I've never actually vaped, so I don't know how they work exactly."

Anita shrugged. "Me, either. We'll look it up." She supposed that was what the internet was for, though her browsing history was going to raise some serious eyebrows after the last couple of days.

"You were pretty straight edge in school, huh?"

"I was always practicing or competing or fitting my schoolwork in around dance. It didn't leave a lot of room for parties or experimentation." Anita shook her head, releasing the memories. "You don't need my life story."

Lucy chewed on her lip and was quiet for a few moments as they drove down the street. "Sounds like you sacrificed a lot for what you wanted to do," she said at last.

Anita shrugged and pulled into the parking lot behind her studio. No other cars, so hopefully Steve Barnes was nowhere to be found. She had canceled that day's classes as a precaution. "It wasn't so much of a sacrifice because I loved it. Dance is all I've ever wanted to do. I wouldn't trade that for anything. I've always had what I needed." Even if it wasn't what she had wanted. A championship. Patrick. Her father's approval.

She and Lucy exited the car, and she unlocked the main door to the studio.

"You're lucky you have Mr. O'Leary, Ms. Goodman," Lucy said.

"Don't I know it." She locked the door again behind them and turned to the teenager. "Also, since we're partners in crime now, you should probably call me Anita."

Lucy's smile brightened. "Okay."

"When do you have to be back at school?"

"Oh." She looked away, at the empty studio and her reflection in the polished mirrors. "My free period ends in about an hour. I can be a little late. I haven't had a tardy in three years."

"Today should not be your first." Anita took the cigar box from her father's desk and placed it on the check-in desk. "So you have testing kits? What do the instructions say we need?"

"Yeah. We need a large open space or something, maybe some towels in case something spills."

"Masks and gloves, too? I don't want anything to get on our skin." Anita pulled a box of each from behind the check-in desk. As she knelt, she caught sight of a pair of thick, black-framed eyeglasses, almost hidden on the back of a shelf. She held them in one hand, smiling.

"Good idea." Lucy pointed to the glasses. "What are those?"

Patrick's Buddy Holly glasses, the ones he'd worn to prom that had made him look so incredibly sexy. She hadn't seen them since he wore them for her about a month before, to make her smile. He would do anything to make her smile.

"Eye protection," Anita said, wiping the tears of nostalgia from her cheeks.

Lucy nodded. "Cool. I have my blue light blocking glasses, too."

Anita and Lucy went into the small rehearsal room with their two bags of vape pens, the cigar box, and sundry supplies.

"What's in the drug test kit? I thought you had to have urine to do that."

Lucy wrinkled her nose and pulled a cardboard box from her messenger bag. "Ew. I hope not. I got this one online. It's a reagent test kit, hopefully like the ones we use in science class." She took out two small plastic trays with six wells each, an assortment of test tubes, a card with the names of multiple drugs on it, and a dropper bottle of reagent. She unfolded the paper instruction packet, which was creased as though it had already been perused multiple times. "So, we take a really small sample, add it to one of the wells or a test tube, then add some reagent, and see if it changes color." She tossed aside the instructions and ran her fingers through her hair, gathering it into a messy bun on top of her head. "It sounds easy enough."

"Chemistry was never my forte," Anita replied. "What should we test first?"

They randomly chose the jar of salve from her dad's cigar box, mostly since they didn't have to crush anything before they added the reagent. Anita went upstairs for a box of cotton-tip applicators while Lucy organized everything, and when she returned, she used the applicator to take a small sample, no more than twenty grains of salt as per the detailed instructions, and placed it into the test tube.

Lucy, with her hair up and her wire-framed glasses and mask in place, focused intently on the solution Anita held. She dropped some of the reagent onto the sample, and her eyes brightened. She squealed. "It's working! Oh my God, look!"

The sample slowly changed color to a pale lemonade color. Anita compared it to the chart attached to the reagent bottle. "Ketamine?"

"This is so cool. Let's test it again with a different reagent." She dug through her box and pulled out another type of reagent and identification chart. She also brandished a foil pack of test strips. "I have fentanyl strips, too. We just need to mix the sample in a little water, then we dip this in."

Anita sat back on her haunches, inspecting the drug-testing debris. "I can't believe you can buy all this on the internet."

Lucy shrugged. "It's not that expensive, either. I used my babysitting money."

Anita shook her head and settled in to the task at hand.

****

Patrick couldn't open his eyes. Someone had covered them with sandpaper or duct tape. Someone had also enchanted his tongue until it was the size of a full-grown summer watermelon in his mouth. He wished it was a watermelon. Delicious, sweet watermelon. His mouth was dry as Death Valley.

His limbs must be made of iron wrapped in pincushions. He couldn't move them, either.

His hearing worked. That was about it.

There were two voices in the darkness—one deep and gruff and angry, the other higher pitched and completely pissed off.

"He was recording you," the deep, male voice said.

He heard a scoff, and the swish of hair being tossed over a shoulder. "He isn't a problem now."

"He's a deputy. You think they're not going to come looking for him?"

"What was I supposed to do? You're the idiot who hid the phone in the antiques shop." There was something eerily familiar about the higher, feminine voice. It burned along the edges of Patrick's brain like teeny needles. "Hopefully you covered up the old woman and the cruiser well enough. You couldn't manage to kill the sheriff. If you blow this operation—"

"I'm not going to blow this operation."

"That's what that idiotic realtor said, too, and she nearly destroyed everything. It's taken us months to rebuild."

Footsteps pounded across the floor. It felt like an earthquake, shaking Patrick's entire body. What was going on? The parts of his body he could control—which was less than ten percent—tensed, preparing for pain.

"If anyone is a loose cannon, it's you," the masculine voice said. "You've taken too many risks, involved too many people."

"We needed those connections."

"Did you need to involve your son?"

"Don't talk about him. You're entirely replaceable."

"Really?" The deeper voice was now more of a growl. "Replaceable?"

The more feminine voice didn't back down. "I'm the one who came up with the recipe. I'm—"

"Shut. Up."

Not that Patrick was speaking, but he held his breath, afraid of releasing even the slightest puff of air to disturb the silence.

Which was a mistake, because he heard moans, pants, the soft lick of tongues against skin.

What the fuck was going on?

Mercifully, the darkness swallowed Patrick again, and he passed back out into a deep, tortured, psychedelic sleep.

****

Anita and Lucy paced around the collection of drug tests on the floor. They had amassed quite the assortment, and the results were…unexpected.

Lucy tapped her pencil along the edge of her notebook page. "So, the jar of salve, the cigar box pills, and some of the vape pens tested positive for ketamine, fentanyl, and cannabinoids."

"I can't believe this many e-cigarettes were contaminated with other drugs," Anita said. At least ten of the discarded pens from the parking lot and the field behind the high school gym had contained the other substances. "Learn something new every day. We don't have test strips for PCP, right?"

"Let me check if there's another way to tell." Lucy opened a website on her phone. "Okay. This website says if you lace a cigarette with PCP, white crystals can grow on brown paper."

Anita grimaced. "Also, super gross."

"True." They high fived. Over the course of their home drug assessment, they had fallen into a good rhythm with each other. "I know what these are." Lucy's voice rose in pitch and frequency, like she was a guitar string during a tense solo. "They're Disco Balls."

"Disco Balls?" Anita asked, incredulous.

"That's the name that's been whispered around school. They get you super trippy and high. The kids who got sick are likely the ones who overdosed." She examined the notes she'd taken about the various drug components from the internet. "Probably from the PCP."

"Disco Balls is a terrible name. It sounds like a euphemism for something I don't want to contemplate."

Lucy ignored her and rolled the eraser end of the pencil against her chin, thinking. "It's weird, though, because some of the pills we tested from the cigar box were naproxen. So the regular ones and the doctored ones were all mixed together."

Anita considered the recurring/relapsing pattern of her dad's behavior over the past few months. "Sometimes you get the doctored drug, sometimes the naproxen. It probably increases the desire for the psychedelic ones, making them more addictive."

"That makes sense." Lucy's tapping increased in frequency. "I feel like we are so close to solving this.

Who do you think is the distributor?"

"I don't know." Anita couldn't shake the memory of her mother's words to her father. What if her dad had cheated with the drug dealer? It would have to be a woman, then. What woman did she know who would drug kids? Mrs. DeVeaux had been problematic, but not completely amoral.

Lucy's expression was sympathetic, as if reading her mind. "I hate to ask, but do you think it could be your dad?"

"Not really." She hoped like hell it wasn't. "Isn't there a thing where the dealers don't use their own product? It cuts into the profits or something."

"I guess that's true."

Anita sighed. "I think we've done all the junior detective work we can. Time to call in the big guns."

"The DEA?" Lucy, no doubt, was picturing herself in a black flak jacket with yellow lettering. She had that dazed, excited expression again.

"Let's start with the Lewis P.D." Anita picked up her cell phone and scrolled through her contacts until she found John's number. "I'll call him, and then I'll drive you back to school."

The excitement fell from Lucy's face like a veil tossed in the wind. "No, please. I want to help."

Anita listened to the ringing with one ear. "I know, and you're amazing. But you're also a teenager and not part of the police force."

"Neither are you."

"No. Which is why I'm calling the actual police." If he would pick up the phone. It went to a message saying his voicemail was full, and the line went dead. Anita opened her messaging app and fired out a text to

John instead.

Lucy peered over her shoulder, clearly in no hurry to return to her classes. "He didn't answer?"

"No. I sent him a text."

Lucy put her hands on the hips of her black Gothic lace leggings. "That's weird. He should answer."

"He's probably busy. He's working on a lot right now, including who attacked the sheriff. He doesn't know what we figured out."

"Wouldn't he want to know?"

"Lucy." Anita covered her face with her hands and screamed inwardly.

"Anita." She mimicked Anita's tone. Which was super irritating, and, she begrudgingly admitted, somewhat justified.

"Okay, I'll call the police station, too. I don't know if you can just call the DEA without them labeling you or something."

Anita looked up the phone number for the police station, but before she could click on it, her phone rang in her hand. She frowned at the caller ID and swiped *accept*. "Katie? Is everything all right?"

Katie's voice ran a mile a minute. "Have you seen John? He's not answering his phone. I've been calling everyone, and no one has heard from him."

The hairs at the back of Anita's neck prickled. "He was here this morning, and he dropped Lucy off at school around nine. I haven't seen him since then."

"Lucy? Who is Lucy?"

Lucy was currently watching Anita like she was the latest installment of a must-see show. She mouthed the words *speaker phone* to Anita, who shook her head.

"Lucy Knight. She's one of the students in

Patrick's ballroom dance club. It's a long story."

"Whatever. I need to talk to John. This isn't like him. Even if he's working, he always calls me back. Always."

Anita knew the feeling, knew the worry that Katie projected intimately. Her gut churned.

"I've been driving around town, trying to find his police cruiser," Katie said. "I've called the department, but they said he hasn't checked in."

"Isn't there GPS on the cruiser?" Anita asked.

"There's supposed to be, but Curtis said it was deactivated this morning. I told him, isn't that evidence of something? But he didn't seem to care." Katie was shouting so loudly that Anita didn't need to turn up the volume so Lucy could hear, too. "I don't know what to do, or who else to call."

Anita paused and bit the inside of her cheek. None of this made sense, but she found none of it reassuring. Without the sheriff or John, the Lewis Police Department was reduced to barely-out-of-the-academy Curtis and another deputy who was on vacation until Sunday. "I understand. Patrick's missing, too. Let's join forces. Maybe we can meet at the police station?"

She felt the wave of relief through the phone cord. "Yes. Yes, let's do that. They can't ignore both of us. I'll see you there in ten minutes."

The call ended, and Anita looked at Lucy, whose eyes were so bright and excited they might as well have been lanterns.

"We're going to the police station? Let me clean up my test kit. I'll go with you. They can copy the results from my notebook there." She took out her phone and walked around the various setups, taking close-up shots of the evidence.

Anita's stomach dropped. "Lucy. Lucy."

The girl paused, the impending heartbreak etched into her face and shoulders. "No. Anita. You can't make me miss this. Please."

"You have to go back to school."

"No." She stomped her foot on the floor, but Anita could see it was halfhearted. Maybe she understood she was in over her head. This wasn't television, and she wasn't a teenage super-sleuth. She could actually get hurt.

"Lucy." Anita opened her hands in a gesture of apology. "If something happens to you, think about how your parents and friends would feel. You don't exist in a vacuum."

Lucy bit her bottom lip, and tears welled in her eyes. She shook them away and busied herself, cleaning up the unused parts of her testing kit. Anita scooped the used portions into a trash bag and knotted it with gloved hands. She would bring all of this with her to the police station, so they could dispose of it or use it as evidence.

When they had finished cleaning up and had washed their hands, Lucy put on her coat and her messenger bag, resigned.

"Okay, you can drop me back off at school," she said, her voice low. "But will you at least record everything?"

"Like on a video?" Anita's technical skills had improved infinitesimally over the past few months, so she at least knew how to work the video recording app.

Lucy dug through a pocket of her messenger bag and pulled out a small mini-recorder. "Try this. It does audio recording, but sometimes the quality is better than my phone. This might not apply to you, but for me, I can't accidentally turn it off if I bump my hip into something."

Anita took the device and slipped it into the side of her purse. "Thank you. I will. And maybe we can meet up tomorrow or tonight and debrief? Or whatever?" She opened the door of the studio, and they both stepped outside. She felt connected to this girl, bound in their mutual desire to find the truth. It was a nice feeling. She didn't have a lot of close female friends, outside of Toni, and since she had poured her time into starting her nonprofit, Anita had been more often alone. It was heartening to be part of a girl band.

"That would be great. Thanks, Anita."

****

Anita parked on the street in front of the police station fifteen minutes later. Katie stood on the sidewalk, pacing back and forth, her chestnut hair coiled on her head in a messy bun. Fury and anguish rose from her like steam.

"I'm sorry I'm late, Katie. I had to drop Lucy back at school." Anita went around to the trunk of her sedan and unloaded the bags of evidence.

"What is all of that?" Katie asked, joining her.

"Don't ask. It's a long story." Though after the drive and her conversation with Lucy, clues were dropping into place. A woman, someone with access to her dad, someone with access to drugs. Someone who thought she knew more than everyone else. Someone with a wonky moral compass. Though she would need an accomplice.

"Are you okay, Anita?" Katie held the door to the police station open for her.

Conviction knitted itself around her spine. She only needed someone else to believe her. "I'm great."

They entered the station together.

****

"So, that's everything," Anita said. She handed the bags of evidence to Curtis. "I don't know what to do with these. Lucy said maybe to call the DEA?"

Curtis Wyczenczak's kind eyes were crossed, and he had the look of someone in desperate need of a seventy-two ounce jolt of caffeine. "Let me get this straight. You tested vape pens and your dad's meds with a sixteen-year-old and a home testing kit."

Okay, yes, when he put it that way, it sounded bad. Anita flushed. She should defend Lucy, particularly since she was recording this entire conversation on the device the girl had given her. "Lucy figured out that this is how they've been distributing the Disco Balls to the kids. Through vapes, pills probably labeled as something else, and laced joints."

"Uh huh." Curtis steepled his fingers together and then cracked his neck.

Katie sighed, and Anita noted how her posture shifted into Teacher Mode. "Curtis, you're missing the point. John is missing. Patrick is missing. The cruiser should have its tracker on, but it's been deactivated. Patrick's phone ended up in the antiques shop. I think it's pretty clear from Anita's story that this Steve Barnes guy and Patrick's mom are in drug cahoots together. We need to go to Diane O'Leary's house and find John and Patrick. We're wasting time."

Anita shivered, but she was grateful Katie had validated her interpretation. Though it meant Patrick's mom and her dad had…Ew. Triple ew.

She nodded in agreement. "Katie's right. We need to go." The sooner they moved, the sooner Patrick and John would be safely home.

Curtis sighed and gestured around the station, where he was currently the only employee apart from the eighty-year-old secretary. "It's not that I don't agree with you. Honestly. How am I supposed to organize a sting with just me?"

Katie leaned forward, all business, so Anita mimicked her posture. "We have a plan."

Chapter Twenty-Six

Patrick couldn't feel his broken leg. Which, upon reflection, was not a terrible thing, just a concerning thing. Normally when he woke, it made its presence known, as though the cells knitting themselves back together had spent the entire night waiting for him to wake up to say, "Hey, look at all the work we did!"

The fact that he was picturing these cells knitting themselves back together in various colors of thick, fluffy yarn was also not a good sign.

He groaned and opened his eyes. Was he in the fucking desert? Everything was dry: his hair, his mouth, his eyes, his damned stomach.

Stomach. Meatloaf?

Patrick groaned again, and a wave of nausea rippled through him.

He blinked several times, willing his tear ducts to work. Where was he?

The light was dim in his corner, but it was enough to see, even if his vision was blurred. Shapes coalesced before him. A table. A lamp with a dark blue scarf thrown over the shade. That must be where the eerie, undersea-style light was coming from. A couch. He was on a couch.

He ran his fingers along the fabric. It wasn't scratchy, but wasn't soft, either. Like new denim.

"Hello?" His voice belonged to a cicada. Patrick

shook his head. He wasn't a cicada. He was Patrick O'Leary. He had a deadline for an article due. He had to get to work. He had to get to Anita.

He swung his numb, broken leg and his numb, good leg onto the floor. Pins and needles rocketed through his feet and up his legs. He stifled a scream.

Panic bloomed in his chest, tightening its hold around his heart, his lungs.

No. He had to focus. He wasn't tied up. Christina Blake was in prison. He was safe.

Though this situation didn't feel safe. The dim blue light made him claustrophobic, like he was trapped in a shark cage with one of those ancient forty-pound scuba diving helmets clamped on his head.

He shut his eyes so tightly his forehead burned. Focus. He had to focus. Two-three-four-and-one. Anita. Two-three-four-and-one. Anita. If he forgot his own name, he couldn't forget the rhythm.

The panic receded, leaving him shivering and cold.

His throat raw, he opened his eyes again.

This time, his vision was clearer. It was a basement. He was in a finished basement. Beside him was a large, uncomfortable-looking armchair, with a huge man folded into it, his long arms and legs stretched out to the side like he was a marionette.

Shit. Was that guy dead?

"Hey." Patrick kept his voice low, and he scooted his butt closer to the armchair. "Hey. Are you okay?"

He was on the armrest now, close enough to touch the man, but his vision hadn't cleared enough to make out his face. He poked at the marionette's arm. It was warm, not dead, but the man didn't move. "Hey. Are you okay?" Patrick repeated. A deep part of him knew this was stupid, but he couldn't think of anything else at the moment. He must have taken something, but why?

He poked the man again, and this time the body shifted, the head lolling to the right, bringing the features into the dim light.

John Flaherty. What was he doing here? "John?"

Patrick was paralyzed. Something was very, very wrong. He had to remember what had happened, but his memory felt like a giant black hole. Anita. He remembered Anita. Rodrigo tangoing with Lydia Swann. Will and Bobby at the hospital. It was a patchwork quilt of bizarre images, nothing cohesive, nothing to explain where he was or why.

Standing, he balanced between the armrest and his numb, good leg, and used his other hand to shake John. John's eyelids fluttered once, twice, but then his breathing slowed, and he fell back asleep.

Shit.

Now that he was standing, Patrick took the opportunity to look around the basement. There was something so familiar about it, about the unused couch, the style of the lanterns, the stacks of unopened boxes from online marketplaces.

The truth rushed upon him and broke like a typhoon.

He was in his mother's basement. Oh fuck. Fuckity mcfuck fuck.

He knew his mother was problematic, at best. She had berated him his entire life. But this?

Sinking grief chilled him. He believed it. She would have absolutely done this. She would have drugged her son and a six-foot-plus sheriff's deputy and locked them in the basement to protect herself. He couldn't even cry about it. Maybe some part of him had always expected her to go that one step too far.

He checked the door at the top of the basement stairwell. It was closed, which was good. She wasn't down here. There wasn't anywhere to hide, or so she thought.

He willed feeling into his good leg and used a combination of furniture and bric-a-brac until he was in the far corner of the basement. A cobwebbed bookshelf languished there, still holding musty copies of his childhood Hardy Boys mysteries. He had scrimped and saved to buy those for himself, and here they were, resigned to beetle food.

With every ounce of strength, he pushed aside the small bookshelf, revealing the outline of a tiny door. His mother had not known this small cavern was here. When she was acting particularly heinous, he used to hide down here, reading by flashlight.

He pushed on the door, and it unlatched, creaking open on rusty hinges. A nostalgic wave of sadness passed through him. There it was. A moth-eaten blanket, a flashlight, a box of long-expired snack foods. He had stopped hiding here in high school, when he was old enough to hide at the soccer field, or ballroom dance practice, or at Anita's house. He had pushed this place from his mind, locked it behind a brick wall covered with razor wire, and thrown himself into outside relationships.

Memory was a tricky thing, though, and at least it helped him this time. He crouched down and picked up the flashlight. Did fifteen-year-old batteries still work?

He twisted the top half of the light, and a weak stream erupted from it. That would be enough.

He cast the weak light around the darkened basement. One of the stacks of boxes had been opened, then clumsily re-sealed. He would check that out first.

Dehydration and the activity on an empty stomach made him woozy, but he fought through it. He had to know what his mom was up to. Then he would focus on waking John and getting them both the hell out of there. They were lucky to be alive, but who knew how long that would last? Patrick walled up the last part of his heart that had been sympathetic to his mom.

He opened the top box and pulled out a plastic bag of empty vape cartridges. He was seeing far too many of these lately. He put it back and dug farther, finding empty, brown, prescription-type bottles and brown cigarette paper. Dread sunk its claws into him.

He whistled through brittle lips. "Oh, Mom, you fucked up big."

"You're awake."

Her voice cut through him like a machete.

He looked up from the box and found her staring ice-daggers into him. His skin prickled where she glared, but he steeled himself against it. She would not hurt him or his friends anymore.

"Hi, Mom."

"What are you doing? Do you have any idea what a mess you're making?"

Patrick chuckled, a low, cruel laugh. "Really? That's what you're upset about? The mess I'm making?"

Diane pointed behind him at the open door. "That's disgusting. What is that back there? Now I'm going to have to clean that up. You have no respect, Patrick. It's only gotten worse since you started dating that Anita."

Patrick laughed loudly now, the voice high-pitched and desperate and replete with grief and anguish and rage. "Are you fucking kidding me?"

She had the gall to look revolted. "Don't speak to me that way. I'm your mother."

"Mother?" Patrick dropped the packet of brown rolling papers back into the box and advanced. "My mother? You want to be my mother now?"

"I've always been your mother."

"Fuck you."

Her body contorted with rage. "How dare you speak to me that way!"

Patrick was done being gaslit. "How dare you drug me and John and lock us in the basement? Do you have any concept of how fucking bonkers that is?" He shook his head, the anger and self-guilt making his muscles tingle. "You know what Christina Blake did to me. And you went and did the exact same fucking thing. You selfish, self-absorbed, sociopathic bitch. So I will talk to you any way I like."

"This is completely inappropriate."

"Really?" Patrick shoved the open box off the stack, spilling its incriminating contents on the floor. "What have you been up to, *Diane*?"

Her eyes narrowed at the scattered drug paraphernalia on her finished basement floor. "It's none of your business."

"I'm pretty sure you made it my business when you drugged my fucking meatloaf."

"Stop swearing. It isn't polite."

This was too much, too bizarre. He could do nothing but laugh, laugh so hard tears rose from his eyes and he had to prop himself upright by leaning his palms against his thighs.

His mother's voice screeched through the basement, so loud it shook the walls. "Stop *laughing*!"

The laughter died in his chest, leaving only grief. Grief over a lost childhood, over lost potential. "What have you been doing, Mom? How did you afford that new car? All this shit?"

He hit one of the other boxes from an online clothes shop, wanting to hurt himself, wanting to make a mess, wanting to hit something, anything. Wanting to hit her, to wound her as she had wounded him.

A high-pitched squeal escaped her, and Patrick followed her wrath-filled gaze to the box he had knocked over, its contents now strewn across the floor.

"Oh, Diane. You bitch."

All across his mother's basement floor were small plastic baggies of drugs, small white pills, and tiny packets of white powder. All labeled Disco Balls. He would recognize that handwriting anywhere. It was hers, her neat, nurse's script.

Everything clicked into place for him. The drugs, the new car. Even seeing her at the hospital with Dr. Goodman. "It's your fault." He knew he was speaking, but his voice was distant, like he was a ventriloquist projecting from a different room. "You gave the drugs to those poor kids at Lewis High. You gave drugs to Anita's dad, and it made him act like a beast. What if he loses his job? What if those kids die?"

She didn't have the decency to look guilty. "It's my recipe. I had to test it, to make sure I had the dosing right before we rolled out to the big cities."

The shed. The newly renovated one out back. "You're cooking in your backyard? Do you have any idea how stupid that is?"

"It's my property. I can do with it what I want."

The image of the drugs swam in front of him, a tidal wave of crazy and awful and amorality.

"So the kids who ended up in the hospital—"

"Their mistake. A slight adjustment in the concentration of PCP, and everything is fine." She sounded…proud. She was fucking proud. She was bragging to him about how she had nearly killed *children*. With PCP. Probably an opioid, too, if he was going off his own physical symptoms. The sociopathic bitch.

Patrick's hand clenched around the flashlight in his hand, its weak heat burning through him. If he looked at her on the staircase, he would see the moon-shaped glow of her face. If only he could have seen her devil horns earlier. "So what are you going to do? Are you going to kill John? Are you going to kill me?"

"Honey, no." She rushed down the stairs, and he steeled himself, wishing he had a protective shield around him that would keep her as far away as possible. He didn't want her toxicity tainting him. "Honey," she repeated, all solicitousness. It was fake, all fake. He weighed the flashlight in his hand. "We don't want to hurt you. You can help us. We need someone like you. Someone with connections. We lost our fence a few months ago. But we're rebuilding. Building back better."

His blood stilled in his veins, and he raised his gaze to her empty, soulless one. "We?" he repeated.

The door at the top of the stairs opened, spilling light down the steps and limning his mother like a monstrous specter.

Then, because Patrick's nightmare was not complete, Steve fucking Barnes stomped down the stairs, his face a mask of wrath. "Keep your fucking voices down. Don't you hear the doorbell?"

Chapter Twenty-Seven

While Anita admired Katie, this was a terrible idea. Curtis Wyczenczak appeared similarly concerned.

"I really don't know about this," he said from the window of his cruiser. He had parked a few houses down from Diane O'Leary's, far enough not to draw attention, but close enough he had a good line of sight. Or so Anita hoped. Desperately. With fingers and toes crossed. "We should wait for the feds."

"How long are they going to take?" Katie swung her cross-body purse over her shoulder, the weight of the Taser inside slapping slightly against her hip. Anita had slipped hers into the back pocket of her leggings, covering the bulk with her long, belted cardigan. "We don't have time to wait. She could have done something terrible to John or Patrick by now."

Curtis frowned and clutched the steering wheel of the car. "It's just, I gave Tasers to civilians."

Katie rolled her eyes. "Curtis, what would the sheriff say?" she said it in a tone of "Do I need to send you to the principal?" which clearly brooked no argument.

Curtis just nodded.

Anita might not be a soldier, but she was ready. If Diane had hurt Patrick, Anita wouldn't hold back her punches. While she typically viewed kickboxing as a way to release her inner demons, it had the super-helpful fringe benefit of disabling bitchy Munchausen nurses.

Curtis tapped out a text on his phone and frowned. "All right. The DEA isn't far. Keep in contact, please." He sighed loudly. "John is going to kill me for this."

"Hardly." Anita patted him on the shoulder and flipped on the recording device in her pocket. She had promised Lucy, after all, and Lucy had apparently kept her promise to stay at school and not put herself in mortal peril.

"Come on," she said to Katie.

She supposed they looked innocuous, two young, pretty women strolling the sidewalk on a chilly October day. If it weren't for the venomous look on Katie's face, they might be mistaken for innocent bystanders.

Her heart raced as they walked up the path toward the single-story house. "The lights are on in the shed," Anita said, keeping the movement of her mouth small, undetectable.

She noticed Katie's gaze flick to the wooden shed behind the house. It had been expanded since Anita had last seen it, years before. Diane wasn't the type to invite her son's girlfriend into her home.

Son. Diane had *never* treated Patrick as a parent should.

Anita let the anger flare through her, let it hone her rage until her body felt like a weapon. If she and Patrick ever had kids—

But this was not the time for that line of thinking.

She and Katie reached the door. They exchanged a glance, painted identical innocuous smiles on their faces, and then Anita rang the doorbell.

Several minutes passed, but neither she nor Katie

moved a single muscle. They didn't look toward the cruiser, or the shed. She didn't check the recorder in her pocket. She didn't blink when a gust of October wind rushed past them.

After an age, she heard the locks thunk on the door, and it swung open, revealing Diane O'Leary, in all her terrible glory. Her hair was slightly mussed, and her nostrils flared as though she had just run up several flights of stairs.

"What do you want?" Diane clipped, her focus lasered on Anita.

Anita could do this. She softened her posture, knowing it made her look a little ditsy. It was what Diane expected of her, after all. "Hi, Ms. O'Leary. So sorry to bother you."

Diane narrowed her eyes at Anita. "Who is she? What are you doing here?"

Katie had the air about her of an efficient, perky elementary school teacher. "Hi, Ms. O'Leary, I'm Katie Bannion, John Flaherty's fiancée. You haven't seen him, by any chance?"

Diane crossed her arms over her chest. "I have not." She looked as though she were going to check the street behind them, and Anita moved to cover her line of sight. She wasn't quite sure where the DEA was going to park, but she didn't want Diane seeing Curtis, either.

"Really?" Anita asked. "Rats. The last location from Deputy Flaherty's GPS tracker was from, well, here."

"I don't know anything about that. There's a lot of people on this street. I'm sure several of them are up to no good."

Anita felt Katie about to break, and the door about to slam in their faces, both metaphorically and literally speaking. She cowed a bit. "Our mistake. Look, I hate to ask, but can I use your bathroom?"

She saw the cold darkness in Diane's eyes flicker, as though debating the best way to appear normal.

"Please." She hoped like hell Katie had her Taser at the ready. She lowered her voice, like they were sharing a secret. "It's an emergency."

Keeping the door half-open, Diane turned to inspect the interior of her home, and apparently found it devoid of clues. "You have to take off your purse."

"Why?" It was a good thing she had her Taser secreted in the back of her leggings, but she didn't want to give Katie away. Anita clutched her purse apologetically. "Is something wrong, Diane? I only need to use your bathroom." She rolled her eyes slightly for emphasis. "Women troubles."

Please, all that is holy, forgive her for playing the period card when the man she loved was in danger.

Anita knew Patrick was here. In her heart of hearts, she knew it. It was like the thread that connected them had drawn taut and pulled her inexorably toward him.

Diane's face clouded over, then cleared, as though deciding it was better to play everything as normal. "Only a moment. I'm very busy today." Diane opened the door a little wider, and Katie and Anita slid into the house.

Anita had been in Diane's house exactly twice, and the latest of those times had been sophomore year in college, when Patrick's mom had not been home. It was best to pretend Anita didn't know where anything was.

She felt Katie tense beside her, like a predator

ready for a battle. Where could Patrick and John be? The living room where they stood didn't look like a war zone. Besides, Diane wouldn't have let them in here if the men were sitting at the kitchen table.

She glanced around, feigning helplessness.

Diane rolled her eyes and gestured down the hallway by the kitchen. There were two doors along the side of the wall, one leading to the bathroom, and one to the basement.

The nerves along Anita's spine prickled. She sent brain waves to Katie, hoping she picked up on it, too.

"You have a lovely home, Ms. O'Leary," Katie said, jumping into distraction mode. She exchanged a quick glance with Anita, then moved into the kitchen. "I love these curtains. Did you make them yourself?"

Once Katie had Diane's back turned, Anita walked down the hallway, forcing her steps to be unconcerned. Just a bathroom emergency, nothing more. Women's troubles, you know.

When she reached the two doors, she checked to make sure Diane was otherwise occupied with Katie in banal small talk, then she turned the knob on the door to the basement and stepped down the stairs.

An arm immediately went around her neck, squeezing the breath from her, but it wasn't enough to drown out the stench of expensive male cologne. She coughed and fidgeted, reaching for the Taser, hoping to grab it before she lost consciousness or her attacker registered its presence.

"You." A low voice breathed across her neck, leaving behind a sticky residue. "You can't keep your nose out of other people's business." A low growl steamed against her skin. *Ew ew ew.*

She tried to shift her weight, but her attacker redoubled his grip. This wasn't working. The stairwell was so dark, she couldn't see anything, either, except for the empty hallway above her. She didn't want to call attention to herself, as it might endanger Katie.

Enough.

She slipped her palms between the arm holding her and her neck, gripped the flesh, pulled down, and stepped to the side. With a practiced series of moves, she elbowed her attacker in the sternum, then connected her fist to his balls. He groaned but didn't release her. Asshole.

At the top of the stairs, Diane appeared, holding Katie with one arm around the woman's neck. Zip ties held Katie's wrists together at her waist. "Steve. What are you doing?"

Right. Of course the swamp growl belonged to Steve Barnes. Anita should have known.

Steve tried to tighten his hold on Anita, but she was ready for him. She snapped her head back, her occiput connecting with the tender cartilage of his nasal bone. He made a wet shriek and stumbled. She helped his momentum by stepping from his grasp and kicking him tight and fast against the side of his shin. Something snapped, echoing sickeningly in the stairwell, and Steve Barnes tumbled backward down the staircase before collapsing in a groaning heap.

Anita reached for the Taser beneath her sweater, but at the same time, Diane swung a pistol toward her. "Get downstairs," Diane said, her voice clipped.

Shit. Maybe she had time—

Diane cocked the safety on the pistol, the sound echoing in the stairwell.

"I won't say it again, you awful, pretentious bitch. Get downstairs."

Anita glanced behind her, then stepped backward down the stairs, watching as Diane followed her, pistol still raised and ready. Anita hated guns. So messy. So complicated.

At the base of the stairs, Anita stumbled over Steve Barnes's broken body, deliberately stepping on his fingers as he reached for her ankles.

"Look what you did," Diane growled. "Do you know how difficult it was to find a competent partner?"

Technically, yes, though not in the sense Diane meant. Anita glanced toward Katie, and the teacher's eyes were not full of fear, but rage.

If only Anita could borrow some of her strength.

She moved into the basement, and that was when she saw them. Patrick, tied up and gagged on the couch. John, passed out in an armchair. Her heart clenched in her chest. "What did you do to them?"

Diane shoved Katie in front of her, using her almost as a barricade. Katie's eyes widened as she saw her fiancé, limp and drugged, but to Anita, it seemed the vision only firmed her resolve. It certainly did for Anita.

Anita caught sight of the spilled boxes of drugs and paraphernalia on the basement floor. Of all the— "So it is you," she said.

Diane rolled her eyes, the gun still trained on Anita. Anita's gaze flicked between Katie and Patrick and John. Katie had moved beside John, running her bound hands over her fiancé's bald pate, as if to announce her presence to him. It might have been a trick of the dim light, but she thought she saw John's hand twitch.

The recording device weighed heavy in her pocket. They could do this. They had to do this. Anita could distract Diane long enough. She would have to, if they were all going to live.

Diane did not seem to notice what Katie was doing, an unexpected boon. "Why does no one believe in me? I am a goddamned queen pin. I am building an empire on the precipice of wild success."

"Are you building it on the backs of children?" Anita asked. "Because I'm a thousand percent sure that makes you a monster."

Diane narrowed her gaze. "People get hurt on the path to greatness."

Steve Barnes tried to stand, leaning against the stair railing, his face and chest covered with blood, but he screamed as he put weight on his broken leg. Lightweight shithead.

Diane's attention faltered, for a fraction of a moment.

Anita took the instant of her distraction to calculate what to do. How far away were the feds? The recording device had a 5G connection, and hopefully Curtis was listening to everything this narcissistic bitch was saying. She had to keep her talking.

"People shouldn't have to get hurt." Anita's hand flinched for the Taser, but Diane snapped the pistol toward her.

"Keep your hands up. I'm older and smarter than you, Anita." She narrowed her eyes and sang Anita's voice like a three-year-old's playground taunt.

Anita saw Patrick on the couch, his eyes wide and pleading. He was trying to tell her something. She followed his gaze. There was a small room behind a bookshelf, barely a clearing of space. Something metallic glinted on the floor. What was it?

"Babe, we need to finish this." Steve Barnes had managed to pull himself to a standing position, and to Anita's great distress, he had his own pistol out and held against his thigh. Shit.

She wished she had a secret distress button to call the feds immediately.

Diane nodded. "I want to start with *her*." She leveled the gun at Anita. Anita's blood chilled in her veins, and her attention narrowed to a tiny frame, like she was looking through goggles that restricted her peripheral vision.

She edged backward, toward the small room Patrick had indicated. She needed the Taser. She needed Curtis and the feds to arrive. She searched desperately through her haze of adrenaline for some clarity, some last shred to hold on for another few moments. The feds had to be here soon. "How did you do it? How did you get my dad to take those drugs? He never would have done it on his own."

Diane pursed her lips, as if to say, "poor baby." Fuck her. "Your dad is too easy, Anita. We have a history, you know. It only took a small suggestion, some pillow talk, when he was feeling guilty. His knees bother him so much." She rolled her eyes. "As if he's the only one."

Anita flicked her gaze to Steve Barnes, whose attention had focused on Diane. Maybe she could spin this. "Does your creepy shitbag lover over there know you were sleeping with my dad?"

Nope, by the steel in his eyes, he had no idea. She

could play this out. Steve's attention was now on Diane, rather than her or the others. This could work. She could use the old green-eyed monster in her favor.

"Let me guess," Anita said, inching infinitesimally closer to the wall. "You picked this meathead from the home shopping channel because you thought you could sell the drugs that way. People buy something online, you shove the drugs into a chair or armoire or inside a makeup case, and no one's the wiser. It would be the post office's fault for delivering it, right?" She could see Diane's features morph and harden, like a rattlesnake, cold-blooded and fanged. She just needed to distract her long enough. That was all. "That's why you used the antiques shop, too. Were you storing the drugs in the furniture? In drawers and hollowed-out legs? Did Mrs. DeVeaux find out? Is that why you killed her? Or maybe she was in on it from the start and wanted to slow it down once she realized kids were getting hurt?" Anita would really like to think well of her neighbor, though that was an inner monologue for another time.

"I didn't kill anyone," Diane said, her tone almost sweet. Anita glimpsed Steve, his face red and bloodied and beaded with sweat.

"Ah. You made him do it. That's smart." Anita waggled her raised hands and stepped one more inch backward. "Gotta keep your hands clean."

She glanced again between the two drug dealers and her friends. Katie had now edged near Patrick and was using her bound hands to work his gag and bindings free.

Resolve steeled her spine. Diane wasn't as smart as she thought she was. Everyone had a weakness. Steve

Barnes's was clearly Diane, and when Anita had a moment when she wasn't terrified for her life, she would be busy scraping those intrusive thoughts from her mind. Not that she minded an age gap, but she didn't need to picture what these two sociopaths did to one another behind closed doors.

"And Sheriff Forbes? She and John were figuring it out, huh?"

Diane's fingers whitened around the handle of her gun. "They were digging into Rita Forest and her contacts. I couldn't have that. Rita sold Steve his condo. The sheriff went back to the creek. She would have found the used vape cartridges we gave those kids. I tie up my loose ends, Anita."

Dread coiled around Anita's lower spine.

The top of the basement sat a few inches above the ground line and was lined with a few inches of windows. Shadows of black boots clouded the grimy glass, and a wave of calm washed over her. This was the moment. She could do this. She had floor craft and reflexes, not to mention the Taser. She knew how to put on a show.

She dropped her hands a fraction of an inch and smiled. "Diane, come on. You know this can't last. The bodies are piling up, right? I'll admit, Curtis isn't John in terms of investigative skills, but Sheriff Forbes is going to wake up soon. How well did you cover your tracks? Are you sure you can trust your lover to get the job done?"

Diane's body radiated anger, but Anita was taut and ready, too. She could do this.

"No one is going to find me," Diane said.

"Really? If you kill us, won't people notice?

Granted, no one really liked Mrs. DeVeaux, but a respected deputy and his fiancée, who is a beloved schoolteacher?" Anita hardened her gaze and pressed her lips into a thin line. "Are you going to kill your son?" Over her dead body.

"I want what's mine." Diane's voice was made of thin, sharp daggers. Anita knew stilettos well.

She leaned in toward Diane, pressing herself closer to the end of the pistol. "So do I," Anita whispered.

In one motion, she ducked low, into the space of the tiny room behind the bookshelf, pulled the Taser from her back pocket, and shot the electrodes at Diane.

Diane's body tensed as the electricity seized through her, and she dropped the gun.

Anita screamed as the pistol went off, covering her ears and her head. Goddamn guns and safeties. The bullet thudded into the wall near her, splintering the faux wood siding with a deafening roar. Why had Patrick wanted her to hide in this tiny target? She would have to ask later.

"Bitch!" Steve Barnes cried. He raised his own pistol, but two huge arms wrapped around him, knocking the gun from his hand.

John Flaherty restrained Barnes, his muscular body dwarfing the drug dealer. "You're both under arrest," he said, his voice thick and hazy.

"Really?" Barnes sneered. "You and what army?"

Boots thundered across the basement ceiling. "That army," Katie said, her usually placid face filled with wrath and justification.

Relief flooded through Anita, casting aside the adrenaline like a wave on the sand.

A team of federal agents in full tactical gear, guns

held in front of them, barreled down the stairs. "DEA. Hands up."

Barnes slumped against John Flaherty, who let the man collapse on the ground.

Diane was still riding out the last few twitches from the Taser, so did not answer the agent.

Anita raised her hands slowly from her tiny hideaway. From across the room, her gaze found Patrick's. The faint hints of a smile tickled around his lips, reddened from the duct tape. Despite the adrenaline, warmth bloomed in her chest. He could always find her in a crowd.

Hey, he mouthed.

Hey, she mouthed back.

Around them, DEA agents secured Diane and Barnes. Katie launched herself into John's arms, looping her still-bound wrists around his neck. Distant sirens neared, and blue and red flashing lights illuminated the basement.

Anita didn't care. Patrick was there. Patrick was alive.

Chapter Twenty-Eight

Patrick slipped under the water in the bath, careful to keep his plastic-wrapped cast out of the tub.

He should have hit his mom with the flashlight. He had waited too long. If he had only—

He opened his mouth underwater and screamed, then popped back upright, spluttering water and sloshing liquid over the sides of Anita's tub.

He was an idiot if he thought that one bath could wash away twenty-seven years of maternal gaslighting. Not to mention the PCP and ketamine that was probably still in his system.

He rested the back of his head against the bath pillow Anita had stuck to the wall of the tub with tiny plastic gaskets. What a day. What a fucking day.

"Hey."

He opened his eyes, and his heart fluttered. She didn't take away the ache, but she softened it.

Anita leaned against the doorjamb, the light from the bedroom haloing her golden hair. She wore fuzzy blue pajamas emblazoned with farm animals, cartoon ducks and pigs and cows.

"Hey," he said.

She smiled, holding up her phone. "Will called. His mom is awake. The doctors said she needs to take it easy for a few weeks, but they think she will be all right with physical and occupational therapy." She bit her bottom lip. "Will also said his mom identified Steve Barnes as the one who attacked her. He rammed her with his car then hit her with a baseball bat. What a dick."

"I knew he was a slimy asshole." He closed his eyes, hoping in vain to keep the revelations at bay. His mom had been having sex with that slimy asshole. Ew. And Dr. Goodman. Double ew.

"How's your dad?" he asked.

She sighed before walking over to the edge of the tub and perching along the porcelain rim. "I don't know. My mom is furious. I'm not sure if she's more upset about the drugs or about the affair. Neither is good. He supposedly is going to rehab." She shook her head, her gaze fixed on some far distant point. "I can't believe he cheated on her. I always thought they had such a good relationship." She swallowed, and he saw a film of tears settle over her eyes, but she blinked them away. "I guess you never really know what goes on in a family." His stomach churned as she looked directly at him.

She had seen. She had seen the things he hid from her. The things that made him broken, that made him…less. He crouched lower in the tub.

When she spoke, her voice was gentle. "Thanks for showing me your hiding spot. In retrospect, it didn't provide the best cover." She dipped her fingertips into the water and swirled, doodling rainbows and eddies. "It looked like you used to spend a lot of time down there."

His heart shattered into a thousand tiny pieces. She was going to break up with him. Who would want someone whose mother treated them like his had?

Patrick sniffed. "I was trying to show you the knife on the floor, my old utility knife. I didn't know you had a Taser with you, you badass."

She smiled, and to his immense relief, there was no pity in it. "How are you feeling?"

"You mean after finding out my mom is basically the Antichrist?" The past weeks had drained his mental filter, leaving only the dregs of truth. "I'm tired of being the one who gets drugged and kidnapped."

A smile pulled at the corner of her lips. He wished he could kiss it, could kiss her and all of the bad memories and feelings away, and spackle all the holes with Anita.

"Should I be the one who gets drugged and kidnapped the next time?" She stood from the rim of the bathtub and pulled her top over her head, revealing inch after inch of her perfect skin.

"No," Patrick replied, his voice hoarse. She was so freaking beautiful. "Never. Please, never."

She hooked her thumbs around the waistband of her pajama pants and slipped them down her legs. She had *incredible* legs.

While part of his anatomy responded as nature had intended, at the back of his mind he realized this wasn't sexual. They had been apart for far too long, out of rhythm, separated by circumstances and their own inability to voice their history.

She slipped into the tub across from him, the water parting for her.

He ran his fingertips along her skin, each brush feeling like the swipe of an eraser across his mind.

"I'm sorry," he whispered, not sure the words had actually left his mouth, because now, he was crying.

She leaned forward, pressing her chest to his, nestling her head in the crook of his neck and shoulder. "You've done nothing to be sorry for."

"I'm such an idiot. All of these years, I made excuses for her. I couldn't see what was right in front of me the whole time. Everyone else saw. Everyone. They tried to tell me. Will tried to tell me, and I didn't listen—"

"Shh." Anita pressed her warm lips to the arch of his collarbone, and a cool, soothing trill ran from her touch to his heart. "You were gaslit by your mother. You did nothing wrong. You were a kid."

"I'm not a kid now."

Anita sighed and squeezed his shoulder with her hand. "Our parents will always be our parents, no matter how juvenile or idiotic or sociopathic they act. They make their own choices, and we make ours. You can't hold yourself responsible for her actions. You are good. You are honorable. You are loyal."

Patrick wanted to lean into her, to lean into this, because it felt like the only real thing in his life. "I don't deserve you." He didn't. He had lost the ring box, somewhere at his mother's house. Or his mother had hidden it. Either way, he couldn't even hold on to an engagement ring, let alone propose properly.

Her smile blossomed against his skin. "I don't deserve you, either."

A sob wracked through him. He should hold it back, but he couldn't, not anymore. He broke, and she held him, and if anything that made him feel worse. "You must hate me," he said through thick tears.

"Never." She said it with such conviction.

"I'm supposed to be the strong one, the one who

helps you. And I'm not. I'm not who you need. I'm broken and...I'm still that little kid hiding in the wall behind a bookshelf, afraid of his own mother."

Anita pulled back slightly. This was it. They were done. She would agree and leave, and he would have to figure all of this out again. He would have to move. He couldn't stay in Lewis if they broke up. Fiji. He had always heard nice things about Fiji.

Instead, she cupped his face between her palms. "Look at me." He found her, her gaze inches from him. What did she see? His flaws, every part of himself he had tried to hide.

Even the broken parts of him had to admit, she didn't look like she was enumerating his flaws.

"Patrick, I love you. I don't need you to be strong. I don't need you to be the leader, or some societal stereotype of masculinity." She slid her hips forward until she was straddling his abdomen, water sloshing around them, sluicing from her skin. His affection-hungry heart reached for her. "All I need, is for you to be you. In all your Patrick glory. I love you just as you are, funny or sweet or caring. Broken or needy or angry or tired or frustrated." She pulled his face to hers and kissed one eyebrow, then the next, the warmth of her lips impressing her words into his skin. "I want you to be yourself. I want you to love yourself, because I love you."

For the first time in a very, very long time, the truth of those words sunk into him, healing his wounds, sealing the cracks his mother had made.

He leaned against her, skin to skin, and kissed her, massaging her lips between his. This was the apology, the forgiveness, and the moving on all in one.

She broke the kiss, and her smile fluttered across his cheek. "I also want you to go to therapy. I'll go, too."

"Okay." He wrapped his arms around her, pulling her close. Anything.

They lay together like that, cocooned in the scented perfume of the bathtub, until the water chilled and they were happily forced to go to bed.

Chapter Twenty-Nine

Patrick perched on the edge of the chair, squinting at John as he straightened the knot on his navy-blue tie and brushed aside a stray piece of lint. His boutonniere was crooked. He adjusted the little sailcloth-wrapped bundle of white rose and baby's breath.

"How are you doing, John?" Personally, Patrick was fucking tired of answering that question, but today was about his friend. His friend and his beloved bride.

"John!" Will, always one to interrupt a quiet moment, slapped him on the shoulder. "You're getting married today! I can't believe it. Do you need a drink?" He waved a silver flask embossed with the Philadelphia Eagles logo under the groom's nose.

John smiled, which softened his chiseled features. "I'm good. This is amazing. It's finally happening."

Patrick nodded with approval. "You look great, man."

"Thanks, guys."

Katie's brothers, who made up the remainder of John's side of the wedding party, whooped and hollered into the preparation suite. "John!" Declan called, holding up a bottle of beer. "If you hurt my sister, I'll kill you!"

"Noted." John rolled his eyes.

Patrick still wasn't sure which Bannion brother had shot the paintball at him, and it wasn't like they had confessed, but he doubted it was Declan. He seemed like he wouldn't swat a fly that buzzed too close.

Still, it was best to keep his distance from the clan of chestnut-haired hellions.

"Off to St. Thomas tomorrow?" Katie's brother Damon handed Patrick a beer, but he turned it down. He needed to keep his faculties about him, if he was going to stand beside his friend.

Will clapped John on the shoulder again with whiskey-fueled strength, the slap resounding through the room. "John has earned a long, loooooong honeymoon." Will had been in decidedly better spirits since his mother had woken up in the hospital. Sheriff Forbes had even been able to go home the day before.

Patrick sank into a chair, resting the heel of his cast on the floor in front of him. "Especially since when he gets back, he'll be interim sheriff. Couldn't go to a better guy. Unanimous approval from the township. I mean, seriously. Can you stop over-achieving?"

John hit him in the deltoid.

Katie's aunt Elle, in a mauve and gold full-length gown, appeared at the doorway, champagne flute in hand. "It's time," she said in a singsong voice.

Patrick flushed, his spine warming. What if this was his and Anita's wedding day? Who would be a part of it? Who would stand with him?

It didn't matter since he had lost the ring.

The Bannion brothers and Will left the preparation suite first, but as Patrick stood and balanced, John stayed him with a hand on his arm.

"You okay, John?" John had to be well. He was a rock.

John's face creased, his eyes soft. "Are you okay?

We haven't had a chance to talk these last few days. Everything happened so fast."

His supposed parent had already fired two defense attorneys, but the prosecution had a good case against her, especially with the evidence Anita and Lucy Knight had compiled. Bobby had whispered to him at the rehearsal dinner that the families of the affected high schoolers were also planning a civil suit. It was going to be a shit show over the next year.

Whoopee.

Patrick's grin faded, but he managed to keep his composure. "It's been a lot. I'm trying to work through it all." Understatement. He already had twice weekly sessions scheduled with a counselor, who kept prodding him for a third.

"I wanted to tell you, Barnes told us where they buried Mrs. DeVeaux. You were right, all along. Thank you. I'm sorry I didn't believe you at first."

Cold comfort. Patrick shivered. He wished he hadn't been right, that maybe she really had gone for a spontaneous Rehoboth Beach vacation. Patrick scuffed the end of his crutch against the thin rug of the preparation suite. "I did sound completely insane. Particularly with the whole picking up vape pens from the parking lot thing."

"It was good you did. It gave Lucy the idea for testing the ones at her school. Before that, we weren't sure how the kids were getting the drugs."

Ah, Lucy. "You going to take her on staff, future sheriff?"

John's face tightened, and Patrick had that sinking sensation that more bad news was on the way.

"Look, I know you don't need more reasons to be

pissed at your mom. But Anita found this unmarked bottle of pills in her drawer. We got the test results back last night. The lab says it's almost straight PCP. It could have killed you or Anita."

Patrick nodded, his entire body blank and unfocused. Super. Great. Just…fucking great.

"So, you're telling me that in addition to my horrible DNA donor drugging teenagers, she also tried to kill my girlfriend?" He wanted to spit and scream and rant, but he might ruin his suit. "Fucking narcissist. No one takes drugs from an unlabeled bottle."

"Are you and Anita okay?"

A soft smiled curved across Patrick's face. Of all the things he was grateful for, Anita topped every list. He hoped she knew it. "Yeah. We will be okay." The sun would rise and set. They would sit on her couch and eat grilled chicken salad and watch terrible movies. Life would go on.

He was the luckiest asshole in the whole world. Fuck his mom for trying to take that.

"Patrick, there is one more thing." John reached into the pocket of his tuxedo pants and pulled out a small black ring box. All the air squeezed out of Patrick's chest. No way. It wasn't possible.

"Where did you get that?' His voice was too hoarse, barely above a whisper.

"We found it in the house, in your mom's jewelry box. I figured it wasn't her style."

A flush ran up Patrick's spine. He slipped the box into the pocket of his pants, the light weight anchoring him. It felt like hope. "Thanks, John."

"Any time."

They slapped each other twice on the back, which

to Patrick meant, "I'm here for you always, friend." He needed it to mean that.

"Let's get you married," Patrick said.

****

Patrick was sure the wedding had been lovely. He was certain the bride had teared up at all the appropriate moments, and that John had said his vows dutifully and with just the right amount of feeling. Patrick simply hadn't paid attention to any of that. He had spent the entire ceremony staring at Anita, her hair piled on her head in a cool updo, smiling and chatting next to Bobby.

He was sure the reception was lovely, too. The alcohol flowed freely, and there was an air in the hall of a near-disaster averted. People laughed and smiled, and congratulations were thrown like rice. After his groomsman duties were complete, all he wanted to see was Anita.

He sat beside her now, his legs angled toward her, his hand wrapped in hers.

She sipped from her glass of champagne. "They look really happy."

Patrick followed her gaze to John and Katie in the midst of their first dance. The long train of Katie's wedding dress had been bustled, but it wouldn't have mattered. John lifted her off her feet and danced with her like she was floating on air. Katie laughed and rested her head on his broad shoulder, as though she wanted to live there. They moved through the steps Anita had choreographed as one, finding their rhythm in each other.

Patrick knew that feeling, when one had the right partner. As if the whole world narrowed to enclose the pair of you in a special warm hug of soft light. Like time stopped and the two of you moved in a parallel dimension.

What a week. What a world.

Will and Bobby dropped into the seats beside them. "This U2 cover band is pretty awesome." Will set a bourbon on the rocks in front of Patrick and sipped from his beer. Bobby had his arm around Will's shoulders, and the two of them beamed.

"Definitely."

"How's your mom?" Anita asked Will.

Will drained half his beer and rolled his eyes affectionately. "She's already fighting us about when she wants to return to work, so I'd say she's doing pretty well."

Bobby kissed his cheek. "This one's being all shy. He's doting on his mom like the good son he is. Homemade soups, nonstop teas and coffees, and herbal remedies. He even went to the library and got her a bunch of audiobooks since she's supposed to be on complete technological rest for the next few days."

Patrick watched the two of them banter playfully and tightened his hold on Anita. The band had switched to "The Sweetest Thing," which was Katie's favorite song. The bride stood front and center, using her bouquet as a microphone, and crooning very loudly. When the song ended, John led the applause, and Katie leapt into his arms again. She was pretty spry in those wedding shoes.

The wait staff dropped off a Caprese salad in front of the guests.

The lead singer of the cover band caught Patrick's eye and gave him a subtle nod. Patrick's pulse raced, and the ring box in his pocket burned like a beacon.

Anita's face lit up. "Oh! They're playing "All I Want Is You." That's my favorite U2 song."

Patrick affected a quizzical expression. "Really? You don't say. You've never mentioned it before." He was a romantic genius, if he did say so himself.

She slapped him playfully, a glorious smile on her face. "Please. You comment on it every time we go on a road trip, and have since we were in college."

"I'm nothing if not predictable."

He watched her as she swayed in her seat, the movement of her body in time with the music. "I really want to dance with you," he said.

She cocked her head and stood. "Then dance with me."

"Anita—"

"If you mention your leg, I'll cry." She faked a pout. "Come on. Lean on me. I can take it."

Patrick stood, using one hand on the chair. Anita took his arms and looped them around her waist, while she locked her wrists behind the nape of his neck.

They swayed softly back and forth, the gentle rhythm guiding the roll of their hips. Anita nuzzled into his neck.

"Best night ever."

Patrick laughed softly into her hair. "Really? Better than that time we got standing room tickets to *Hamilton*?"

She tilted her head, considering. "Okay, yeah, that was awesome, too." She breathed against his skin, and he was warm and home. "We've had so many best nights."

Patrick tightened his hold on her, pressing his body

to hers. "We have time for more."

"I love you, Patrick."

This was it. This was the moment. It was her favorite song, there was soft lighting, flowers everywhere, and happy couples. He had a ring in his pocket. Patrick was not a king of timing, but this was the moment.

"Anita, I want—"

The song ended, and there was a staticky tap on the microphone.

Anita lifted her head from his shoulder and glanced up toward the stage.

Will stood in the spotlight, microphone in hand. "Um, hello? Hi, everyone. Sorry to interrupt. Let's give a hand to this incredible band." Patrick joined in the applause, unsure if he should sit or keep standing. "You guys really are great. For those of you who don't know me, I'm Will Forbes. I'm not that great at speeches. I usually leave that to Bobby. He's the pro. But, here I am. John and I have known each other since, what, seventh grade? When his family first moved here. I'm not going to lie, we got into some youthful shenanigans—" There was a polite titter of laughter. Patrick figured the stories about Will and John's rambunctious past were practically urban legends by now. "But, even when we were twelve, I knew John was a guy you can count on. One who knows what he wants, and he gets it done in a way that makes everyone feel like there is still good in this world." He coughed slightly and sipped at the beer in the hand not holding the mic. "I think he knew Katie Bannion was for him the moment he saw her. I remember him telling me, I think we were juniors or something, he saw you across the playing field. You were in your field hockey uniform, and he turned to me and said, 'That's her. That's the girl for me.' " Patrick turned to see Katie, whose eyes had misted, her hands clasped to her chest. "He spent the next decade of his life becoming the man he thought you deserved, Katie. He would spend an eternity. You two, you are so inspiring. The way you care about each other. The support you have." Patrick noticed Will's gaze shift, away from the happy couple and now to Bobby, sitting beside Anita. "This last week has been…a lot of things. What it's shown me, though, is that life is short. We need to spend it with the people who support us and make us want to be better versions of ourselves. The ones who will stay up all night with us in the hospital, just to hold our hands." His voice choked, and he wiped at his face with the back of his wrist. "Bobby, I love you. I'll always love you. And this might not be the best time, but I don't want to wait another moment without telling you how I feel. Bobby, will you marry me?"

The entire ballroom erupted in cheers and hoots. Bobby rose from his chair so quickly it toppled over and dashed into Will's waiting arms.

Patrick kept his own ring box in his pocket. He saw Anita, tears streaming down her cheeks. "Patrick, wasn't that just beautiful? It was so romantic. I can't believe they're engaged!"

Patrick clapped along with everyone else for his friend, but he knew it lacked a bit of luster.

Yup. Patrick was not the king of timing.

Epilogue

One Month Later

Anita stepped out of Patrick's car and closed the door. "How does it feel to be driving again?" she asked.

She watched Patrick step from the driver's side door and test out the weight on his newly cast-free leg. "It feels pretty good." He walked around to her side, wrapped his hands around her waist, and kissed her. She leaned into it, into him. Things had been good the past month. Therapy had been helping both of them, Patrick with his deprogramming, and Anita with her family issues. She and Patrick were both finally back in a rhythm.

She slipped her hand into his. Across the parking lot, the antiques store had been sold and emptied. The pretty antique vanity she had admired had been bought before she could make an offer on it. When she had come home the evening of the auction, though, there it was, waiting for her at her apartment. Patrick always knew how to surprise her.

He squeezed her hand and followed her gaze. "Hopefully somebody cool will move in."

"Yeah." She eyed him, a little warily. He had been a little off all evening, restless. They had been at a social dance party in a neighboring town, and while he had been attentive, sweet, jovial, he wasn't his usual self. "Are you okay?"

He unlocked the door to the studio, an odd smile on his face, like it was Christmas morning and he was Santa Claus.

A prickle of nerves tingled at Anita's spine. There was no fear this time, only sweet anticipation. "Patrick? What's going on?"

He stepped in front of her, blocking her entrance to the studio, and took her wrists in his hands. "Close your eyes."

"Why?"

He pressed tiny kisses to her eyebrows and nose. "Do you trust me?"

Butterflies erupted in her stomach. "Yes. Of course."

He kissed her lightly on her lips, and warmth bloomed through her. "Then close your eyes."

As she shut her lids, the grin started from her toes and spread through her body like branches sprouting from a tree trunk. The studio was dim, lit only by the streetlights, but she felt warm and safe, like she was surrounded by fuzzy towels straight from the dryer.

"Wait for it," Patrick said.

One by one, lights overhead flicked on, bathing her face in their cozy glow. Behind her eyelids, she saw a prism of colors. Soft music played over the stereo speakers, Adele's "Make You Feel My Love."

Anita's jaw dropped open, and her heart throbbed in her chest.

Oh. My. God. Ohmygod ohmygod ohmygod.

"Okay," Patrick said. "Open your eyes."

Anita bit her lip and opened her eyes slowly, wanting to savor this moment. Her breath caught in her chest, and delirious happiness warmed her limbs.

Her studio had been transformed into a dreamscape. Fairy lights twinkled from the ceiling, their soft, happy light reflected in the mirrors and making their luminescence endless. The floor was a carpet of white, pink, and lavender rose petals, their scent perfuming the air.

Anita couldn't hold back the tears, though she tried by clasping her hands over her mouth.

"I can't believe you did all this." She couldn't stop staring. It was like something out of a movie. She found Patrick's gaze. "You did this for me?"

He had his hands in his pockets, and his smile was lopsided and perfect. "I had help. Lucy and the ballroom dance club volunteered to set this up while we were out. And, before you ask, they will clean it up tomorrow morning." He laughed a little, his eyes shining.

Anita didn't want to wait. She rushed into his arms and wrapped herself around him. "It's incredible. Thank you."

Patrick pulled away a few inches and tucked a strand of her hair behind her ears. "I had this whole speech planned." He kissed her lightly, the warmth of his soft lips against hers intoxicating. "I was going to tell you all about the rose colors, and how lavender means love at first sight, and white means new beginnings." Anita cupped his face between her hands. That was all she ever wanted, to have Patrick with her. He leaned into her palms. "I can't remember it all now."

They both laughed, reinforcing the happy bubble that cocooned them in this gorgeous setting. If Anita never woke up from this dream, so much the better.

Patrick rested his forehead against hers, and she listened, imprinting his words on her heart. "The truth is that I've loved you since I was a teenager and didn't know any better. My childhood was…not the best. The moment you entered my life, I finally felt like I had a purpose, a home. I was finally worth something. I mattered to someone. And every moment since then has solidified that feeling. When I'm with you, I'm home. I'm whole. Even broken and neglected, you find me. There's a thread that connects us, that keeps us in rhythm, and I never want to lose that. I love you. I love that you will not upgrade your cell phone because you're terrified you won't be able to figure out the newer technology. I love that your favorite music is a tie between 1980s power ballads and showtunes. I love that you are freaking amazing at your job. I love how you believe in people. Like me."

Anita's heart, already fluttering, completely ceased its beat when he dropped to one knee, taking her hand in his.

"Anita, will you marry me?"

He removed a black ring box from his pocket, but before she gave him the chance to show her the ring, she launched herself into his arms. She wrapped herself around him, melting into him, her ecstatic heart meeting his.

"Is that a yes?" he asked. She felt his smile against her hair.

"Yes. Yes, yes, and yes. You're my home, too." The culmination of all those years of longing and wanting, and now here she was, a rose gold band on her finger, a diamond sparkling in the soft fairy lights. Most of all there was Patrick. Sweet, wonderful, sexy, talented, smart Patrick. The love of her life.

Patrick kissed her then, sealing their agreement with the intimacy of touch. With his arms around her, she knew that whatever life had in store, they could face it together.

A word about the author...

A lifelong lover of the written word, Natalie used to spend her school recess hours reading Michael Crichton and Jane Austen. Not much has changed, except now she writes stories about smart, kickass women and the people who adore them. Sometimes there are even pirates involved. Natalie lives in Los Angeles, where she is married to a man who literally brings life into the world. She is mom to two lovely young munchkins who despise brushing their hair and eat way too much cake. She is unapologetically terrible at taking selfies. www.nataliecrosswrites.com

Also by Natalie Cross...

Ballroom Blitz